A Round Dozen

STORIES BY

Louisa May Alcott

A Round Dozen

STORIES BY

Louisa May Alcott

SELECTED AND WITH A FOREWORD BY

Anne Thaxter Eaton

ILLUSTRATED BY

Tasha Tudor

NEW YORK

The Viking Press

SC 1. Short stories

Library of Congress catalog card number: 63–18366
PRINTED IN THE U.S.A.

594-1

Contents

6   *Contents*

Foreword

About the middle of the nineteenth century a charming toy called a Peep Show was devised. When the top cover of a small cardboard tablet (usually six by three inches) was pulled out, the observer looked through a series of paper arches to see a small gaily colored picture at the end. It might be a garden with children playing under the rose trees, a street with people walking, or a boat on a river with a castle, or, perhaps, the Tower of London in the background.

To read Louisa Alcott's stories, written a hundred years ago, is like looking into one of these nineteenth-century peep shows, with the difference that what is seen at the end is not a stationary scene but people in action; for youthful readers looking through this tunnel of years will see boys and girls like themselves enjoying the same things, amused or touched by the same kind of happenings.

What reader of any age can resist, in "Tabby's Tablecloth," spirited little Tabitha of Revolutionary times who, hidden by the folds of the best damask tablecloth, put on to do honor to three British officers, overheard what those officers were plotting and reported it to the colonial authorities.

Children who love animals will sympathize with Tilda and Patty who worked so hard to carry water to the stock train where the sheep and cows were suffering from dust and heat and thirst; while children who like to imagine the unseen doings of inanimate things will take delight in "The Silver Party" when the forks and spoons assembled on the dining table indulge in their own festivities (with a touch of Hans Christian Andersen's fancy) before the family appears for Thanksgiving Dinner.

Something of the integrity, loyalty, and warm affection that make the March family (actually the Alcott family) in *Little Women* so real and so lovable has found its way into these lesser stories.

"Tabby's Tablecloth" is a story of the American Revolution, but perhaps Miss Alcott wrote with more zest of the little girl's determination to help the colonists because a later war was so close to her heart. In 1863 Louisa Alcott went to the Union Hospital in Georgetown as a nurse. She knew the work would be difficult and dangerous but could not be dissuaded. Out of the six weeks she was there—for a serious illness made it necessary for her to return home—came *Hospital Sketches,* almost exact reproductions of her letters home, a book which has been reprinted recently and which because of its vivid picture of a wartime hospital in those days, its freshness, originality, and human quality is well worth reading today. For these letters with their warm sympathy for the wounded, their appreciation of the humor as well as the pathos of life in a wartime hospital, round out for us the character of Jo whom we loved in *Little Women* until we see her as the loyal, determined, unselfish woman she came to be.

These qualities—loyalty, determination, unselfishness—are all reflected in greater or less degree in these twelve stories, which show as well the delightful appreciation of character and personality that makes the people in *Little Women* so timelessly alive. It is true, as the adult reader is likely to observe, that Louisa May Alcott emphasizes the moral in her stories; but children like clear definition of right and wrong, and this pleases rather than disturbs them. And it may well be that in addition to giving pleasure for their own sake, these tales, loved and remembered by their mothers and grandmothers, will bring to the children of today a feeling of continuity and understanding between generations.

—ANNE THAXTER EATON

A Round Dozen

STORIES BY

Louisa May Alcott

ONE

A Hole in the Wall

PART I

If anyone had asked Johnny Morris who were his best friends, he would have answered, "The sun and the wind, next to Mother."

Johnny lived in a little court that led off from one of the busiest streets in the city—a noisy street, where horsecar bells tinkled and omnibuses rumbled all day long, going and coming from several great depots nearby. The court was a dull place, with only two or three shabby houses in it and a high blank wall at the end.

The people who hurried by were too busy to do more than glance at the lame boy who sat in the sunshine against the wall, or to guess that there were a picture gallery and a circulating library in the court. But Johnny had both, and took such comfort in them that he never could be grateful enough to the wind that brought him his books and pictures, or to the sun that made it possible for him to enjoy them in the open air, far more than richer folk enjoy their fine galleries and libraries.

A bad fall, some months before the time this story begins, did something to Johnny's back which made his poor legs nearly useless and changed the lively, rosy boy into a pale cripple. His mother took in fine washing and worked hard to pay doctors' bills and feed and clothe her boy, who could no longer run errands, help with the heavy tubs, or go to school. He could only pick out laces for her to iron, lie on his bed in pain for hours, and, each fair day, hobble out to sit in a little old chair between the water butt and the leaky tin boiler in which he kept his library.

But he was a happy boy, in spite of poverty and pain, and the day a great gust came blowing fragments of a gay placard and a dusty newspaper down the court to his feet was the beginning of good fortune for patient Johnny. There was a theatre in the street beyond, and other pictured bits found their way to him, for the frolicsome wind liked to whisk the papers around the corner and chase them here and there till they settled under the chair or flew wildly over the wall.

Faces, animals, people, and big letters—all came to cheer

the boy, who was never tired of collecting these waifs and strays, cutting out the big pictures to paste on the wall with the leavings of his mother's starch and the smaller, in the scrapbook he made out of stout brown wrappers or newspapers, when he had read the latter carefully. Soon it was a very gay wall, for mother helped, standing on a chair, to put the large pictures up, when Johnny had covered all the space he could reach. The books were laid carefully away in the boiler, after being smoothly ironed out and named to suit Johnny's fancy by pasting letters on the back. This was the circulating library, for not only did the papers whisk about the court to begin with, but the books they afterward made went the rounds among the neighbors till they were worn out.

The old cobbler next door enjoyed reading the anecdotes on Sunday when he could not work; the pale seamstress upstairs liked to look over advertisements of the fine things which she longed for; and Patsey Flynn, the newsboy, who went by each day to sell his papers at the station, often paused to look at the playbills, for he adored the theatre and entertained Johnny with descriptions of the splendors there to be beheld, till he felt as if he had really been and had known all the famous actors, from Humpty Dumpty to the great Salvini.

Now and then a flock of dirty children would stray into the court and ask to see the "pretty picters." Then Johnny was a proud and happy boy, for, armed with a clothespole, he pointed out and explained the beauties of his gallery, feeling that he was a public benefactor when the poor babies thanked him warmly and promised to come again and bring all the nice papers they could pick up.

These were Johnny's pleasures, but he had two sorrows:

one, a very real one, his aching back; and the other, a boyish longing to climb the wall and see what was on the other side, for it seemed a most wonderful and delightful place to the poor child, shut up in that dismal court, with no playmates and few comforts.

He amused himself with imagining how it looked over there and nearly every night added some new charm to this unseen country, when his mother told him fairy tales to get him to sleep. He peopled it with the dear old characters all children know and love. The white cat that sat on the wall was Puss in Boots to him, or Whittington's good friend. Bluebeard's wives were hidden in the house of whose upper windows the boy could just catch glimpses. Red Ridinghood met the wolf in the grove of chestnuts that rustled over there, and Jack's beanstalk grew up just such a wall as that, he was sure.

But the story he liked best was the "Sleeping Beauty in the Wood"; for he was sure some lovely creature lived in that garden, and he longed to get in to find and play with her. He actually planted a bean in a bit of damp earth behind the water barrel and watched it grow, hoping for as strong a ladder as Jack's. But the vine grew very slowly, and Johnny was so impatient that he promised Patsey his best book "for his ownty-donty," if he would climb up and report what was to be seen in that enchanted garden.

"Faith, and I will, thin." And up went good-natured Pat, after laying an old board over the hogshead to stand on, for there were spikes all along the top of the wall, and only cats and sparrows could walk there.

Alas for Johnny's eager hopes, and alas for Pat's Sunday best! The board broke, and splash! went the climber, with a wild Irish howl that startled Johnny half out of his wits and brought both Mrs. Morris and the cobbler to the rescue.

After this sad event Pat kept away for a time in high dudgeon, and Johnny was more lonely than ever. But he was a cheery little soul, so he was grateful for what joys he had and worked away at his wall—for the March winds had brought him many treasures, and, after April rains were over, May sunshine made the court warm enough for him to be out nearly all day.

"I'm so sorry Pat is mad, 'cause he saw this piece and told me about it, and he'd like to help me put up these pictures," said Johnny to himself, one breezy morning, as he sat examining a big poster which the wind had sent flying into his lap a few minutes before.

The play was *Monte Cristo,* and the pictures represented the hero getting out of prison by making holes in the wall, among other remarkable performances.

"This is a jolly red one! Now, where will I put it to show best and not spoil the other beauties?"

As he spoke, Johnny turned his chair around and surveyed his gallery with as much pride and satisfaction as if it held all the wonders of art.

It really *was* quite splendid, for every sort of picture shone in the sun—simpering ladies, tragic scenes, circus parades, and labels from tin cans—rosy tomatoes, yellow peaches, and purple plums—funny advertisements and gay bills of all kinds. None were perfect, but they were arranged with care, and the effect was very fine, Johnny thought.

Presently his eyes wandered from these treasures to the budding bushes that nodded so tantalizingly over the wall. A grapevine ran along the top, trying to hide the sharp spikes; lilacs tossed their purple plumes above it, and several tall chestnuts rose over all, making green tents with their broad leaves, where spires of blossom began to show like candles on a mammoth Christmas tree. Sparrows were chirping gaily everywhere; the white cat, with a fresh blue bow, basked on the coping of the wall, and from the depths of the enchanted garden came a sweet voice singing,

> "And she bids you to come in,
> With a dimple in your chin,
> Billy boy, Billy boy."

Johnny smiled as he listened and put his finger to the little dent in his own chin, wishing the singer would finish this pleasing song. But she never did, though he often heard that, as well as other childish ditties, sung in the same gay voice, with bursts of laughter and the sound of lively feet tripping up and down the boarded walks. Johnny longed intensely to know who the singer was, for her music cheered his solitude, and the mysterious sounds he heard in the garden increased his wonder and his longing day by day.

Sometimes a man's voice called, "Fay, where are you?" and Johnny was sure "Fay" was short for Fairy. Another voice was often heard talking in a strange, soft language, full of exclamations and pretty sounds. A little dog barked and answered to the name Pippo. Canaries carolled, and some elfish bird scolded, screamed, and laughed so like a human being that Johnny felt sure that magic of some sort was at work next door.

A delicious fragrance was now wafted over the wall as of flowers, and the poor boy imagined untold loveliness behind that cruel wall, as he tended the dandelions his mother brought him from the Common, when she had time to stop and gather them, for he loved flowers dearly and tried to make them out of colored paper, since he could have no sweeter sort.

Now and then a soft, rushing sound excited his curiosity

to such a pitch that once he hobbled painfully up the court till he could see into the trees, and once his eager eyes caught glimpses of a little creature, all blue and white and gold, who peeped out from the green fans and nodded and tried to toss him a cluster of chestnut flowers. He stretched his hands to her with speechless delight, forgetting his crutches, and would have fallen if he had not caught the shutter of a window so quickly that he gave the poor back a sad wrench; and when he could look up again, the fairy had vanished, and nothing was to be seen but the leaves dancing in the wind.

Johnny dared not try this again for fear of a fall, and every step cost him a pang, but he never forgot it and was thinking of it as he sat staring at the wall on that memorable May day.

"How I *should* like to peek in and see just how it all really looks! It sounds and smells so summery and nice in there. I know it must be splendid. I say, pussy, can't you tell a feller what you see?"

Johnny laughed as he spoke, and the white cat purred politely, for she liked the boy who never threw stones at her, or disturbed her naps. But puss could not describe the beauties of the happy hunting ground below, and, to console himself for the disappointment, Johnny went back to his new picture.

"Now, if this man in the play dug his way out through a wall ten feet thick with a rusty nail and a broken knife, I don't see why I couldn't pick away one brick and get a peek. It's all quiet in there now; here's a good place, and nobody will know, if I stick a picture over the hole. And I'll try it; I declare I will!"

Fired with the idea of acting *Monte Cristo* on a small scale, Johnny caught up the old scissors in his lap and began to dig out the mortar around the brick already loose and crumbling at the corners. His mother smiled at his energy, then sighed and said, as she clapped her laces with a heavy heart. "Ah, poor dear, if he only had his health he'd make his way in the world. But now he's like to find a blank wall before him while he lives, and none to help him over."

Puss, in her white boots, sat aloft and looked on, wise as the cat in the story, but offered no advice. The toad who lived behind the water barrel hopped under a few leaves of the struggling bean, like Jack waiting to climb, and just then the noon bells began to ring as if they sang clear and loud, "Turn again, Whittington, Lord Mayor of London."

So, cheered by his friends, Johnny scraped and dug vigorously till the old brick fell out, showing another behind it. Only pausing to take breath, he caught up his crutch and gave two or three hearty pokes, which soon cleared the way and let the sunshine stream through, while the wind tossed the lilacs like triumphal banners, and the jolly sparrows chirped, "Hail, the conquering hero comes!"

Rather scared by his unexpected success, the boy sat silent for a moment to see what would happen. But all was still, and, presently, with a beating heart, Johnny leaned forward to enjoy the long desired "peek." He could not see much, but that little increased his curiosity and delight, for it seemed like looking into fairyland after the dust and noise and dingy houses of the court.

A bed of splendid tulips tossed their gay garments in the middle of a grass plot; a strange and brilliant bird sat dressing its feathers on a golden cage; a little white dog dozed in the sun; and on a red carpet under the trees lay the Princess, fast asleep.

"It's all right," said Johnny, with a long sigh of pleasure, "that's the Sleeping Beauty, sure enough. There's the blue gown, the white fur cloak sweeping round, the pretty hair, and—yes—there's the old nurse, spinning and nodding, just as she did in the picture book Mother got me when I cried because I couldn't go to see the play."

This last discovery really did bewilder Johnny and make him believe that fairy tales *might* be true, after all, for how could he know that the strange woman was an Italian servant, in her native dress, with a distaff in her hand? After pausing a moment, to rub his eyes, he took another look and made fresh discoveries by twisting his head about. A basket of oranges stood near the Princess; a striped curtain hung from a limb of the tree to keep the wind off, and several books fluttered their pictured leaves temptingly before Johnny's longing eyes.

"Oh, if I could only go in and eat 'em and read 'em and speak to 'em and see all the splendid things!" thought the poor boy as he looked from one delight to another and felt shut out from all. "I can't go and wake her like the Prince did, but I do wish she'd get up and do something, now I *can* see. I daren't throw a stone—it might hit someone—or holler —it might scare her. Pussy won't help, and the sparrows are too busy scolding one another. I know! I'll fly a kite over, and that will please her anyway. Don't believe she has kites; girls never do."

Eager to carry out his plan, Johnny tied a long string to his gayest poster, and then, fastening it to the pole with which he sometimes fished in the water cask, held it up to catch the fresh breezes blowing down the court. His good friend, the wind, soon caught the idea and with a strong breath sent the red paper whisking over the wall, to hang a moment on the trees and then drop among the tulips, where its frantic struggles to escape waked the dog and set him to racing and barking, as Johnny hurriedly let the string go and put his eye to his peephole.

The eyes of the Princess were wide open now, and she clapped her hands when Pippo brought the gay picture for her to see, while the old woman, with a long yawn, went away, carrying her distaff, like a gun, over her shoulder.

"She likes it! I'm so glad. Wish I had some more to send

over. This will come off; I'll poke it through, and maybe she'll see it."

Very much excited, Johnny recklessly tore from the wall his most cherished picture, a gay flower-piece, just put up; and folding it, he thrust it through the hole and waited to see what followed.

Nothing but a rustle, a bark, and a queer croak from the splendid bird, which set the canaries to trilling sweetly.

"She don't see; maybe she will hear," said Johnny. And he began to whistle like a mockingbird, for this was his one accomplishment, and he was proud of it.

Presently he heard a funny burst of laughter from the parrot, and then a voice said, "No, Polly, you can't sing like that bird. I wonder where he is? Among the bushes over there, I think. Come, Pippo, let us go and find him."

"Now she's coming!" And Johnny grew red in the face trying to give his best trills and chirrups.

Nearer and nearer came the steps, the lilacs rustled as if shaken, and presently the roll of paper vanished. A pause, and then the little voice exclaimed, in a tone of great surprise, "Why, there's a hole! I never saw it before. Oh! I can see the street. How nice! How nice!"

"She likes the hole! I wonder if she will like me?" And, emboldened by these various successes, Johnny took another peep. This was the most delicious one of all, for he looked right into a great blue eye, with glimpses of golden hair above, a little round nose in the middle, and red lips below. It was like a flash of sunshine, and Johnny winked, as if dazzled, for the eye sparkled, the nose sniffed daintily, and the pretty mouth broke into a laugh as the voice cried out delightedly, "I see someone! Who are you? Come and tell me!"

"I'm Johnny Morris," answered the boy, quite trembling with pleasure.

"Did you make this nice hole?"

"I just poked a brick, and it fell out."

"Papa won't mind. Is that your bird?"

"No, it's me. I whistled."

"It's very pretty. Do it again," commanded the voice, as if used to giving orders.

Johnny obeyed and when he paused, out of breath, a small hand came through the hole, grasping as many lilies of the valley as it could hold, and the Princess graciously expressed her pleasure by saying, "I like it; you shall do it again, by and by. Here are some flowers for you. Now we will talk. Are you a nice boy?"

This was a poser, and Johnny answered meekly, with his nose luxuriously buried in the lovely flowers, "Not very—I'm lame; I can't play like other fellers."

"Poverino!" sighed the little voice, full of pity, and, in a moment, three red-and-yellow tulips fell at Johnny's feet, making him feel as if he really had slipped into fairyland through that delightful hole.

"Oh, thank you! Aren't they just elegant? I never see such beauties," stammered the poor boy, grasping his treasures as if he feared they might vanish away.

"You shall have as many as you like. Nanna will scold, but Papa won't mind. Tell me more. What do you do over there?" asked the child, eagerly.

"Nothing but paste pictures and make books, when I don't ache too bad. I used to help Mother, but I got hurt, and I can't do much now," answered the boy, ashamed to mention how many laces he patiently picked or clapped, since it was all he could do to help.

"If you like pictures, you shall come and see mine some day. I do a great many. Papa shows me how. His are splendid. Do you draw or paint yours?"

"I only cut 'em out of papers and stick 'em on this wall or put 'em in scrapbooks. I can't draw, and I haven't got no paints," answered Johnny.

"You should say 'haven't any paints.' I will come and see you some day, and, if I like you, I will let you have my old paintbox. Do you want it?"

"Guess I do!"

"I think I *shall* like you, so I'll bring it when I come. Do you ache much?"

"Awfully, sometimes. Have to lay down all day and can't do a thing."

"Do you cry?"

"No! I'm too big for that. I whistle."

"I *know* I shall like you, because you are brave!" cried the impetuous voice, with its pretty accent, and then an orange came tumbling through the hole, as if the new acquaintance longed to do something to help the "ache."

"Isn't that a rouser! I do love 'em, but Mother can't afford 'em often." And Johnny took one delicious taste on the spot.

"Then I shall give you many. We have loads at home, much finer than these. Ah, you should see our garden there!"

"Where do you live?" Johnny ventured to ask, for there was a homesick sound to the voice as it said those last words.

"In Rome. Here we only stay a year, while Papa arranges his affairs; then we go back, and I am happy."

"I should think you'd be happy in there. It looks real splendid to me, and I've been longing to see it ever since I could come out."

"It's a dull place to me. I like better to be where it's always warm, and people are more beautiful than here. Are *you* beautiful?"

"What queer questions she does ask!" And poor Johnny was so perplexed he could only stammer, with a laugh, "I guess not. Boys don't care for looks."

"Peep, and let me see. I like pretty persons," commanded the voice.

"Don't she order around?" thought Johnny, as he obeyed. But he liked it and showed such a smiling face at the peep-hole that Princess Fay was pleased to say, after a long look at him, "No, you are not beautiful, but your eyes are bright, and you look pleasant, so I don't mind the freckles on your nose and the whiteness of your face. I think you are good. I am sorry for you, and I shall lend you a book to read when the pain comes."

"I couldn't wait for that if I had a book. I do *love* so to read!" And Johnny laughed out from sheer delight at the thought of a new book, for he seldom got one, being too poor to buy them and too helpless to enjoy the free libraries of the city.

"Then you shall have it *now*." And there was another quick rush in the garden, followed by the appearance of a fat little book, slowly pushed through the hole in the wall.

"This is the only one that will pass. You will like Hans Andersen's fairy tales, I know. Keep it as long as you please. I have many more."

"You're so good! I wish I had something for you," said the boy, quite overcome by this sweet friendliness.

"Let me see one of *your* books. They will be new to me. I'm tired of all mine."

Quick as a flash, off went the cover of the old boiler, and out came half a dozen of Johnny's best works, to be crammed through the wall, with the earnest request, "Keep 'em all; they're not good for much, but they're the best I've got. I'll do some prettier ones as soon as I can find more nice pictures and pieces."

"They look very interesting. I thank you. I shall go and read them now, and then come talk again. *Addio,* Giovanni."

"Good-by, Miss."

Thus ended the first interview of little Pyramus and Thisbe through the hole in the wall, while Puss sat up above and played moonshine with her yellow eyes.

PART II

After that day a new life began for Johnny, and he flourished like a poor little plant that has struggled out of some dark corner into the sunshine. All sorts of delightful things happened, and good times really seemed to have come. The mysterious papa made no objection to the liberties taken with his wall, being busy with his own affairs and glad to have his little girl happy. Old Nanna, being more careful, came to see the new neighbors and was disarmed at once by the affliction of the boy and the gentle manners of the mother. She brought all the curtains of the house for Mrs. Morris to do up, and in her pretty broken English praised Johnny's gallery and library, promising to bring Fay to see him someday.

Meantime the little people prattled daily together, and all manner of things came and went between them. Flowers, fruit, books, and bonbons kept Johnny in a state of bliss and inspired him with such brilliant inventions that the Princess never knew what agreeable surprise would come next. Astonishing kites flew over the wall and tissue ballons exploded in the flower beds. All the birds of the air seemed to live in that court, for the boy whistled and piped till he was hoarse, because she liked it. The last of the long hoarded cents came out of his tin bank to buy paper and pictures for the gay little books he made for her. His side of the wall was ravaged that hers might be adorned, and, as the last offering his grateful heart could give, he poked the toad through the hole, to live among the lilies and eat the flies that began to buzz about Her Highness when she came to give her orders to her devoted subjects.

She always called the lad Giovanni, because she thought it a prettier name than John, and she was never tired of telling stories, asking questions, and making plans. The favorite one was what they would do when Johnny came to see her, as she had been promised he should when Papa was not too busy to let them enjoy the charms of the studio, for Fay was a true artist's child and thought nothing so lovely as pictures. Johnny thought so, too, and dreamed of the happy day when he should go and see the wonders his little friend described so well.

"I think it will be tomorrow, for Papa has a lazy fit coming on, and then he always plays with me and lets me rummage where I like, while he goes out or smokes in the garden. So be ready, and, if he says you can come, I will have the flag up early and you can hurry."

These agreeable remarks were breathed into Johnny's willing ear about a fortnight after the acquaintance began; and he hastened to promise, adding soberly, a minute after, "Mother says she's afraid it will be too much for me to go around and up steps and see new things, for I get tired so easy, and then the pain comes on. But I don't care how I ache if I can only see the pictures—and you."

"Won't you ever be any better? Nanna thinks you might."

"So does Mother, if we had money to go away in the country and eat nice things and have doctors. But we can't, so it's no use worrying." And Johnny gave a great sigh.

"I wish Papa was rich; then he would give you money. He works hard to make enough to go back to Italy, so I cannot ask him, but perhaps I can sell *my* pictures also and get a little. Papa's friends often offer me sweets for kisses; I will have money instead, and that will help. Yes, I shall do it." And Fay clapped her hands decidedly.

"Don't you mind about it. I'm going to learn to mend shoes. Mr. Pegget says he'll teach me. That doesn't need legs, and he gets enough to live on very well."

"It isn't pretty work. Nanna can teach you to braid straw as she did at home; that is easy and nice, and the baskets sell very well, she says. I shall speak to her about it, and you can try tomorrow when you come."

"I will. Do you really think I *can* come, then?" And Johnny stood up to try his legs, for he dreaded the long walk, as it seemed to him.

"I will go at once and ask Papa."

Away flew Fay and soon came back with a glad, "Yes!" that sent Johnny hobbling in to tell his mother and beg her to mend the elbows of his only jacket; for suddenly, his old clothes looked so shabby he feared to show himself to the neighbors he so longed to see.

"Hurrah! I'm really going tomorrow. And you, too, Mammy dear," cried the boy, waving his crutch so vigorously that he slipped and fell.

"Never mind; I'm used to it. Pull me up, and I'll rest while we talk about it," he said cheerily, as his mother helped him to the bed, where he forgot his pain in thinking of the delights in store for him.

Next day, the flag was flying from the wall, and Fay early at the hole, but no Johnny came; and when Nanna went to see what kept him, she returned with the sad news that the poor boy was suffering much and would not be able to stir for some days.

"Let me go and see him," begged Fay imploringly.

"*Cara mia,* it is no place for you. So dark, so damp, so poor, it is enough to break the heart," said Nanna decidedly.

"If Papa was here, he would let me go. I shall not play; I shall sit here and make some plans for my poor boy."

Nanna left her indignant little mistress and went to cook a nice bowl of soup for Johnny, while Fay concocted a fine plan and, what was more remarkable, carried it out.

For a week it rained, for a week Johnny lay in pain, and for a week Fay worked quietly at her little easel in the corner of the studio, while her father put the last touches to his fine picture, too busy to take much notice of the child. On Saturday the sun shone, Johnny was better, and the great picture was done. So were the small ones, for, as her father sat resting after his work, Fay went to him with a tired but happy face, and, putting several drawings into his hand, told her cherished plan.

"Papa, you said you would pay me a dollar for every good copy I made of the cast you gave me. I tried very hard, and here are three. I want some money very, very much. Could you pay for these?"

"They are excellent," said the artist, after carefully looking at them. "You *have* tried, my good child, and here are your well-earned dollars. What do you want them for?"

"To help my boy. I want him to come in here and see the pictures and let Nanna teach him to plait baskets; and he can rest, and you will like him, and he might get well if he had some money, and I have three quarters the friends gave me instead of bonbons. Would that be enough to send poor Giovanni into the country and have doctors?"

No wonder Fay's papa was bewildered by this queer jumble, because, being absorbed in his work, he had never heard half the child had told him and had forgotten all about Johnny. Now he listened with half an ear, studying the effect of sunshine upon his picture meantime, while Fay told him the little story and begged to know how much money it would take to make Johnny's back well.

"Bless your sweet soul, my darling, it would need more than I can spare or you earn in a year. By and by, when I am at leisure, we will see what can be done," answered Papa, smoking comfortably, as he lay on the sofa in the large studio at the top of the house.

"You say that about a great many things, Papa. 'By and by' won't be long enough to do all you promise then. I like *now* much better, and poor Giovanni needs the country more than you need cigars or I new frocks," said Fay, stroking her father's tired forehead and looking at him with an imploring face.

"My dear, I cannot give up my cigar, for in this soothing smoke I find inspiration, and, though you are a little angel, you must be clothed; so wait a bit, and we will attend to the boy—later." He was going to say "by and by" again, but paused just in time, with a laugh.

"Then *I* shall take him to the country all myself. I cannot wait for this hateful 'by and by.' I know how I shall do it, and at once. Now, now!" cried Fay, losing patience, and with an indignant glance at the lazy papa, who seemed going to sleep, she dashed out of the room, down many stairs, through the kitchen, startling Nanna and scattering the salad as if a whirlwind had gone by, and never paused for breath till she stood before the garden wall with a little hatchet in her hand.

"This shall be the country for him till I get enough money to send him away. I will show what *I* can do. He pulled out two bricks. *I* will beat down the wall, and he *shall* come in at once," panted Fay, and she gave a great blow at the bricks, bent on having her will without delay—for she was an impetuous little creature, full of love and pity for the poor boy pining for the fresh air and sunshine, of which she had so much.

Bang, bang, went the little hatchet, and down came one brick after another, till the hole was large enough for Fay to thrust her head through, and, being breathless by that time, she paused to rest and take a look at Johnny's court.

Meanwhile Nanna, having collected her lettuce leaves and her wits, went to see what the child was about and, finding her at work like a little fury, the old woman hurried up to tell "the Signor," Fay's papa, that his little daughter was about to destroy the garden and bury herself under the ruins of the wall. This report, delivered with groans and wringing of the hands, roused the artist and sent him to the rescue, as he well knew that his angel was a very energetic one and capable of great destruction.

When he arrived, he beheld a cloud of dust, a pile of bricks among the lilies, and the feet of his child sticking out of a large hole in the wall, while her head and shoulders were on the other side. Much amused, yet fearful that the stone coping might come down on her, he pulled her back with the assurance that he would listen and help her now immediately, if there was such need for haste.

But he grew sober when he saw Fay's face, for it was bathed in tears; her hands were bleeding, and dust covered her from head to foot.

"My darling, what afflicts you? Tell Papa, and he will do anything you wish."

"No, you will forget, you will say 'Wait,' and now that I have seen it all, I cannot stop till I get him out of that dreadful place. Look, look, and see if it is not sad to live there all in pain and darkness, and so poor."

As she spoke, Fay urged her father toward the hole. And to please her he looked, seeing the dull court, the noisy street beyond, and close by the low room, where Johnny's mother worked all day, while the poor boy's pale face was dimly seen as he lay on his bed waiting for deliverance.

"Well, well, it *is* a pitiful case and easily mended, since Fay is so eager about it. Hope the lad is all she says, and nothing catching about his illness. Nanna can tell me."

Then he drew back his head, and, leading Fay to the seat, took her on his knee, all flushed, dirty, and tearful as she was, soothing her by saying tenderly, "Now let me hear all about it, and be sure I'll not forget. What shall I do to please you, dear, before you pull down the house about my ears?"

Then Fay told her tale all over again; and, being no longer busy, her father found it very touching, with the dear, grimy little face looking into his, and the wounded hands clasped beseechingly as she pleaded for poor Johnny.

"God bless your tender heart, child; you shall have him in here tomorrow, and we will see what can be done for those pathetic legs of his. But listen, Fay, I have an easier way to do it than yours, and a grand surprise for the boy. Time is short, but it can be done; and to show you that I am in earnest, I will go this instant and begin the work. Come and wash your face while I get on my boots, and then we will go together."

At these words Fay threw her arms about Papa's neck and

gave him many grateful kisses, stopping in the midst to ask, "Truly *now?*"

"See if it is not so." And putting her down, Papa went off with great strides, while she ran laughing after him, all her doubts set at rest by this agreeable energy on his part.

If Johnny had not been asleep in the back room, he would have seen strange and pleasant sights that afternoon and evening, for something went on in the court that delighted his mother, amused the artist, and made Fay the happiest child in Boston. No one was to tell till the next day, that Johnny's surprise might be quite perfect, and Mrs. Morris sat up till eleven to get his old clothes in order, for Fay's papa had been to see her, and became interested in the boy, as no one could help being when they saw his patient little face.

So hammers rang, trowels scraped, shovels dug, and wonderful changes were made, while Fay danced about in the moonlight, like Puck intent upon some pretty prank, and Papa quoted Snout [1] the tinker's parting words, as appropriate to the hour,

> "Thus have I, Wall, my part dischargèd so;
> And, being done, thus Wall away doth go."

PART III

A lovely Sunday morning dawned without a cloud, and even in the dingy court the May sunshine shone warmly, and the spring breezes blew freshly from green fields far away. Johnny begged to go out, and, since he was much better, his mother consented, helping him to dress with such a bright face and eager hands that the boy said innocently, "How glad

[1] A character in Shakespeare's *Midsummer Night's Dream.*

you are when I get over a bad turn! I don't know what you'd
do if I ever got well."

"My poor dear, I begin to think you *will* pick up, now the
good weather has come and you have got a little friend to
play with. God bless her!"

Why his mother should suddenly hug him tight and then
brush his hair so carefully, with tears in her eyes, he did not
understand but was in such a hurry to get out, he could only
give her a good kiss and hobble away to see how his gallery
fared after the rain and to take a joyful "peek" at the enchanted garden.

Mrs. Morris kept close behind him, and it was well she did,
for he nearly tumbled down, so great was his surprise when
he beheld the old familiar wall after the good fairies Love
and Pity had worked their pretty miracle in the moonlight.

The ragged hole had changed to a little arched door,
painted red. On either side stood a green tub with a tall
oleander in full bloom; from the arch above hung a great
bunch of gay flowers, and before the threshold lay a letter
directed to "Signor Giovanni Morris," in a childish hand.

As soon as he recovered from the agreeable shock of this
splendid transformation scene, Johnny sank into his chair,
where a soft cushion had been placed, and read his note, with
little sighs of rapture at the charming prospect opening before him.

DEAR GIOVANNI,

Papa has made this nice gate so you can come in when you
like and not be tired. We are to have two keys, and no one else
can open it. A little bell is to ring when we pull the cord, and
we can run and see what we want. The paint is wet. Papa did it,
and the men put up the door last night. I helped them and did

not go in my bed till ten. It was very nice to do it so. I hope
you will like it. Come in as soon as you can; I am all ready.

Your friend,

FAY

"Mother, she must be a real fairy to do all that, mustn't
she?" said Johnny, leaning back to look at the dear door behind which lay such happiness for him.

"Yes, my sonny, she is the right sort of good fairy, and I
just wish I could do her washing for love the rest of her blessed
little life," answered Mrs. Morris, in a burst of grateful ardor.

"You shall! You shall! Do come in! I cannot wait another
minute!" cried an eager little voice as the red door flew open;
and there stood Fay, looking very like a happy elf in her
fresh white frock, a wreath of spring flowers on her pretty
hair, and a tall green wand in her hand, while the brilliant

bird sat on her shoulder, and the little white dog danced about her feet.

> "So she bids you to come in,
> With a dimple in your chin,
> Billy boy, Billy boy,"

sang the child, remembering how Johnny liked that song. And waving her wand, she went slowly backward as the boy, with a shining face, passed under the blooming arch into a new world, full of sunshine, liberty, and sweet companionship.

Neither Johnny nor his mother ever forgot that happy day, for it was the beginning of help and hope to both just when life seemed hardest and the future looked darkest.

Papa kept out of sight, but enjoyed peeps at the little party as they sat under the chestnuts, Nanna and Fay doing the honors of the garden to their guests with Italian grace and skill, while the poor mother folded her tired hands with unutterable content, and the boy looked like a happy soul in heaven.

Sabbath silence, broken only by the chime of bells and the feet of church-goers, brooded over the city; sunshine made golden shadows on the grass; the sweet wind brought spring odors from the woods; and every flower seemed to nod and beckon, as if welcoming the new playmate to their lovely home.

While the women talked together, Fay led Johnny up and down her little world, showing all her favorite nooks, making him rest often on the seats that stood all about and amusing him immensely by relating the various fanciful plays with which she beguiled her loneliness.

"Now we can have much nicer ones, for you will tell me yours, and we can do great things," she said, when she had displayed her big rocking horse; her grotto full of ferns; her mimic sea, where a fleet of toy boats lay at anchor in the basin of an old fountain; her fairyland under the lilacs, with paper elves sitting among the leaves; her swing, that tossed one high up among the green boughs; and the basket of white kittens, where Topaz, the yellow-eyed cat, now purred with maternal pride. Books were piled on the rustic table, and all the pictures Fay thought worthy to be seen.

Here also appeared a nice lunch, before the visitors could remember it was noon and tear themselves away. Such enchanted grapes and oranges Johnny never ate before; such delightful little tarts and Italian messes of various sorts; even the bread and butter seemed glorified because served in a plate trimmed with leaves and cut in dainty bits. Coffee that perfumed the air put heart into poor Mrs. Morris, who half starved herself that the boy might be fed, and he drank milk till Nanna said, laughing, as she refilled the pitcher, "He takes more than both the blessed lambs we used to feed for Saint Agnes in the convent at home. And he is truly welcome, the dear child, to the best we have, for he is as innocent and helpless as they."

"What does she mean?" whispered Johnny to Fay, rather abashed at having forgotten his manners in the satisfaction which three mugfuls of good milk had given him.

So, sitting in the big rustic chair beside him, Fay told the pretty story of the lambs who are dedicated to Saint Agnes, with ribbons tied to their snowy wool, and then raised with care till their fleeces are shorn to make garments for the Pope. A fit tale for the day, the child thought, and went on to tell about the wonders of Rome till Johnny's head was filled with a splendid confusion of new ideas, in which Saint Peter's and appletarts, holy lambs and red doors, ancient images and dear little girls were delightfully mixed. It all seemed like a fairy tale, and nothing was too wonderful or lovely to happen on that memorable day.

So when Fay's papa at last appeared, finding it impossible to keep away from the happy little party any longer, Johnny decided at once that the handsome man in the velvet coat was the king of the enchanted land and gazed at him with reverence and awe. A most gracious king he proved to be, for, after talking pleasantly to Mrs. Morris, and joking Fay on storming the walls, he proposed to carry Johnny off and, catching him up, strode away with the astonished boy on his shoulder, while the little girl danced before to open doors and clear the way.

Johnny thought he couldn't be surprised any more, but when he had mounted many stairs and found himself in a great room with a glass roof, full of rich curtains, strange armor, pretty things, and pictures everywhere, he just sat in the big chair where he was placed and stared in silent delight.

"This is Papa's studio, and that, the famous picture, and here is where I work, and isn't it pleasant? And aren't you glad to see it?" said Fay, skipping about to do the honors of the place.

"I don't believe heaven is beautifuller," answered Johnny, in a low tone, as his eyes went from the green treetops peeping in at the windows to the great sunny picture of a Roman garden, with pretty children at play among the crumbling statues and fountains.

"I'm glad you like it, for we mean to have you come here a great deal. I sit to Papa very often and get *so* tired; and you can talk to me, and then you can see me draw and model in clay, and then we'll go in the garden, and Nanna will show you how to make baskets, and *then* we'll play."

Johnny nodded and beamed at this charming prospect and for an hour explored the mysteries of the studio, with Fay for a guide and Papa for an amused spectator. He liked the boy more and more and was glad Fay had so harmless a play-mate to expend her energies and compassion upon. He as-sented to every plan proposed and really hoped to be able to help these poor neighbors, for he had a kind heart and loved his little daughter even more than his art.

When at last Mrs. Morris found courage to call Johnny away, he went without a word and lay down in the dingy room, his face still shining with the happy thoughts that filled his mind, hungry for just such pleasures and never fed before.

After that day everything went smoothly, and both children blossomed like the flowers in that pleasant garden, where the magic of love and pity, fresh air and sunshine, soon worked miracles. Fay learned patience and gentleness from Johnny; he grew daily stronger on the better food Nanna gave him and the exercise he was tempted to take; and both spent very happy days working and playing, sometimes under the trees, where the pretty baskets were made, or in the studio, where both pairs of small hands modeled graceful things in clay or daubed amazing pictures with the artist's old brushes and discarded canvases.

Mrs. Morris washed everything washable in the house and did up Fay's frocks so daintily that she looked more like an elf than ever when her head shone out from the fluted frills, like the yellow middle of a daisy with its white petals all spread.

As he watched the children playing together, the artist, hav-ing no great work in hand, made several pretty sketches of them and then had a fine idea of painting the garden scene where Fay first talked to Johnny. It pleased his fancy, and the little people sat for him nicely; so he made a charming thing of it, putting in the cat, dog, bird, and toad as the various characters in Shakespeare's lovely play, while the flowers were the elves, peeping and listening in all manner of merry, pretty ways.

He called it "Little Pyramus and Thisbe," and it so pleased a certain rich lady that she paid a large price for it, and then, discovering that it told a true story, she generously added enough to send Johnny and his mother to the country, when Fay and her father were ready to go.

But it was to a lovelier land than the boy had ever read of in his fairy books, and to a happier life than mending shoes in the dingy court. In the autumn they all sailed gaily away together, to live for years in sunny Italy, where Johnny grew tall and strong and learned to paint with a kind master and a faithful friend, who always rejoiced that she found and delivered him, thanks to the wonderful hole in the wall.

Baa! Baa!

BAA THE FIRST

They didn't look at all like heroines, those two shabby little
girls, as they trotted down the hill, leaving a cloud of dust
behind them. Their bare feet were scratched and brown, their
hands were red with berry stains, and their freckled faces
shone with heat under the flapping sunbonnets. But Patty
and Tilda were going to do a fine piece of work, although
they did not know it then, and were very full of their own

small affairs as they went briskly toward the station to sell berries.

The tongues went as fast as the feet, for this was a great expedition, and both were much excited about it.

"Don't they look lovely?" said Tilda, proudly surveying her sister's load as she paused to change a heavy pail from one arm to the other.

"Perfectly de-licious! I know folks will buy 'em, if we ain't too scared to offer 'em," answered Patty, stopping also to settle the two dozen little birch baskets full of red raspberries which she carried, prettily set forth, on an old waiter,[1] trimmed with scarlet bunchberries, white everlasting, and green leaves.

"I shan't be. I'll go right along and holler real loud, see if I don't. I'm bound to have our books and boots for next winter, so just keep thinking how nice they'll be and push ahead," said stouthearted Tilda, the leader of the expedition.

"Hurry up. I want to have time to sprinkle the posies, so they'll look fresh when the train comes. I hope there'll be lots of children in it; they always want to eat, Ma says."

"It was real mean of Elviry Morris to go and offer to sell cheaper up to the hotel than we did and spoil our market. Guess she'll wish she'd thought of this when we tell what we've done down here." And both children laughed with satisfaction as they trudged along, never minding the two hot, dusty miles they had to go.

The station was out of the village, and the long trains carrying summer travellers to the mountains stopped there once a day to meet the stages for different places. It was a pleasant spot, with a great pond on one side, deep forests on the other, and in the distance glimpses of gray peaks or green slopes inviting the weary city people to come and rest.

[1] That is, a tray. *Ed.*

Everyone seemed glad to get out during the ten minutes' pause, even if their journey was not yet ended; and while they stood about, enjoying the the fresh air from the pond, or watching the stages load up, Tilda and Patty planned to offer their tempting little baskets of fresh fruit and flowers. It was a great effort, and their hearts beat with childish hope and fear as they came in sight of the station, with no one about but the jolly stage drivers lounging in the shade.

"Plenty of time. Let's go to the pond and wash off the dust and get a drink. Folks won't see us behind those cars," said Tilda, glad to slip out of sight till the train arrived, for even her courage seemed to ooze away as the important moment approached.

A long cattle train stood on a side track waiting for the other one to pass, and, while the little girls splashed their feet in the cool water or drank from their hands, a pitiful sound filled the air. Hundreds of sheep, closely packed in the cars and suffering agonies from dust and heat and thirst, thrust their poor noses through the bars, bleating frantically, for the sight of all that water, so near yet so impossible to reach, drove them wild. Those farther down the track, who could not see the blue lake, could smell it and took up the cry till the woods echoed with it, and even the careless drivers said, with a glance of pity, "Hard on the poor critters this hot day, ain't it?"

"Oh, Tilda, hear 'em baa, and see 'em crowd this side to get at the water! Let's take 'em some in our pickin' dishes. It's so dreadful to be dry," said tenderhearted Patty, filling her pint cup and running to offer it to the nearest pathetic nose outstretched to meet it. A dozen thirsty tongues tried to lap it and in the struggle the little cup was soon emptied, but Patty ran for more, and Tilda did the same, both getting so excited over the distress of the poor creatures that they never heard the far-off whistle of their train and continued running to and fro on their errand of mercy, careless of their own weary feet, hot faces, and the precious flowers withering in the sun.

They did not see a party of people sitting nearby under the trees, who watched them and listened to their eager talk with smiling interest.

"Run, Patty; this poor little one is half dead. Throw some water in his face while I make this big one stop walking on him. Oh, dear! There are so many! We can't help half, and our mugs are so small!"

"I know what I'll do, Tilda; tip out the berries into my apron and bring up a nice lot at once," cried Patty, half beside herself with pity.

"It will spoil your apron and mash the berries, but never mind. I don't care if we don't sell one if we can help these poor dear lammies," answered energetic Tilda, dashing into the pond up to her ankles to fill the pail, while Patty piled up the fruit in her plaid apron.

"Oh, my patience me! The train is coming!" cried Patty, as a shrill shriek woke the echoes and an approaching rumble was heard.

"Let it come. I won't leave this sheep till it's better. You go and sell the first lot; I'll come as quick as I can," commanded Tilda, so busy reviving the exhausted animal that she could not stop even to begin the cherished new plan.

"I don't dare go alone; you come and call out, and I'll hold the waiter," quavered poor Patty, looking sadly scared as the long train rolled by with a head at every window.

"Don't be a goose. Stay here and work, then; I'll go and sell every basket. I'm so mad about these poor things, I ain't afraid of anybody," cried Tilda, with a last refreshing splash among the few favored sheep, as she caught up the tray and marched off to the platform—a very hot, wet, shabby little girl, but with a breast full of the just indignation and tender pity that go to redress half the wrongs of this great world.

"Oh, Mamma, see the pretty baskets! Do buy some, I'm so thirsty and tired," exclaimed more than one eager little traveller, as Tilda held up her tray, crying bravely, "Fresh berries! Fresh berries! Ten cents! Only ten cents!"

They were all gone in ten minutes, and, if Patty had been with her, the pail might have been emptied before the train left. But the other little Samaritan was hard at work, and, when her sister joined her, proudly displaying a handful of silver, she was prouder still to show her woolly invalid feebly nibbling grass from her hand.

"We might have sold every one—folks liked 'em ever so much, and next time we'll have two dozen baskets apiece. But we'll have to be spry, for some of the children fuss about picking out the one they like. It's real fun, Patty," said Tilda, tying up the precious dimes in a corner of her dingy little handkerchief.

"So's this," answered the other, with a last loving pat of her patient's nose, as the train began to move, and car after car of suffering sheep passed them with plaintive cries and vain efforts to reach the blessed water of which they were in such dreadful need.

Poor Patty couldn't bear it. She was hot, tired, and unhappy because she could do so little, and, when her pitying eyes lost sight of that load of misery, she just sat down and cried.

But Tilda scolded as she carefully put the unsold berries back into the pail, still unconscious of the people behind the elder bushes by the pond.

"That's the wickedest thing that ever was, and I just wish I was a man, so I could see about it. I'd put all the railroad folks in those cars and keep 'em there hours and hours and hours, going by ponds all the time; and I'd have ice cream, too, where they couldn't get a bit, and lots of fans, and other folks all cool and comfortable, never caring how hot and tired and thirsty they were. Yes, I would! And then we'd see how *they* like it."

Here indignant Tilda had to stop for breath, and refreshed herself by sucking berry juice off her fingers.

"We *must* do something about it. I can't be happy to think of those poor lammies going so far without any water. It's awful to be dry," sobbed Patty, drinking her own tears as they fell.

"If I had a hose, I'd come every day and hose all over the cars; that would do some good. Anyway, we'll bring the other big pail and water all we can," said Tilda, whose active brain was always ready with a plan.

"Then we shan't sell our berries," began Patty, despondently, for all the world was saddened to her just then by the sight she had seen.

"We'll come earlier, and both work real hard till our train is in. Then I'll sell, and you go on watering with both pails. It's hard work, but we can take turns. What ever shall we do with all these berries? The under ones are smashed, so we'll eat 'em, but these are nice; only who will buy 'em?" And Tilda looked soberly at the spoiled apron and the four quarts of raspberries picked with so much care in the hot sun.

"I will," said a pleasant voice, and a young lady came out from the bushes just as the good fairy appears to the maidens in old tales.

Both little girls started and stared and were covered with

confusion when other heads popped up, and a stout gentleman came toward them, smiling so good-naturedly that they were not afraid.

"We are having a picnic in the woods and would like these nice berries for our supper, if you want to sell them," said the lady, holding out a pretty basket.

"Yes, ma'am, we do. You can have 'em all. They're a little mashed, so we won't ask but ten cents a quart, though we expected to get twelve," said Tilda, who was a real Yankee and had an eye to business.

"What do you charge for watering the sheep?" asked the stout gentleman, looking kindly at Patty, who at once retired into the depths of her sunbonnet, like a snail into its shell.

"Nothing, sir. Wasn't it horrid to see those poor things? That's what made her cry. She's real tenderhearted, and she couldn't bear it, so we let the berries go and did what we could," answered Tilda, with such an earnest little face that it looked pretty in spite of tan and freckles and dust.

"Yes, it was very sad, and we must see about it. Here's something to pay for the berries, also for the water." And the gentleman threw a bright half-dollar into Tilda's lap and another into Patty's, just as if he were used to tossing money about in that delightful manner.

The little girls didn't know what to say to him, but they beamed at everyone and surveyed the pretty silver pieces as if they were very precious in their sight.

"What will you do with them?" asked the lady, in the friendly sort of voice that always gets a ready answer.

"Oh, we are saving up to buy books and rubber boots, so we can go to school next winter. We live two miles from school and wear out lots of boots and get colds when it's wet. We had *Pewmonia* last spring, and Ma said we *must* have rubber boots, and we might earn 'em in berry time," said Tilda eagerly.

"Yes, and *she's* real smart, and *she's* going to be promoted and *must* have new books, and they cost so much, and Ma ain't rich, so we get 'em ourselves," added sister Patty, forgetting bashfulness in sisterly pride.

"That's brave. How much will it take for the boots and the books?" asked the lady, with a glance at the old gentleman, who was eating berries out of her basket.

"As much as five dollars, I guess. We want to get a shawl for Ma, so she can go to meetin'. It's a secret, and we pick every day real hard, 'cause berries don't last long," said Tilda wisely.

"*She* thought of coming down here. We felt so bad about losing our place at the hotel and didn't know what to do, till Tilda made this plan. I think it's a splendid one." And Patty eyed her half-dollar with immense satisfaction.

"Don't spoil the plan, Alice. I'm passing every week while you are up here, and I'll see to the success of the affair," said the old gentleman, with a nod, adding, in a louder tone, "These are very fine berries, and I want you to take four quarts every other day to Miller's farm over there. You know the place?"

"Yes, sir! Yes, sir!" cried two eager voices, for the children felt as if a rain of half-dollars was about to set in.

"I come up every Saturday and go down Monday; and I shall look out for you here, and you can water the sheep as much as you like. They need it, poor beasts!" added the old gentleman.

"We will, sir! We will!" cried the children, with faces so full of innocent gratitude and good will that the young lady stooped and kissed them both.

"Now, my dear, we must be off, and not keep our friends waiting any longer," said the old gentleman, turning toward the heads still bobbing about behind the bushes.

"Good-by, good-by. We won't forget the berries and the sheep," called the children, waving the stained apron like a banner and showing every white tooth in the beaming smiles they sent after these new friends.

"Nor I my lambs," said Alice to herself, as she followed her father to the boat.

"What will Ma say when we tell her and show her this heap of money!" exclaimed Tilda, pouring the dimes into her lap and rapturously chinking the big half-dollars before she tied them all up again.

"I hope we shan't be robbed going home. You'd better hide it in your breast, else someone might see it," said prudent Patty, oppressed by the responsibility of so much wealth.

"There goes the boat!" cried Tilda. "Don't it look lovely? Those are the nicest folks I ever saw."

"She's perfectly elegant. I'd like a white dress and a hat just like that. When she kissed me, the long feather was as soft as a bird's wing on my cheeks, and her hair was all curling round like the picture we cut out of the paper." And Patty gazed after the boat as if this little touch of romance in her hard-working life was delightful to her.

"They must be awful rich, to want so many berries. We shall have to fly round to get enough for them and the car folks, too. Let's go right off now to that thick place we left this morning, else Elviry may get ahead of us," said practical Tilda, jumping up, ready to make hay while the sun shone. But neither of them dreamed what a fine crop they were to get in that summer, all owing to their readiness in answering that pitiful "Baa! Baa!"

BAA THE SECOND

A very warm and very busy week followed, for the berries were punctually delivered at the farm and successfully sold at the station; and, best of all, the sheep were as faithfully watered as two little pails and two little girls could do it. Everyone else forgot them. Mr. Benson was a busy old gentleman far away in the city; Miss Alice was driving, boating, and picnicking all day long; and the men at the depot had no orders to care for the poor beasts. But Tilda and Patty never forgot, and, rain or shine, they were there when the long train came in, waiting to do what they could, with dripping pails, handfuls of grass, or green branches to refresh these suffering travellers for whom no thought was taken.

The rough stage drivers laughed at them, the brakemen ordered them away, and the station master said they were "little fools"; but nothing daunted the small sisters of charity, and in a few days they were let alone. Their arms were very tired lifting the pails, their backs ached with lugging so much water, and mother would not let them wear any but their oldest clothes for such wet work, so they had their trials but bore them bravely and never expected to be thanked.

When Saturday came around, and Miss Alice drove to meet her father, she remembered the little girls and looked for them. Up at the farm she enjoyed her berries and ordered them to be promptly paid for, but was either asleep or away when they arrived and so had not seen the children. The sight of Patty, hastily scrambling a clean apron over her old frock, as she waited for the train with her tray of fruit, made the young lady leave the phaeton and go to meet the child, asking, with a smile, "Where is the black-eyed sister? Not ill, I hope?"

"No, ma'am; she's watering the sheep. She's so strong she does it better'n I do, and I sell the baskets," answered Patty, rejoicing secretly in the clean faded apron that hid her shabbiness.

"Ah, I forgot *my* lambs, but you were faithful to yours, you good little things! Have you done it every day?"

"Yes, ma'am. Ma said, if we promised, we *must* do it, and we like it. Only there's such a lot of 'em, and we get pretty tired." And Patty rubbed her arms as if they ached.

"I'll speak to Papa about it this very day. It will be a good time, for Mr. Jacobs, the president of the railroad, is coming up to spend Sunday, and they must do something for the poor beasts," said Miss Alice, ashamed to be outdone by two little girls.

"That will be so nice. We read a piece in a paper our teacher lends us, and I brought it down to show Mr. Weed, the depot man. He said it was a shame, but nobody could help it, so we thought we'd tell him about the law we found." And Patty eagerly drew a worn copy of "Our Dumb Animals" from her pocket to show the little paragraph to this all-powerful friend who knew the railroad king.

Miss Alice read, "An act of Congress provides that at the end of every twenty-eight hours' journey animals shall be given five hours' rest, and duly fed and watered, unless shipped in cars having accommodations for the care of livestock on board."

"There!" cried Patty. "That's the law, and Ma says these sheep come ever so far and ought to be watered. Do tell the president, and ask him to see to it. There was another piece about some poor pigs and cows being ninety-two hours without water and food. It was awful."

"I *will* tell him. Here's our train. Run to your berries. I'll find Papa, and show him this."

As Miss Alice spoke, the cars thundered into the little station and a brief bustle ensued, during which Patty was too busy to see what happened.

Mr. Benson and another stout old gentleman got out; and the minute Miss Alice had been kissed, she said very earnestly, "Wait a little, please; I want to settle a very important piece of business before we go home."

Then, while the gentlemen listened indulgently, she told the story, showed the bit in the paper, and, pointing out Patty, added warmly, "That's one good child. Come and see the other, and you will agree with me that something ought to be done to relieve their kind little hearts and arms, if not out of mercy to the animals, who can't be called dumb in this case, though *we* have been deaf too long."

"My wilful girl must have her way. Come and get a whiff of fresh air, Jacobs." And Mr. Benson followed his daughter across the track, glad to get out of the bustle.

Yes, Tilda was there and at work so energetically that they dared not approach but stood looking and laughing for a moment. Two pails of water stood near her, and with a long-handled dipper she was serving all she could reach. Those which were packed on the upper tier she could only refresh by a well-aimed splash, which was eagerly welcomed and much enjoyed by all parties—for Tilda got well showered herself but did not care a bit, for it was a melting July day.

"That is a very little thing to do, but it is the cup of cold water which *we* have forgotten, said Miss Alice softly, while the air was full of cries of longing as the blue lake shone before the thirsty beasts.

"Jacobs, we must attend to this."

"Benson, we will. I'll look into the matter and report at the next meeting."

That was all they said, but Alice clapped her hands, for she knew the thing would be done and smiled like sunshine on the two old gentlemen, who presently watched the long train rumble away, with shakes and nods of the gray heads, which expressed both pity and determination.

The other train soon followed, and Patty came running over with her empty tray and a handful of silver to join Tilda, who sat down upon her upturned pail, tired out.

"Papa will see to it, children, and, thanks to you, the sheep will soon be more comfortable," said Miss Alice, joining them.

"Oh, goody! I hope they'll be quick; it's so hot, there's ever so many dead ones today, and I can't help 'em," answered Tilda, fanning herself with her bonnet and wiping the drops off her red face.

Miss Alice took a pretty straw fan out of her pocket and handed it to her, with a look of respect for the faithful little soul who did her duty so well.

"Ask for me when you come to the farm tonight. I shall have some hats and aprons for you, and I want to know you better," she said, remembering the broadbrimmed hats and ready-made aprons in the village store.

"Thank you, ma'am. We'll come. Now we won't have to do this wet work, we'd like to be neat and nice," said Patty gratefully.

"Do you always sell all your berries down here?" asked Miss Alice, watching Tilda tie up the dimes.

"Yes, indeed, and we could sell more if both of us went. But Ma said we were making lots of money, and it wasn't best to get rich too fast," answered Tilda wisely.

"That's a good thing for us to remember, Benson, especially just now, and not count the cost of this little improvement in our cattle cars too closely," said Mr. Jacobs, as the old gentlemen came up in time to hear Tilda's speech.

"Your mother is a remarkable woman; I must come and see her," added Mr. Benson.

"Yes, sir; she is. She'd be pleased to see you any day." And Tilda stood up respectfully as her elders addressed her.

"Getting too rich are you? Then I suppose it wouldn't do to ask you to invest this in your business for me?" asked Mr. Jacobs, holding up two silver dollars, as if he felt bashful about offering them.

Two pairs of eyes sparkled, and Patty's hand went out involuntarily as she thought how many things she could get with all that money.

"Would they buy a lamb? And would you like to use it that way?" asked Tilda, in a business-like tone.

"I guess Miller would let you have one for that sum if Miss Alice makes the bargain, and I *should* very much like to start a flock if you would attend to it for me," answered Mr. Jacobs, with a laughing nod at the young lady, who seemed to understand that way of making bargains.

"We'd like it ever so much! We've wanted a lamb all summer, and we've got a nice rocky pasture, with lots of pennyroyal and berry bushes and a brook, for it to live in. We could get one ourselves now we are so rich, but we'd rather buy more things for Ma and mend the roof 'fore the snow comes. It's so old, rain runs down on our bed sometimes."

"That's bad, but you seem fond of water and look as if it agreed with you," said Mr. Jacobs, playfully poking Tilda's soaked apron with his cane.

They all laughed, and Mr. Benson said, looking at his watch, "Come, Alice, we must go. I want my dinner and so does Jacobs. Good-by, little water-witches. I'll see you again."

"Do you s'pose they'll remember the lambs and hats, and all they promised?" asked Patty, as the others turned away.

"I don't believe they will. Rich folks are so busy having good times they are apt to forget poor folks, seems to me," answered Tilda, shaking her head like a little Solomon.

"Bless my heart, what a sharp child that is! We must not disappoint her; so remind me, Alice, to make a memorandum of all this business," whispered Mr. Benson, who heard every word.

"The president is a *very* nice man, and I know *he*'ll keep his word. See! He dropped the money in my tray, and I never saw him do it," cried Patty, pouncing on the dollars like a robin on a worm.

"There's a compliment for you, and well worth the money. Such confidence is beautiful," said Mr. Jacobs, laughing.

"Well, I've learned a little lesson, and I'll lay it to heart so well I won't let either of you forget," added Alice, as they drove away, while Tilda and Patty trudged home, quite unconscious that they had set an example which their elders were not ashamed to follow.

So many delightful things happened after this that the children felt as if they had got into a fairy tale. First of all, two nice rough straw hats and four useful aprons were given them that very night. Next day Miss Alice went to see their mother and found an excellent woman, trying to bring up her girls, with no one to help her.

Then somehow the roof got mended, and the fence, so that passing cattle could not devastate the little beds where the children carefully cultivated wild flowers from the woods and hills. There seemed to be a sudden call for berries in the neighborhood, for the story of the small Samaritans went about, and, even while they laughed, people felt an interest in the children and were glad to help them; so the dimes in the spoutless teapot rose like a silver tide, and visions of new gowns, and maybe sleds, danced through the busy little brains.

But best and most wonderful of all, the old gentlemen did *not* forget the sheep. It was astonishing how quickly and easily it was all done, when once those who had the power found both the will and the way. Everyone was interested now: the stage drivers joked no more, the brakemen lent a hand with the buckets while waiting for better means of relief, and cross Mr. Weed patted Tilda and Patty on the head and pointed them out to strangers as the "nice little girls who stirred up the railroad folks." Children from the hotel came to look at them, and Elviry Morris was filled with regret that she had no share in this interesting affair.

Thus the little pail of water they offered for pity's sake kept the memory of this much-needed mercy green till the lake poured its full tide along the channel made for it, and there was no more suffering on that road.

The first day the new pumps were tried everyone went to see them work; and earliest of all were Tilda and Patty, in pink aprons and wreaths of evergreens round their new hats in honor of the day. It was sweet to see their intense satisfaction as the water streamed into the troughs, and the thirsty sheep drank so gratefully. The innocent little souls did not know how many approving glances were cast upon them as they sat on a log, with the tired arms folded, two trays of berries at their feet now, and two faces beaming with the joy of a great hope beautifully fulfilled.

Presently a party from the hotel appeared, and something

was evidently going to happen, for the boys and girls kept dodging behind the cars to see if they were coming. Tilda and Patty wondered who or what but kept modestly apart upon their log, glad to see that the fine folks enjoyed the sight about as much as they did.

A rattle was heard along the road; a wagon stopped behind the station; and an excited boy came flying over the track to make the mysterious announcement to the other children, "They've got 'em, and they are regular beauties."

"More pumps or troughs, I guess. Well, we can't have too

many," said Tilda, with an eye to the business under way.

"I wish those folks wouldn't stare so. I s'pose it's the new aprons with pockets," whispered bashful Patty, longing for the old sunbonnet to retire into.

But both forgot pumps and pockets in a moment as a striking procession appeared around the corner. Mr. Benson, trying not to laugh but shining with heat and fun, led a very white lamb with a red bow on its neck; behind him came Miss Alice, leading another lamb with a blue bow. She looked very much in earnest, and more like a good fairy than ever, as she carried out her little surprise. People looked and laughed; but everyone semed to understand the joke at once, and was very quiet when Mr. Benson held up his hand and said, in a voice which was earnest as well as merry, "Here, my little girls, are two friends of those poor fellows yonder come to thank you for your pity and to prove, I hope, that rich people are not always too busy with their own good times to remember their poorer neighbors. Take them, my dears, and God bless you!"

"I didn't forget my lambs this time but have been taming these for you, and Mr. Jacobs begs you will accept them, with his love," added Miss Alice, as the two pretty creatures were led up to their new owners, wagging their tails and working their noses in the most amiable manner, though evidently much amazed at the scene.

Tilda and Patty were so surprised that they were dumb with delight and could only blush and pat the woolly heads, feeling more like storybook girls than ever. The other children, charmed with this pleasant ending to the pretty story, set up a cheer; the men joined in it with a will, while the ladies waved their parasols, and all the sheep seemed to add to the chorus their grateful "Baa! Baa!"

The Silver Party

"Such a long morning! Seems as if dinnertime would *never* come!" sighed Tony, as he wandered into the dining room for a third pick at the nuts and raisins to beguile his weariness with a little mischief.

It was Thanksgiving Day. All the family were at church, all the servants busy preparing for the great dinner; and so poor Tony, who had a cold, had not only to stay at home, but to amuse himself while the rest said their prayers, made calls, or took a brisk walk to get an appetite. If he had been allowed in the kitchen, he would have been quite happy, but cook was busy and cross and rapped him on the head with a poker when he ventured near the door. Peeping through the slide [that opened to the kitchen] was also forbidden, and John, the man, bribed him with an orange to keep out of the way till the table was set.

That was now done. The dining room was empty and quiet, and poor Tony lay down on the sofa to eat his nuts and admire the fine sight before him. All the best damask, china, glass, and silver was set forth with great care. A basket of flowers hung from the chandelier, and the sideboard was beautiful to behold with piled-up fruit, dishes of cake, and many-colored finger bowls and glasses.

"That's all very nice, but the eating part is what *I* care for. Don't believe I'll get my share today, because Mamma found out about this horrid cold. A fellow can't help sneezing, though he *can* hide a sore throat. Oh, hum! Nearly two more hours to wait," and, with a long sigh, Tony closed his eyes for a luxurious yawn.

When he opened them, the strange sight he beheld kept him staring without a thought of sleep. The big soup ladle stood straight up at the head of the table with a face plainly to be seen in the bright bowl. It was a very heavy, handsome old ladle, so the face was old, but round and jolly, and the long handle stood very erect, like a tall, thin gentleman with a big head.

"Well, upon my word that's queer!" said Tony, sitting up also and wondering what would happen next.

To his great amazement the ladle began to address the assembled forks and spoons in a silvery tone very pleasant to hear.

"Ladies and gentlemen, at this festive season it is proper that we should enjoy ourselves. As we shall be tired after dinner, we will at once begin our sports by a grand promenade. Take partners and fall in!"

At these words a general uprising took place, and before Tony could get his breath a long procession of forks and spoons stood ready. The finger bowls struck up an airy tune as if invisible wet fingers were making music on their rims, and, led by the stately ladle like a drum major, the grand march began. The forks were the gentlemen, tall, slender, and with a fine curve to their backs; the spoons were the ladies, with full skirts, and the scallops on the handles stood up like silver combs; the large ones were the mamas, the teaspoons were the young ladies, and the little salts, the children. It was sweet to see the small things walk at the end of the procession, with the two silver rests for the carving knife and fork trotting behind like pet dogs. The mustard spoon and pickle fork went together, and quarreled all the way, both being hot-tempered and sharp-tongued. The steel knives looked on, for this was a very aristocratic party, and only the silver people could join in it.

"Here's fun!" thought Tony, staring with all his might, and so much interested in this remarkable state of things that he forgot hunger and time altogether.

Round and round went the glittering train, to the soft music of the many-toned finger bowls, till three turns about the long oval table had been made; then all fell into line for a country-dance, as in the good old times before everyone took to spinning like tops. Grandpa Ladle led off with his oldest daughter, Madam Gravy Ladle, and the little salts stood at the bottom prancing like real children impatient for their turn. When it came, they went down the middle in fine style, with a cling! clang! that made Tony's legs quiver with a longing to join in.

It was beautiful to see the older ones twirl round in a stately way, with bows and courtesies at the end, while the teaspoons and small forks romped a good deal, and Mr. Pickle and Miss Mustard kept everyone laughing at their smart speeches. The silver butter knife, who was an invalid, having broken her back and been mended, lay in the rack and smiled sweetly down upon her friends, while the little Cupid on the lid of the butter dish pirouetted on one toe in the most delightful manner.

When everyone had gone through the dance, the napkins were arranged as sofas, and the spoons rested, while the polite forks brought sprigs of celery to fan them with. The little salts got into Grandpa's lap, and the silver dogs lay down panting, for they had frisked with the children. They all talked, and Tony could not help wondering if real ladies said such things when they put *their* heads together and nodded and whispered, for some of the remarks were so personal that he was much confused. Fortunately they took no notice of him, so he listened and learned something in this queer way.

"I have been in this family a hundred years," began the soup ladle, "and it seems to me that each generation is worse than the last. My first master was punctual to a minute, and madam was always down beforehand to see that all was ready. Now master comes at all hours, mistress lets the servants do as they like, and the manners of the children are very bad. Sad state of things, very sad!"

"Dear me, yes!" sighed one of the large spoons; "we don't see such nice housekeeping now as we did when we were young. Girls were taught all about it then, but now it is all books or parties, and few of them know a skimmer from a gridiron."

"Well, I'm sure the poor things are much happier than if they were messing about in kitchens as girls used to do in your day. It is much better for them to be dancing, skating, and studying than wasting their young lives darning and preserving and sitting by their mammas as prim as dishes. *I* prefer the present way of doing things, though the girls in this family *do* sit up too late, and wear too high heels to their boots."

The mustard spoon spoke in a pert tone, and the pickle fork answered sharply, "I agree with you, cousin. The boys also sit up too late. I'm tired of being waked to fish out olives or pickles for those fellows when they come in from the theatre or some dance; and as for that Tony, he is a real pig —eats everything he can lay hands on and is the torment of the maid's life."

"Yes," cried one little salt spoon, "we saw him steal cake out of the sideboard, and he never told when his mother scolded Norah."

"So mean!" added the other, and both the round faces were so full of disgust that Tony fell flat and shut his eyes as if asleep to hide his confusion. Someone laughed, but he dared not look and lay blushing and listening to remarks which plainly proved how careful we should be of our acts and words even when alone, for who knows what apparently dumb thing may be watching us.

"I have observed that Mr. Murry reads the paper at table instead of talking to his family, that Mrs. Murry worries about the servants, the girls gossip and giggle, the boys eat and plague one another, and that small child Nelly teases for all she sees and is never quiet till she gets the sugar bowl," said Grandpa Ladle, in a tone of regret. "Now, useful and pleasant chat at table would make meals delightful, instead of being scenes of confusion and discomfort."

"I bite their tongues when I get a chance, hoping to make them witty or to check unkind words, but they only sputter and get a lecture from Aunt Maria, who is a sour old spinster, always criticizing her neighbors."

As the mustard spoon spoke, the teaspoons laughed as if they thought *her* rather like Aunt Maria in that respect.

"I gave the baby a fit of colic to teach her to let pickles alone, but no one thanked me," said the pickle fork.

"Perhaps if we keep ourselves so bright that those who use us can see their faces in us, we shall be able to help them a little, for no one likes to see an ugly face or a dull spoon. The art of changing frowns to smiles is never old-fashioned, and lovely manners smooth away the little worries of life beautifully." A silvery voice spoke, and all looked respectfully at Madam Gravy Ladle, who was a very fine old spoon, with a coat of arms and a polish that all envied.

"People can't always be remembering how old and valuable and bright they are. Here in America we just go ahead and make manners and money for ourselves. *I* don't stop to ask what dish I'm going to help to; I just pitch in and take all I can hold and don't care a bit whether I shine or not. My grandfather was a kitchen spoon, but I'm smarter than he was, thanks to my plating, and look and feel as good as anyone, though I haven't got stags' heads and big letters on my handle."

No one answered these impertinent remarks of the sauce spoon, for all knew that she was not pure silver and was only used on occasions when many spoons were needed. Tony was ashamed to hear her talk in that rude way to the fine old silver he was so proud of and resolved he'd give the saucy spoon a good rap when he helped himself to the cranberry.

An impressive silence lasted till a lively fork exclaimed, as the clock struck, "Everyone is coasting out of doors. Why not have our share of the fun inside? It is very fashionable this winter, and ladies and gentlmen of the best families do it, I assure you."

"We will!" cried the other forks, and, as the dowagers did not object, all fell to work to arrange the table for this agreeable sport. Tony sat up to see how they would manage and was astonished at the ingenuity of the silver people. With a great clinking and rattling they ran to and fro, dragging the stiff white mats about; the largest they leaned up against the tall caster, and laid the rest in a long slope to the edge of

the table, where a pile of napkins made a nice snowdrift to
tumble into.

"What *will* they do for sleds?" thought Tony, and the next
minute chuckled when he saw them take the slices of bread
laid at each place, pile on, and spin away, with a great scattering of crumbs like snowflakes and much laughter as they
landed in the white pile at the end of the coast.

"Won't John give it to 'em if he comes in and catches 'em
turning his nice table topsy-turvy!" said the boy to himself,
hoping nothing would happen to end this jolly frolic. So he
kept very still and watched the gay forks and spoons climb up
and whiz down till they were tired. The little salts got Baby
Nell's own small slice and had lovely times on a short coast of
their own made of one mat held up by Grandpa, who smiled
benevolently at the fun, being too old and heavy to join in it.

They kept it up until the slices were worn thin, and one
or two upsets alarmed the ladies; then they rested and con-
versed again. The mammas talked about their children, how
sadly the silver basket needed a new lining, and what there
was to be for dinner. The teaspoons whispered sweetly together, as young ladies do—one declaring that rouge powder
was not as good as it used to be, another lamenting the sad
effect upon her complexion, and all smiled amiably upon the
forks, who stood about discussing wines and cigars, for both
lived in the sideboard and were brought out after dinner, so
the forks knew a great deal about such matters and found
them very interesting, as all gentlemen seem to do.

Presently someone mentioned bicycles, and what fine rides
the boys of the family told about. The other fellows proposed
a race; and before Tony could grasp the possibility of such a
thing, it was done. Nothing easier, for there stood a pile of
plates, and just turning them on their edges, the forks got

astride, and the big wheels spun away as if a whole bicycle club had suddenly arrived.

Old Pickle took the baby's plate, as better suited to his size. The little salts made a tricycle of napkin rings and rode gaily off, with the dogs barking after them. Even the carving fork, though not invited, could not resist the exciting sport, and tipping up the wooden bread platter, went whizzing off at a great pace, for his two prongs were better than four, and his wheel was lighter than the china ones. Grandpapa Ladle cheered them on, like a fine old gentlemen as he was, for, though the new craze rather astonished him, he liked manly sports and would have taken a turn if his dignity and age had allowed. The ladies chimed their applause, for it really was immensely exciting to see fourteen plates with forks astride racing around the large table with cries of, "Go it, Pickle! Now, then, Prongs! Steady, Silver-top! Hurrah for the twins!"

The fun was at its height when young Prongs ran against Pickle, who did not steer well, and both went off the table with a crash. All stopped at once and crowded to the edge to see who was killed. The plates lay in pieces; old Pickle had a bend in his back that made him groan dismally; and Prongs had fallen down the register.

Wails of despair arose at that awful sight, for he was a favorite with everyone, and such a tragic death was too much for some of the tenderhearted spoons, who fainted at the idea of that gallant fork's destruction in what to them was a fiery volcano.

"Serves Pickle right! He ought to know he was too old for such wild games," scolded Miss Mustard, peering anxiously over at her friend, for they were fond of each another in spite of their tiffs.

"Now let us see what these fine folks will do when they get off the damask and come to grief. A helpless lot, I fancy, and those fellows deserve what they've got," said the sauce spoon, nearly upsetting the twins as she elbowed her way to the front to jeer over the fallen.

"I think you will see that gentle people are as brave as those who make a noise," answered Madam Gravy, and, leaning over the edge of the table, she added in her sweet voice, "Dear Mr. Pickle, we will let down a napkin and pull you up if you have strength to take hold."

"Pull away, ma'am," groaned Pickle, who well deserved his name just then, and, soon, thanks to Madam's presence of mind, he was safely laid on a pile of mats, while Miss Mustard put a plaster on his injured back.

Meanwhile brave Grandpapa Ladle had slipped from the table to a chair, and so to the floor without too great a jar to his aged frame; then, sliding along the carpet, he reached the register. Peering down that dark, hot abyss he cried, while all listened breathlessly for a reply, "Prongs, my boy, are you there?"

"Aye, aye, sir; I'm caught in the wire screen. Ask some of the fellows to lend a hand and get me out before I'm melted," answered the fork, with a gasp of agony.

Instantly the long handle of the patriarchal Ladle was put down to his rescue, and, after a moment of suspense, while Prongs caught firmly hold, up he came, hot and dusty, but otherwise unharmed by that dreadful fall. Cheers greeted them, and everyone lent a hand at the napkin as they were hoisted to the table to be embraced by their joyful relatives and friends.

"What did you think about down in that horrid place?" asked one of the twins.

"I thought of a story I once heard master tell, about a child who was found one cold day sitting with his feet on a newspaper, and when asked what he was doing, answered, 'Warming my feet on the "Christian Register." ' I hoped my register would be Christian enough not to melt me before help came. Ha! Ha! See the joke, my dears?" and Prongs laughed as gaily as if he never had taken a header into a volcano.

"What did you see down there?" asked the other twin, curious, as all small people are.

"Lots of dust and pins, a baby-doll's head put there, Norah's thimble, and the big red marble that boy Tony was raging about the other day. It's a regular catchall and shows how the work is shirked in this house," answered Prongs, stretching his legs, which were a little damaged by the fall.

"What shall we do about the plates?" asked Pickle, from his bed.

"Let them lie, for we can't mend them. John will think the boy broke them, and he'll get punished, as he deserves, for he broke a tumbler yesterday and put it slyly in the ash barrel," said Miss Mustard spitefully.

"Oh! I say, that's mean," began Tony, but no one listened.

In a minute Prongs answered bravely, "I'm a gentleman, and I don't let other people take the blame of my scrapes. Tony has enough of his own to answer for."

"I'll have that bent fork for mine and make John keep it as bright as a new dollar to pay for this. Prongs is a trump, and I wish I could tell him so," thought Tony, much gratified at this handsome behavior.

"Right, Grandson. I am pleased with you, but allow me to suggest that the Chinese mandarin on the chimney piece be politely requested to mend the plates. He can do that sort of thing nicely and will be charmed to oblige us, I am sure."

Grandpapa's suggestion was a good one, and Yam Ki Lo consented at once, skipped to the floor, tapped the bits of china with his fan, and in the twinkling of an eye was back on his perch, leaving two whole plates behind him, for he was a wizard and knew all about blue china.

Just as the silver people were rejoicing over this fine escape from discovery, the clock struck, a bell rang, voices were heard upstairs, and it was very evident that the family had arrived.

At these sounds a great flurry arose in the dining room as every spoon, fork, plate, and napkin flew back to its place. Pickle rushed to the jar, and plunged in head first, regardless of his back; Miss Mustard retired to the caster; the twins scrambled into the saltcellar; and the silver dogs lay down by the carving knife and fork as quietly as if they had never stirred a leg; Grandpapa slowly reposed in his usual place; Madam followed his example with dignity; the teaspoons climbed into the holder, uttering little cries of alarm; and Prongs stayed to help them till he had barely time to drop down at Tony's place and lie there with his bent leg in the air, the only sign of the great fall, about which he talked for a long time afterward. All was in order but the sauce spoon, who had stopped to laugh at the mandarin till it was too late to get to her corner, and before she could find any place of concealment, John came in and caught her lying in the middle of the table, looking very common and shabby among all the bright silver.

"What in the world is that old plated thing here for? Missis told Norah to put it in the kitchen, as she had a new one for a present today—real silver—so out you go," and as he spoke, John threw the spoon through the slide—an exile forevermore from the good society which she did not value as she should.

Tony saw the glimmer of a smile in Grandpapa Ladle's face, but it was gone like a flash, and by the time the boy reached the table nothing was to be seen in the silver bowl but his own round rosy countenance, full of wonder.

"I don't think anyone will believe what I've seen, but I mean to tell, it was so *very* curious," he said, as he surveyed the scene of the late frolic, now so neat and quiet that not a wrinkle or a crumb betrayed what larks had been going on.

Hastily fishing up his long-lost marble, the doll's head, and Norah's thimble, he went thoughtfully upstairs to welcome his cousins, still much absorbed by this very singular affair.

Dinner was soon announced, and while it lasted everyone was too busy eating the good things before them to observe how quiet the usually riotous Tony was. His appetite for turkey and cranberries seemed to have lost its sharp edge, and the mince pie must have felt itself sadly slighted by his lack of appreciation of its substance and flavor. He seemed in a brown study and kept staring about as if he saw more than other people did. He examined Nelly's plate as if looking for a crack, smiled at the little spoon when he took salt, refused pickles and mustard with a frown, kept a certain bent fork by him as long as possible, and tried to make music with a wet finger on the rim of his bowl at dessert.

But in the evening, when the young people sat around the fire, he amused them by telling the queer story of the silver party; but he very wisely left out the remarks made upon himself and family, remembering how disagreeable the sauce spoon had seemed, and he privately resolved to follow Madam Gravy Ladle's advice to keep his own face bright, manners polite, and speech kindly, that he might prove himself to be pure silver, and be stamped a gentleman.

FOUR

The Brownie and the Princess

She was not a real Brownie, but a little girl named Betty,
who lived with her father in a cottage near a great forest.
They were poor, so Betty always wore a brown frock, a big

brown hat, and, being out in the sun a great deal, her face was as brown as a berry, though very pretty with its rosy cheeks, dark eyes, and curly hair blowing in the wind. She was a lively little creature, and, having no neighbors, she made friends with the birds and flowers, rabbits and squirrels and had fine frolics with them, for they knew and loved her dearly. Many people drove through the beautiful wood, which was not far from the King's palace; and when they saw the little girl dancing with the daisies in the meadow, chasing squirrels up the trees, splashing in the brook, or sitting under her big hat like an elf under a mushroom, they would say, "There is the Brownie."

Betty was wild and shy and always tried to hide if anyone called to her; and it was funny to see her vanish in a hollow tree, drop down in the tall grass, or skip away into the ferns like a timid rabbit. She was afraid of the fine lords and ladies, who laughed at her and called her names but never thought to bring a book or toy or say a kind word to the lonely little girl.

Her father took care of the deer in the King's park and was away all day, leaving Betty to sweep the little house, bake the brown bread, and milk Daisy, the white cow, who lived in the shed behind the cottage and was Betty's dearest friend. They had no pasture for her to feed in; so, when the work was done, Betty would take her knitting and drive Daisy along the road where she could eat the grass on either side till she had had enough and lay down to rest under some shady tree. While the cow chewed her cud and took naps, the little girl would have fine games among her playmates, the wood creatures, or lie watching the clouds, or swing on the branches of the trees, or sail leaf boats in the brook. She was happy, but she longed for someone to talk to and tried vainly to learn what the birds sang all day long. There were a great many about the cottage, for no one troubled them, and they were so tame they would eat out of her hand and sit on her head. A stork family lived on the roof, swallows built their clay nest under the eaves, and wrens chirped in their little homes among the red and white roses that climbed up to peep in at Betty's window. Wood-pigeons came to pick up the grain she scattered for them, larks went singing up from the grass close by, and nightingales sang her to sleep.

"If I only knew what they said, we could have such happy times together. How can I ever learn?" sighed Betty, as she was driving Daisy home one day at sunset.

She was in the wood, and as she spoke she saw a great gray owl fluttering on the ground as if he was hurt. She ran at once to see what ailed the bird and was not afraid, though his round eyes stared at her, and he snapped his hooked beak as if very angry.

"Poor thing! Its leg is broken," she said, wondering how she could help it.

"No, it isn't; it's my wing. I leaned out of my nest up there to watch a field mouse, and a ray of sunshine dazzled me, so I tumbled down. Pick me up, child, and put me back, and I shall be all right."

Betty was so surprised to hear the owl speak that she did not stir, and, thinking she was frightened at his cross tone, the gray bird said more gently, with a blink of his yellow eyes and a wise nod, "I shouldn't speak to everyone, nor trust any other child, but I know you never hurt anything. I've watched you a long time, and I like you; so I'm going to reward you by giving you the last wish you made, whatever it is. I can; I'm a wizard, and I know all sorts of magic charms. Put me in my nest, tell me your wish, and you shall have it."

"Oh, thank you!" cried Betty joyfully. "I wished to understand what birds say."

"Dear me, that's a wish that may make trouble, but I'll grant it if you won't tell anyone how you learned the secret. I can't have people coming to me, and my neighbors won't want their gossip heard by many ears. They won't mind you, and it will amuse you, poor thing!" said the owl, after a pause.

Betty promised, and, holding the fat bird carefully in her arm, she climbed up the old oak and put him safely in his hole, where he settled himself with a great ruffling of feathers and a hoot of pleasure at being home again.

"Now, pull the tallest bit of down off my right ear and put it in your own; then you will hear what the birds say. Good night; I'm used up and want to rest," said the owl, with a gape.

"Thank you," said Betty and ran after Daisy, who was slowly eating her way home.

The bit of down lay snugly in Betty's ear, and in a moment she heard many sweet voices calling to one another—"Good night!" "Happy dreams!" "A bright tomorrow!" "Lie still, my darlings!" "Hush, my birdie, sleep till day."—and all sorts of pretty things, as the wood-birds were going to bed with the sun. When she came to the cottage the papa stork was standing on one leg, while the mamma tucked the little ones under her wings, scolding now and then as a red bill or a long leg popped out. The doves were cooing tenderly in the pine that rustled nearby; the swallows, skimming over the ground to catch and bring their babies a few more gnats for supper; and the wrens were twittering among the roses like the little gossips they were.

"Now I shall know what they all are saying," cried Betty, trying to hear the different voices, for there were so many going at once it was difficult to understand the sweet new language.

So she milked Daisy, set the table, and made ready for her father, who was often late, then took her bowl of bread and milk and sat on the doorstep listening with all her might. She always strewed crumbs for the wrens, and they flew down to eat without fear. Tonight they came, and as they pecked they talked, and Betty understood every word.

"Here's a fine soft bit, my love," said the papa, as he hopped briskly about, with his bright eye on the little girl. "Have a good supper while I feed the children. The child never forgets us, and saves me many a long journey by giving us these nice crumbs. I wish we could do something for her."

"So do I, and quite tire my wits trying to make some plan

to give her pleasure. I often wonder why the little Princess up at the palace has so much and our dear Betty so little. A few of the books and toys that lie about up there would make this child so happy. It is a pity no one thinks of it." And the kind Mamma Wren sighed as she ate a nice bit close to Betty's bare foot.

"If she was not so shy and would let people speak to her, I think she would soon make friends, she is so pretty and gay," answered the papa, coming back for another load for the hungry babies in the nest.

"The Princess has heard of her and wants to see her. I heard the maids talking about it today when I went to call on Cousin Tomtit in the palace garden. They said Her Highness was to drive through the pine wood early tomorrow morning to breathe the fresh air and hoped to see the Brownie and the pretty white cow. Now, if Betty only knew it, she might gather a posy of cowslips and, when the little lady comes, give them to her. That would please her very much and bring Betty some pretty gift, for her Highness is generous, though sadly spoilt, I'm afraid."

This fine plan of Mamma Wren's pleased Betty so much that she clapped her hands and startled the birds away.

"I'll do it! I'll do it!" she cried. "I always wanted to see the little Princess father has told me about. She is ill and cannot run and play as I do, so I should love to please her, and the cowslips are all out. I'll go early and get a hatful and not run away if she comes."

Betty was so full of this delightful plan that she went early to bed but did not forget to lean out of her window and peep through the roses into the nest where Mamma Wren brooded over her babies while the papa roosted nearby with his head under his wing.

"Good night, dear birds; thank you very much," whispered
Betty, but they did not mind her and only twittered sleepily
as if a dream disturbed them.

> "Up, up, little maid;
> Day has begun.
> Welcome with us
> Our father, the sun!"

sang the larks, as they rose from the grass and waked Betty
with their sweet voices.

> "Tweet, tweet, it is morning;
> Please get up, Mamma.
> Do bring us some breakfast,
> Our dearest Papa,"

twittered the young wrens, with their mouths wide open.

> "Click, clack, here's another day;
> Stretch our wings and fly away
> Over the wood and over the hills,
> Seeking food for our babies' bills;"

and away went the storks with their long legs trailing out
behind, while the little ones popped up their heads and
stared at the sun.

> "Cluck! cluck!
> Here's good luck:
> Old Yellow-legs
> Has laid two eggs,
> All fresh and sweet,
> For our girl to eat,"

cackled the gray hens, picking about the shed where the cock
stood crowing loudly.

> "Coo! coo! coo!
> Come, bathe in the dew;

For the rosy dawn shines
Through our beautiful pines.
So kiss, everyone,
For a new day's begun,"

called the doves softly to one another as they billed and cooed and tripped about on their little pink feet.

Betty looked and listened at her window and was so happy she kissed the roses nodding at her, then ran down to make the porridge, singing like a bird herself. When her father had gone away to work she made haste to milk Daisy, sweep the floor, and make all tidy for the day before she went to wait for the Princess.

"Now, you eat your breakfast here while I get the cowslips, for this is a pretty place to be in, and I want you to look very nice when the fine people come," said Betty, as she left the cow to feed in a little shady nook by the road where the grass was green and an old oak made pleasant shade.

The cowslips were all open and as yellow as gold, so Betty made a great nosegay of some and a splendid cowslip-ball of the rest; then she put them in her hat, well sprinkled with water, and sat on a fallen log knitting busily, while Daisy lay down to chew her cud, with a green wreath of oak leaves around her neck for full dress.

They did not have to wait long. Soon the tramp of horses was heard, and along the wood road came the white ponies tossing their heads, the pretty carriage with coachman and footman in blue and silver coats, and inside the little Princess, with white plumes waving from her hat as she sat by her nurse, wrapt in a soft silken cloak, for the summer air seemed cold to her.

"Oh, there's the Brownie and her pretty white cow! Tell her not to run away; I want to see her and hear her sing," cried the little Princess eagerly, as they came nearer.

Betty was rather scared but did not run away, for the nurse was a kind-looking old woman in a high peasant cap, who smiled and nodded at her with a motherly look and seemed much pleased when she held up the cowslips, saying, "Will the little lady have them?"

"Oh yes, I wanted some: I never had a cowslip-ball before. How pretty it is! Thank you, Brownie," cried the Princess, with both hands full of flowers as she laughed with pleasure.

"I picked them all for you. I have so many, and I heard you cried for some," said Betty, very glad that she had not run away and spoilt the little lady's drive.

"How did you know?" asked the Princess, staring at her.

"The birds told me," said Betty.

"Oh yes! Brownies are fairies, and understand bird-talk; I forget that. I know what parrots say, but not my other birds. Could you tell me?" asked the Princess, leaning down very earnestly, for any new thing pleased her.

"I think so, if tame ones sing like the wild ones," answered Betty, proud to know more than the fine child did.

"Come to the palace and tell me; come now, I can't wait! My canary sings all day, but I never understand a word, and I must. Tell her to come, nurse," commanded the Princess, who always had her own way.

"Can you?" asked the old woman. "We will bring you back at night. Her Highness has a fancy to see you, and she will pay you for coming."

"I can't leave Daisy; we have no field to put her in, and if I shut her up in the shed all day she will be hungry and call for me," answered Betty, longing to go, but not liking to leave her dear cow to suffer.

"Put her in that field till you come back; I give you leave.

All this land is mine, so no one will blame you. Do it!" said the Princess, waving her hand to the footman, who jumped down and had Daisy in the great clover field before Betty could say a word.

"She will like that; and now I can go if you don't mind my old gown and hat—I have no other clothes," she said, as the cow began to eat, and the footman opened the carriage door for her.

"I like it. Come in. Now, go home at once," said the Princess; and there was poor little Betty rolling away in the grand carriage, feeling as if it was all a fairy tale.

The Princess asked a great many questions and liked her new friend more and more, for she had never spoken to a poor child before, or known how they live. Betty was excited by this fine adventure and was so gay and charming in her little ways that the old nurse soon forgot to watch lest she should do or say something amiss.

When they drove up to the great marble palace shining in the sun, with green lawns and terraces and blooming gardens all about it, Betty could only hold her breath and look with all her eyes as she was led through splendid halls and up wide stairs into a room full of pretty things, where six gaily dressed maids sewed and chattered together.

The Princess went away to rest, but Betty was told to stay there and be dressed before she went to play with Her Highness. The room was full of closets and chests and boxes and baskets, and, as the doors opened and the covers flew off, Betty saw piles of pretty frocks, hats, cloaks, and all manner of dainty things for little girls to wear. Never had she dreamed of such splendid clothes, all lace and ribbons, silk and velvet. Hats with flowers and feathers, pretty pink and blue shoes with gold and silver buckles, silk stockings like cobwebs, and muslin and linen petticoats and nightgowns, and little caps all embroidered as if by fairy fingers.

She could only stand and look like one in a dream while the maids very kindly took away her poor brown dress and hat, and, after much gossip over what looked best, at last put on a rosy muslin frock, a straw hat with roses in it, and some neat shoes and stockings. Then, when her hair was smoothed in thick brown curls, they told her to look in the tall mirror and tell what she saw there.

"Oh, what a pretty little girl!" cried Betty, smiling and nodding at the other child, who smiled and nodded back at her. She did not know herself, never having had any glass but a quiet pool in the wood or the brook in the meadow.

The maids laughed, and then she saw who it was and laughed with them and danced and courtesied and was very merry till a bell rang, and she was ordered to go to Her Highness.

It was a lovely room, all hung with blue silk and lace, with a silver bed, and chairs and couches of blue damask, pictures on the walls, flowers in all the windows, and golden cages full of birds. A white cat slept on its cushion, a tiny dog ran about with a golden collar hung with bells, and books and toys were heaped on the tables. The Princess was scolding her nurse because she wanted her to rest longer after the drive; but when Betty came in looking so pretty and gay, the frown changed to a smile, and she cried, "How nice you look! Not like a Brownie now, but I hope you have not forgotten about the birds."

"No," said Betty; "let me listen a minute, and I'll tell you what they say."

So both were silent, and the maid and nurse kept as still
as mice while the canary sang his shrill, sweet song, and Betty's
face grew sad as she heard it.

"He says he is tired of his cage and longs to be free among
the other birds, for a tree is a better home than a golden palace
and a crumb in the wood sweeter than all the sugar in his

silver cup. 'Let me go! Let me go! or my heart will break!'
That is what he says, and the bullfinch sings the same song;
so do the lovebirds and the beautiful gay one whom I don't
know."

"What does Polly say? I understand him when he talks, but
not when he scolds and chatters to himself as he is doing now,"
said the Princess, looking much surprised at what she heard,
for she thought her birds must be happy in such fine cages.

Betty listened to the great red and green and blue parrot,
who sat on a perch wagging his head and chuckling to himself as if he were enjoying some good joke. Presently Betty
blushed and laughed and looked both troubled and amused
at what she heard, for the bird was gabbling away and nodding
his head at her in a very funny manner.

"What does he say?" asked the Princess impatiently.

"Please don't ask. You will not like it. I couldn't tell," said
Betty, still laughing and blushing.

"You *must* tell, or I'll have Polly's neck wrung. I *will* know
every word, and I won't be angry with *you*, no matter what
that saucy bird says," commanded the Princess.

"He says this," began Betty, not liking to obey, but afraid
poor Polly would be hurt if she did not, " 'Now here's a new
pet for Her Highness to torment. Nice pretty little girl! Pity
she came, to be made much of for a day or two and then
thrown away or knocked about like an old doll. She thinks it
all very fine here, poor thing! But if she knew all I know she
would run away and never come back, for a crosser, more
spoilt child than Her Highness never lived.' "

Betty dared not go on, for the Princess looked angry, and
the maid went to slap the parrot, who gave a queer laugh and
snapped at her fingers, squalling out, "She is! She is! And you
all say it behind her back. *I* know your sly ways. You praise

and pet her and pretend that she is the sweetest darling in the world, when you know that this nice, rosy, good little girl out of the wood is worth a dozen silly, tyrannical princesses. Ha! Ha! I'm not afraid to speak the truth, am I, Betty?"

Betty was frightened but could not help laughing when the naughty bird winked at her as he hung upside down, with his hooked beak wide open and his spendid wings flapping.

"Tell me! Tell me!" cried the Princess, forgetting her anger in curiosity.

Betty had to tell and was very glad when Bonnibelle laughed also and seemed to enjoy the truth told in this funny way.

"Tell him you know what he says and ask him, since he is so wise, what I shall do to be as good as you are," said the Princess, who really had a kind little heart and knew that she was petted far too much.

Betty told the parrot she understood his language, and he was so surprised that he got on his perch at once and stared at her, as he said eagerly, "Don't let me be punished for telling truth; there's a dear child. I can't take it back, and, since you ask my advice, I think the best thing you can do for Her Highness is to let her change places with you and learn to be contented and useful and happy. Tell her so, with my compliments."

Betty found this a hard message to give, but it pleased Bonnibelle, for she clapped her hands and cried, "I'll ask Mamma. Would you like to do it, Brownie, and be a princess?"

"No, thank you," said Betty; "I couldn't leave my father and Daisy, and I'm not fit to live in a palace. It's very splendid, but I think I love the little house and the wood and my birds better."

The nurse and the maid held up their hands, amazed at such a fancy, but Bonnibelle seemed to understand and said kindly, "Yes, I think it is very dull here and much pleasanter in the fields to do as one likes. May I come and play with you and learn to be like you, dear Betty?"

She looked a little sad as she spoke, and Betty pitied her, so she smiled and answered gladly, "Yes, that will be lovely. Come and stay with me, and I will show you all my playmates, and you shall milk Daisy, and feed the hens, and see the rabbits and the tame fawn, and run in the daisy field, and pull cowslips, and eat bread and milk out of my best blue bowl."

"Yes, and have a little brown gown and a big hat like yours, and wooden shoes that clatter, and learn how to knit, and climb trees, and what the birds say!" added Bonnibelle, so charmed at the plan that she jumped off the couch and began to skip about as she had not done for days before.

"Now come and see my toys and choose any you like, for I'm fond of you, dear, because you tell me new things and are not like the silly little lords and ladies who come to see me and only quarrel and strut about like peacocks till I'm tired of them."

Bonnibelle put her arm around Betty and led her away to a long hall so full of playthings that it looked like a splendid toy shop. Dolls by the dozen were there—dolls that talked and sang and walked and went to sleep, fine dolls, funny dolls, big and little doll queens and babies, dolls of all nations. Never was there such a glorious party of these dear creatures seen before, and Betty had no eyes for anything else, being a real little girl, full of love for dollies, and never yet had she owned one.

"Take as many as you like," said Bonnibelle. "I'm tired of them."

It nearly took Betty's breath away to think that she might have a dozen dolls if she chose. But she wisely decided that

one was enough and picked out a darling baby-doll in its
pretty cradle, with blue eyes shut, and flaxen curls under the
dainty cap. It would fill her motherly little soul with joy to
have this lovely thing to lie in her arms by day, sleep by her
side at night, and live with her in the lonely cottage, for baby
could say "Mamma!" quite naturally, and Betty felt that she
would never be tired of hearing the voice call her by that
sweet name.

It was hard to tear herself from the cradle to see the other
treasures, but she went to and fro with Bonnibelle, admiring
all she saw, till nurse came to tell them that lunch was ready
and Her Highness must play no more.

Betty hardly knew how to behave when she found herself
sitting at a fine table with a footman behind her chair and all
sorts of curious glass and china and silver things before her.
But she watched what Bonnibelle did, and so got on pretty
well, and ate peaches and cream and cake and dainty white
rolls and bonbons with a good appetite. She would not touch
the little birds in the silver dish, though they smelt very nice,
but said sadly, "No, thank you, sir; I couldn't eat my friends."

The footman tried not to laugh, but the Princess pushed
away her own plate with a frown, saying, "Neither will I.
Give me some apricot jelly and a bit of angel cake. Now
that I know more about birds and what they think of me, I
shall be careful how I treat them. Don't bring any more to my
table."

After lunch the children went to the library, where all the
best picture books ever printed were ranged on the shelves,
and cozy little chairs stood about where one could sit and
read delicious fairy tales all day long. Betty skipped for joy
when her new friend picked out a pile of the gayest and best
for her to take home, and then they went to the music room,

where a band played beautifully, and the Princess danced with her master in a stately way that Betty thought very stupid.

"Now you must dance. I've heard how finely you do it, for some lords and ladies saw you dancing with the daisies and said it was the prettiest ballet they ever looked at. You *must!* No, please do, dear Betty," said Bonnibelle, commanding at first; then, remembering what the parrot said, she spoke more gently.

"I cannot, here before these people. I don't know any steps and need flowers to dance with me," said Betty.

"Then come on the terrace; there are plenty of flowers in the garden, and I am tired of this," answered Bonnibelle, going through one of the long windows to the wide marble walk where Betty had been longing to go.

Several peacocks were sitting on the steps, and they at once spread their splendid tails and began to strut before the children, making a harsh noise as they tossed the crowns of shining feathers on their heads.

"What do they say?" asked the Princess.

" 'Here comes the vain little creature who thinks her fine clothes handsomer than ours and likes to show them off to poorer people and put on proud airs. We don't admire her, for we know how silly she is, for all her fine feathers.' "

"I won't listen to any more rude words from these bad birds, and I won't praise their splendid tails as I meant to. Go along, you vain things! No one wants you here," cried Betty, chasing the peacocks off the terrace, while the Princess laughed to see them drop their gorgeous trains and go scurrying away with loud squawks of fear.

"It was true. I *am* vain and silly, but no one ever dared to tell me so, and I shall try to do better now I see how foolish those birds look and how sweet you are," she said, when Betty came skipping back to her.

"I'll make a peacock dance for you. See how well I do it!" and Betty began to prance, with her full pink skirt held up, and her head tossed, and her toes turned out, so like the birds that the old nurse and the maid, who had followed, began to laugh as well as Bonnibelle.

It was very funny, and, when she had imitated the vain strutting and fluttering of the peacocks, Betty suddenly dropped her skirt and went hurrying away, flapping her arms like wings and squawking dismally.

She wanted to please the Princess and make her forget the rude things she had been forced to tell, so when she came running back she was glad to find her very merry and anxious for more fun.

"Now, I'll do the tulip dance," said Betty and began to bow and courtesy to a bed full of splendid flowers, all gold and scarlet, white and purple; and the tulips seemed to bow and courtesy back again like stately lords and ladies at a ball. Such dainty steps, such graceful sweeps and elegant wavings of the arms one never saw before, for Betty imitated the tall blossoms waving in the wind and danced a prettier minuet with them than any ever seen at court.

"It is wonderful!" said the maid.

"Bless the dear! She must be a real fairy to do all that," said the old nurse.

"Dance again! Oh, please dance again, it is so pretty!" cried the Princess, clapping her hands as Betty rose from her farewell courtesy and came smiling toward her.

"I'll give you the wind dance; that is very gay, and this fine floor is so smooth I feel as if my feet had wings."

With that Betty began to flutter to and fro like a leaf blown

by the wind; now she went down the terrace as if swept by
a strong gust, now she stood still, swaying a little in the soft
breath of air, then off she spun as if caught in a storm, eddy-
ing round and round till she looked like a stray rose leaf
whisked over the ground. Sometimes she whirled close to the
Princess, then blew up against the stout old nurse, but was
gone before she could be caught. Once she went down the
marble steps at a bound and came flying over the railing as
if in truth she did have wings on her nimble feet. Then the
gale seemed to die away, and slowly the leaf floated to the
ground at Bonnibelle's feet, to lie there rosy, breathless, and
tired.

Bonnibelle clapped her hands again, but before she could
tell half her delight, a beautiful lady came from the window,
where she had seen the pretty ballet. Two little pages carried
her long train of silvery silk; two ladies walked beside her,
one holding a rose-colored parasol over her head, the other
with a fan and cushion; jewels shone on her white hands and
neck and in her hair, and she was very splendid, for this was
the Queen. But her face was sweet and lovely, her voice very
soft, and her smile so kind that Betty was not afraid and made
her best courtesy prettily.

When the red damask cushion was laid on one of the carved
stone seats, and the pages had dropped the train, and the maids
had shut the parasol and handed the golden fan, they stepped
back, and only the Queen and nurse and little girls were left
together.

"Does the new toy please you, darling?" asked the shining
lady, as Bonnibelle ran to climb into her lap and pour out
a long story of the pleasant time she had been having with the
Brownie. "Indeed I think she is a fairy, to make you so rosy,
gay, and satisfied."

"Who taught you to dance so wonderfully, child?" asked the Queen when she had kissed her little daughter, glad to see her look so unlike the sad, cross, or listless creature she usually found.

"The wind, Lady Queen," answered Betty, smiling.

"And where did you get the fine tales you tell?"

"From the birds, Lady Queen."

"And what do you do to have such rosy cheeks?"

"Eat brown bread and milk, Lady Queen."

"And how is it that a lonely child like you is so happy and good?"

"My father takes care of me, and my mother in heaven keeps me good, Lady Queen."

When Betty said that, the Queen put out her hand and drew the little girl closer, as if her tender heart pitied the motherless child and longed to help if she only knew how.

Just then the sound of horses' feet was heard in the great courtyard below, trumpets sounded, and everyone knew that the King had come home from hunting. Presently, with a jingling of spurs and trampling of boots, he came along the terrace with some of his lords behind him.

Everyone began to bow except the Queen, who sat still with the Princess on her knee, for Bonnibelle did not run to meet her father as Betty always did when he came home. Betty thought she would be afraid of the King, and so she would, perhaps, if he had worn his crown and ermine cloak and jewels everywhere; but now he was dressed very like her father, in hunter's green, with a silver horn over his shoulder, and no sign of splendor about him but the feather in his hat and a great ring that glittered when he pulled off his glove to kiss the Queen's hand; so Betty smiled and bobbed her little courtesy, looking boldly up in his face.

He liked that and knew her, for he had often seen her when he rode through the wood.

"Come hither, Brownie; I have a story you will like to hear," he said, sitting down beside the Queen and beckoning to Betty with a friendly nod.

She went and stood at his knee, eager to hear, while all the lords and ladies bent forward to listen, for it was plain that something had happened beside the killing of a stag that day.

"I was hunting in the great oak wood two hours ago, and had knelt down to aim at a splendid stag," began the King, stroking Betty's brown head, "When a wild boar, very fierce and large, burst out of the ferns behind me just as I fired at the deer. I had only my dagger left to use, but I sprang up to face him, when a root tripped my foot, and there I lay quite helpless, as the furious old fellow rushed at me. I think this little maid here would have been Queen Bonnibelle tomorrow if a brave woodman had not darted from behind a tree and with one blow of his axe killed the beast as he bent his head to gore me. It was your father, Brownie, and I owe my life to him."

As the King ended, a murmur rose, and all the lords and ladies looked as if they would like to give a cheer, but the Queen turned pale and the old nurse ran to fan her, while Bonnibelle put out her arms to her father, crying, "No, I will never be a queen if you die, dear Papa!"

The King took her on one knee and set Betty on the other, saying gaily, "Now what shall we do for this brave man who saved me?"

"Give him a palace to live in and millions of money," said the Princess, who could think of nothing better.

"I offered him a house and money, but he wanted neither, for he loved his little cottage and had no need of gold, he said. Think again, little maids, and find something he *will* like," said the King, looking at Betty.

"A nice field for Daisy is all he wants, Lord King," she answered boldly, for the handsome brown face with the kind eyes was very like her father's, she thought.

"He shall have it. Now wish three wishes for yourself, my child, and I will grant them if I can."

Betty showed all her little white teeth as she laughed for joy at this splendid offer. Then she said slowly, "I have but one wish now, for the Princess has given me a dear doll and many books, so I am the happiest creature in all the kingdom and have no wants."

"Contented little lass! Who of us can say the same?" said the King, looking at the people around him, who dropped their eyes and looked foolish, for they were always asking favors of the good King. "Well, now let us know the one thing I can do to please brave woodman John's little daughter."

"Please let the Princess come and play with me," said Betty eagerly.

The lords looked horrified and the ladies as if they would faint away at the mere idea of such a dreadful thing. But the Queen nodded; Bonnibelle cried, "Oh, do!"

The King laughed as he asked in a surprised tone, "But why not come and play with her here? What is there at the cottage that we have not at the palace?"

"Many things, Lord King," answered Betty. "She is tired of the palace and everything in it, she says, and longs to run about in the wood and be well and gay and busy all day long, as I am. She wants to bake and milk and sweep and knit, and hear the wind blow, and dance with the daisies, and talk with my birds, and dream happy dreams, and love to be alive, as I do."

"Upon my word, here's a bold Brownie! But she is right, I think, and if my Princess can get a pair of cheeks like these down at the cottage, she shall go as often as she likes," said the King, amused at Betty's free words and struck by the contrast between the two faces before him, one like a pale garden lily and the other like a fresh wild rose.

Then Bonnibelle burst out and told all the story of the day, talking as she had never talked before, and everyone listened, amazed to see how lively and sweet Her Highness could be, and wondered what had made such a sudden change. But the old nurse went about, saying in a whisper, "She is a real Brownie, I know it; for no mortal child would be so bold and bright and do what she has done—bewitched both King and Queen, and made Her Highness a new child."

So all looked at Betty with great respect, and when at last the talk was over and the King rose to go, with a kiss for each little girl, everyone bowed and made way for the Brownie, as if she too were a Princess.

But Betty was not proud, for she remembered the peacocks as she walked hand in hand with Bonnibelle after the royal papa and mamma over the terrace to the great hall, where the feast was spread and music sounding splendidly.

"You shall sit by me and have my golden cup," said Bonnibelle, when the silver horns were still, and all waited for the King to hand the Queen to her place.

"No, I must go home. It is sunset; Daisy must be milked, and father's supper ready when he comes. Let me run away and get my old clothes; these are too fine to wear in the cottage," answered Betty, longing to stay, but so faithful to her duty that even the King's command could not keep her.

"Tell her to stay, Papa; I want her," cried Bonnibelle, going to the great gilded chair where her father sat.

"Stay, child," said the King, with a wave of the hand where the great jewel shone like a star.

But Betty shook her head and answered sweetly, "Please do not make me, dear Lord King. Daisy needs me, and father will miss me sadly if I do not run to meet him when he comes home."

Then the King smiled and said heartily, "Good child! We will not keep you. Woodman John gave me my life, and I will not take away the comfort of his. Run home, little Brownie, and God bless you!"

Betty tripped upstairs and put on her old frock and hat, took one of the finest books and the dear doll, leaving the rest to be sent next day, and then tried to slip away by some back door; but there were so many halls and steps she got lost and came at last into the great hall again. All were eating now, and the meat and wine and spicy pies and piles of fruit smelt very nice, and Betty would have only brown bread and milk for supper; but she did not stay, and no one but the pages saw her as she ran down the steps to the courtyard, like Cinderella hurrying from the hall when the clock struck twelve and all her fine clothes vanished.

She had a very happy walk through the cool, green wood, however, and a happy hour telling her father all about this wonderful day; but the happiest time of all was when she went to bed in her little room, with the darling baby fast asleep on her arm and the wrens talking together among the roses of how much good their wise Brownie would do the Princess in the days to come.

Then Betty fell asleep and dreamed such lovely dreams of the moon with a sweet face like the Queen's smiling at her; of her father looking as proud and handsome as the King, with his axe on his shoulder and the great boar dead at his feet;

and Bonnibelle—rosy, gay, and strong, working and playing
with her like a little sister in the cottage, while all the birds
sang gaily,

"Bonnibelle! Bonnibelle!
Listen, listen, while we tell
A sweet secret all may know,
How a little child may grow
Like a happy wayside flower,
Warmed by sun, fed by shower,
Rocked by wind, loved by elf,
Quite forgetful of itself;
Full of honey for the bee,
Beautiful for all to see,
Nodding to the passers-by,
Smiling at the summer sky,
Sweetening all the balmy air,
Happy, innocent, and fair.
Flowers like these blossom may
In a palace garden gay;
Lilies tall or roses red,
For a royal hand or head.
But be they low, or be they high,
Under the soft leaves must lie
A true little heart of gold,
Never proud or hard or cold,
But brave and tender, just and free,
Whether it queen or beggar be;
Else its beauty is in vain,
And never will it bloom again.
This is the secret we would tell,
Bonnibelle! Bonnibelle!"

Tabby's Tablecloth

On the twentieth day of March 1775, a girl was trudging along a country road with a basket of eggs on her arm. She seemed in a great hurry and looked anxiously about her as she went, for those were stirring times, and Tabitha Tarbell lived in a town that took a famous part in the Revolution. She was a rosy-faced, bright-eyed lass of fourteen, full of vigor, courage, and patriotism, and just then much excited by the frequent rumors which reached Concord that the British were coming to destroy the stores sent there for safekeeping while the enemy occupied Boston. Tabby glowed with wrath at the idea, and (metaphorically speaking) shook her fist at august King George, being a stanch little Rebel, ready to fight and die for her country rather than submit to tyranny of any kind.

In nearly every house something valuable was hidden. Colonel Barrett had six barrels of powder; Ebenezer Hubbard, sixty-eight barrels of flour; axes, tents, and spades were at Daniel Cray's; and Captain David Brown had guns, cartridges, and musket balls. Cannon were hidden in the woods; firearms were being manufactured at Barrett's Mills; cartouch boxes, belts, and holsters, at Reuben Brown's; saltpeter at Josiah Melvin's; and much oatmeal was prepared at Captain Timothy Wheeler's. A morning gun was fired, a guard of ten men patrolled the town at night, and the brave farmers were making ready for what they felt must come.

There were Tories in the town who gave the enemy all the information they could gather; therefore, much caution was necessary in making plans, lest these enemies should betray them. Passwords were adopted, secret signals used, and messages sent from house to house in all sorts of queer ways. Such a message lay hidden under the eggs in Tabby's basket, and the brave girl was going on an important errand from her uncle, Captain David Brown, to Deacon Cyrus Hosmer, who lived at the other end of the town, by the South Bridge. She had been employed several times before in the same way and had proved herself quick-witted, stouthearted, and light-footed. Now, as she trotted along in her scarlet cloak and hood, she was wishing she could still further distinguish herself by some great act of heroism, for good Parson Emerson had patted her on the head and said, "Well done, child!" when he heard how she ran all the way to Captain Barrett's, in the night, to warn him that Doctor Lee, a Tory, had been detected sending information of certain secret plans to the enemy.

"I would do more than that, though it was a fearsome run through the dark woods. Wouldn't those two like to know all I know about the stores? But I wouldn't tell 'em, not if they drove a bayonet through me. I'm not afeard of 'em," and Tabby tossed her head defiantly, as she paused to shift her basket from one arm to the other.

But she evidently was "afeard" of something, for her ruddy cheeks turned pale and her heart gave a thump, as two men came in sight and stopped suddenly on seeing her. They were strangers, and, though nothing in their dress indicated it, the girl's quick eye saw that they were soldiers; step and carriage betrayed it, and the rapidity with which these martial gentlemen changed into quiet travellers roused her suspicions at once. They exchanged a few whispered words; then they came on, swinging their stout sticks, one whistling, the other keeping a keen lookout along the lonely road before and behind them.

"My pretty lass, can you tell me where Mr. Daniel Bliss lives?" asked the younger, with a smile and a salute.

Tabby was sure now that they were British, for the voice was deep and full, the face a ruddy English face, and the man they wanted was a well-known Tory. But she showed no sign of alarm, beyond the modest color in her cheeks, and answered civilly, "Yes, sir, over yonder a piece."

"Thanks, and a kiss for that," said the young man, stooping to bestow his gift. But he got a smart box on the ear, and Tabby ran off in a fury of indignation.

With a laugh they went on, never dreaming that the little Rebel was going to turn spy herself and get the better of them. She hurried away to Deacon Hosmer's and did her errand, adding thereto the news that strangers were in town. "We must know more of them," said the Deacon. "Clap a different suit on her, wife, and send her with eggs to Mrs. Bliss. We have all we want of them, and Tabby can look well about her, while she rests and gossips over there. Bliss must be looked after smartly, for he is a knave and will do us harm."

Away went Tabby in a blue cloak and hood, much pleased with her mission; and, coming to the Tory's house about noon, smelt afar off a savory odor of roasting meat and baking pies.

Stepping softly to the back door, she peeped through a small window and saw Mrs. Bliss and her handmaid cooking away in the big kitchen, too busy to heed the little spy, who slipped around to the front of the house to take a general survey before she went in. All she saw confirmed her suspicions, for in the keeping room a table was set forth in great style, with the silver tankards, best china, and the fine damask tablecloth, which the housewife kept for holidays. Still another peep through the lilac bushes before the parlor windows showed her the two strangers closeted with Mr. Bliss, all talking earnestly, but in too low a tone for a word to reach even her sharp ears.

"I *will* know what they are at. I'm sure it is mischief, and I won't go back with only my walk for my pains," thought Tabby; and marching into the kitchen she presented her eggs with a civil message from Madam Hosmer.

"They are mighty welcome, child. I've used a sight for my custards and need more for the flip. We've company to dinner unexpected, and I'm much put about," said Mrs. Bliss, who seemed to be concerned about something besides the dinner and in her flurry forgot to be surprised at the unusual gift; for the neighbors shunned them, and the poor woman had many anxieties on her husband's account, the family being divided—one brother a Tory, and one a Rebel.

"Can I help ma'am? I'm a master hand at beating eggs, Aunt Hitty says. I'm tired and wouldn't mind sitting a bit if I'm not in the way," said Tabby, bound to discover something more before she left.

"But you be in the way. We don't want any help, so you'd better be steppin' along home, else suthin' besides eggs may git whipped. Talebearers ain't welcome here," said old Puah, the maid, a sour spinster who sympathized with her master and openly declared she hoped the British would put down the Yankee Rebels soon and sharply.

Mrs. Bliss was in the pantry and heard nothing of this little passage of arms, for Tabby hotly resented the epithet "talebearer," though she knew that the men in the parlor were not the only spies on the premises.

"When you are all drummed out of town and this house burnt to the ground, you may be glad of my help, and I wish you may get it. Good-day, old crabapple," answered saucy Tabby, and, catching up her basket, she marched out of the kitchen with her nose in the air.

But as she passed the front of the house, she could not resist another look at the fine dinner table, for in those days few had time or heart for feasting, and the best napery and china seldom appeared. One window stood open, and, as the girl leaned in, something moved under the long cloth that swept the floor. It was not the wind, for the March day was still and sunny, and in a minute out popped a gray cat's head, and puss came purring to meet the newcomer whose step had roused her from a nap.

"Where one tabby hides, another can. Can I dare to do it? What would become of me if found out? How wonderful it would be if I could hear what these men are plotting. I will!"

A sound in the next room decided her, and, thrusting the basket among the bushes, she leaped lightly in and vanished under the table, leaving Puss calmly washing her face on the windowsill.

As soon as it was done Tabby's heart began to flutter, but it was too late to retreat, for at that moment in bustled Mrs. Bliss, and the poor girl could only make herself as small as possible, quite hidden under the long folds that fell on all sides from the wide, old-fashioned table. She discovered nothing from the women's chat, for it ran on sage-cheese, eggnog, roast pork, and lamentations over a burnt pie. By the time dinner was served, and the guests called in to eat it, Tabby was calm enough to have all her wits about her, and pride gave her courage to be ready for the consequences, whatever they might be.

For a time the hungry gentlemen were too busy eating to talk much, but when Mrs. Bliss went out, and the flip came in, they were ready for business. The window was shut, whereat Tabby exulted that she was inside; the talkers drew closer together and spoke so low that she could only catch a sentence now and then, which caused her to pull her hair with vexation; and they swore a good deal, to the great horror of the pious little maiden curled up at their feet. But she heard enough to prove that she was right, for these men were Captain Brown and Ensign De Bernicre, of the British army, come to learn where the supplies were stored and how well the town was defended. She heard Mr. Bliss tell them that some of the "Rebels," as he called his neighbors, had sent him word that he should not leave the town alive, and he was in much fear for his life and property. She heard the

Englishmen tell him that if he came with them they would protect him, for they were armed, and three of them together could surely get safely off, as no one knew the strangers had arrived but the slip of a girl who showed them the way. Here "the slip of a girl" nodded her head savagely and hoped the speaker's ear still tingled with the buffet she gave it.

Mr. Bliss gladly consented to this plan and told them he would show them the road to Lexington, which was a shorter way to Boston than through Weston and Sudbury, the road they came.

"These people won't fight, will they?" asked Ensign De Bernicre.

"There goes a man who will fight you to the death," answered Mr. Bliss, pointing to his brother Tom, busy in a distant field.

The Ensign swore again and gave a stamp that brought his heavy heel down on poor Tabby's hand, as she leaned forward to catch every word. The cruel blow nearly forced a cry from her, but she bit her lips and never stirred, though faint with pain. When she could listen again, Mr. Bliss was telling all he knew about the hiding places of the powder, grain, and cannon the enemy wished to capture and destroy. He could not tell much, for the secrets had been well kept, but, if he had known that our young Rebel was taking notes of his words under his own table, he might have been less ready to betray his neighbors. No one suspected a listener, however, and all Tabby could do was to scowl at three pairs of muddy boots and wish she were a man that she might fight the wearers of them.

She very nearly had a chance to fight or fly, for, just as they were preparing to leave the table, a sudden sneeze nearly undid her. She thought she was lost and hid her face, expecting to be dragged out—to instant death, perhaps—by the wrathful men of war.

"What's that?" exclaimed the Ensign, as a sudden pause followed the fatal sound.

"It came from under the table," added Captain Brown, and a hand lifted a corner of the cloth.

A shiver went through Tabby, and she held her breath, with her eye upon that big, brown hand, but the next moment she could have laughed with joy, for pussy saved her. The cat had come to doze on her warm skirts, and when the cloth was raised, fancying she was to be fed by her master, puss rose and walked out purring loudly, tail erect, with its white tip waving like a flag of truce.

"'Tis but the old cat, gentlemen. A good beast, and, fortunately for us, unable to report our conference," said Mr. Bliss, with an air of relief, for he had started guiltily at the bare idea of an eavesdropper.

"She sneezed as if she were as great a snuff-taker as an old woman of whom we asked our way above here," laughed the Ensign, as they all rose.

"And there she is now, coming along as if our grenadiers were after her!" exclaimed the Captain, as the sound of steps and a wailing voice came nearer and nearer.

Tabby took a long breath and vowed that she would beg or buy the dear old cat that had saved her from destruction. Then she forgot her own danger in listening to the poor woman, who came in crying that her neighbors said she must leave town at once or they would tar and feather her for showing spies the road to a Tory's house.

"Well for me I came and heard their plots, or I might be sent off in like case," thought the girl, feeling that the more perils she encountered, the greater heroine she would be.

Mr. Bliss comforted the old soul, bidding her stay there till the neighbors forgot her, and the officers gave her some money to pay for the costly service she had done them. Then they left the room, and after some delay the three men set off, but Tabby was compelled to stay in her hiding place till the table was cleared, and the women deep in gossip, as they washed dishes in the kitchen. Then the little spy crept out softly, and, raising the window with great care, ran away as fast as her stiff limbs would carry her.

By the time she reached the Deacon's, however, and told her tale, the Tories were well on their way, Mr. Bliss having provided them with horses that his own flight might be speedier.

So they escaped, but the warning was given, and Tabby received great praise for her hour under the table. The towns-people hastened their preparations and had time to remove the most valuable stores to neighboring towns, to mount their cannon and drill their minutemen, for these resolute farmers meant to resist oppression, and the world knows how well they did it when the hour came.

Such an early spring had not been known for years, and by the nineteenth of April fruit trees were in bloom, winter grain was up, and the stately elms that fringed the river and overarched the village streets were budding fast. It seemed a pity that such a lovely world should be disturbed by strife, but liberty was dearer than prosperity or peace, and the people leaped from their beds when young Dr. Prescott came, riding for his life, with the message Paul Revere brought from Boston in the night, "Arm! Arm! The British are coming!"

Like an electric spark the news ran from house to house, and men made ready to fight, while the brave women bade them go and did their best to guard the treasure confided to their keeping. A little later, word came that the British were at Lexington and blood had been shed. Then the farmers shouldered their guns, with few words but stern faces, and by sunrise a hundred men stood ready, with good Parson Emerson at their head. More men were coming in from the neighboring towns, and all felt that the hour had arrived when patience ceased to be a virtue and rebellion was just.

Great was the excitement everywhere, but at Captain David Brown's one little heart beat high with hope and fear, as Tabby stood at the door, looking across the river to the town, where drums were beating, bells ringing, and people hurrying to and fro.

"I can't fight, but I *must* see," she said, and, catching up her cloak, she ran over the North Bridge, promising her aunt to return and bring her word as soon as the enemy appeared.

"What news? Are they coming?" called the people, from the manse and the few houses that then stood along that road. But Tabby could only shake her head and run the faster, in her eagerness to see what was happening on that memorable day. When she reached the middle of the town she found that the little company had gone along the Lexington Road to meet the enemy. Nothing daunted, she hurried in that direction and, climbing a high bank, waited to catch a glimpse of the British grenadiers, of whom she had heard so much.

About seven o'clock they came, the sun glittering on the arms of eight hundred English soldiers marching toward the hundred stouthearted farmers, who waited till they were within a few rods of them.

"Let us stand our ground, and, if we die, let us die here," said brave Parson Emerson, still among his people, ready for anything but surrender.

"Nay," said a cautious Lincoln man, "it will not do for us to *begin* the war."

So they reluctantly fell back to the town, the British following slowly, being weary with their seven-mile march over the hills from Lexington. Coming to a little brown house perched on the hillside, one of the thirsty officers spied a well, with the bucket swinging at the end of the long pole. Running up the bank, he was about to drink, when a girl, who was crouching behind the well, sprang up, and, with an energetic gesture, flung the water in his face, crying, "That's the way we serve spies!"

Before Ensign De Bernicre—for it was he, acting as guide to the enemy—could clear his eyes and dry his drenched face, Tabby was gone over the hill with a laugh and a defiant gesture toward the redcoats below.

In high feather at this exploit, she darted about the town, watching the British at their work of destruction. They cut down and burnt the liberty pole, broke open sixty barrels of flour, flung five hundred pounds of balls into the millpond and wells, and set the courthouse on fire. Other parties were ordered to different quarters of the town to ransack houses and destroy all the stores they found. Captain Parsons was sent to take possession of the North Bridge, and De Bernicre led the way, for he had taken notes on his former visit and was a good guide. As they marched, a little scarlet figure went flying on before them and vanished at the turn of the road. It was Tabby hastening home to warn her aunt.

"Quick, child, whip on this gown and cap and hurry into bed. These prying fellows will surely have pity on a sick girl and respect this room if no other," said Mrs. Brown, briskly helping Tabby into a short nightgown and round cap and tucking her well up when she was laid down, for between the plump featherbeds were hidden many muskets, the most precious of their stores. This had been planned beforehand, and Tabby was glad to rest and tell her tale while Aunty Brown put physic bottles and glasses on the table, set some evil-smelling herbs to simmer on the hearth, and, compromising with her conscience, concocted a nice little story to tell the invaders.

Presently they came, and it was well for Tabby that the Ensign remained below to guard the doors while the men ransacked the house from garret to cellar, for he might have recognized the saucy girl who had twice maltreated him.

"These are feathers; lift the covers carefully or you'll be half smothered, they fly about so," said Mrs. Brown, as the men came to some casks of cartridges and flints, which she had artfully ripped up several pillows to conceal.

Quite deceived, the men gladly passed on, leaving the very things they most wanted to destroy. Coming to the bedroom, where more treasures of the same valuable sort were hidden in various nooks and corners, the dame held up her finger, saying, with an anxious glance toward Tabby, "Step softly, please. You wouldn't harm a poor, sick girl. The doctor thinks it is smallpox, and a fright might kill her. I keep the chamber as fresh as I can with yarbs, so I guess there isn't much danger of catching it."

The men reluctantly looked in, saw a flushed face on the pillow (for Tabby was red with running, and her black eyes wild with excitement), took a sniff at the wormwood and motherwort, and, with a hasty glance into a closet or two where sundry clothes concealed hidden doors, hastily retired to report the danger and get away as soon as possible.

They would have been much disgusted at the trick played upon them if they had seen the sick girl fly out of bed and dance a jig of joy as they tramped away to Barrett's Mills. But soon Tabby had no heart for merriment, as she watched the minutemen gather by the bridge, saw the British march down on the other side, and when their first volley killed brave Isaac Davis and Abner Hosmer, of Acton, she heard Major Buttrick give the order, "Fire, fellow soldiers, for God's sake, fire!"

For a little while shots rang, smoke rose, shouts were heard, and red and blue coats mingled in the struggle on the bridge. Then the British fell back, leaving two dead soldiers behind them. These were buried where they fell, and the bodies of

Acton men were sent home to their poor wives, Concord's first martyrs for liberty.

No need to tell more of the story of that day; all children know it, and many have made a pilgrimage to see the old monument set up where the English fell and the bronze Minuteman, standing on his granite pedestal to mark the spot where the brave Concord farmers fired the shot that made the old North Bridge immortal.

We must follow Tabby and tell how she got her tablecloth. When the fight was over, the dead buried, the wounded cared for, and the prisoners exchanged, the Tories were punished. Dr. Lee was confined to his own farm, on penalty of being shot if he left it, and the property of Daniel Bliss was confiscated by government. Some things were sold at auction, and Captain Brown bought the fine cloth and gave it to Tabby, saying heartily, "There, my girl; that belongs to you, and you may well be proud of it, for, thanks to your quick wits and eyes and ears, we were not taken unawares, but sent the redcoats back faster than they came."

And Tabby *was* proud of it, keeping it carefully, displaying it with immense satisfaction whenever she told the story, and spinning busily to make a set of napkins to go with it. It covered the table when her wedding supper was spread, was used at the christening of her first boy, and for many a Thanksgiving and Christmas dinner through the happy years of her married life.

Then it was preserved by her daughters, as a relic of their mother's youth, and, long after the old woman was gone, the well-worn cloth still appeared on great occasions, till it grew too thin for anything but careful keeping, to illustrate the story so proudly told by the grandchildren, who found it hard to believe that the feeble old lady of ninety could be the lively lass who played her little part in the Revolution with such spirit.

In 1861, Tabby's tablecloth saw another war and made an honorable end. When men were called for, Concord responded "Here!" and sent a goodly number, led by another brave Colonel Prescott. Barretts, Hosmers, Melvins, Browns, and Wheelers stood shoulder to shoulder, as their grandfathers had stood that day to meet the British by the bridge. Mothers said, "Go my son," as bravely as before, and sisters and sweethearts smiled with wet eyes as the boys in blue marched away again, cheered on by another noble Emerson. More than one of Tabby's descendants went, some to fight, some to nurse; and for four long years the old town worked and waited, hoped and prayed, burying the dear dead boys sent home, nursing those who brought back honorable wounds, and sending more to man the breaches made by the awful battles that filled both North and South with a wilderness of graves.

The women knit and sewed Sundays as well as weekdays, to supply the call for clothes; the men emptied their pockets freely, glad to give; and the minister, after preaching like a Christian soldier, took off his coat and packed boxes of comforts like a tender father.

"More lint and bandages called for, and I do believe we've torn and picked up every old rag in the town," said one busy lady to another, as several sat together making comfort-bags in the third year of the long struggle.

"I have cleared my garret of nearly everything in it and only wish I had more to give," answered one of the patriotic Barrett mothers.

"We can't buy anything so soft and good as worn-out sheets and tableclothes. New ones won't do, or I'd cut up every one

of mine," said a newly married Wheeler, sewing for dear
life, as she remembered the many cousins gone to the war.

"I think I shall have to give our Revolutionary tablecloth.
It's old enough, and soft as silk, and I'm sure my blessed
grandmother would think that it couldn't make a better end,"
spoke up white-headed Madam Hubbard, for Tabby Tarbell
had married one of that numerous and worthy race.

"Oh, you wouldn't cut up that famous cloth, would you?"
cried the younger woman.

"Yes, I will. It's in rags, and when I'm gone no one will
care for it. Folks don't seem to remember what the women
did in those days, so it's no use keeping relics of 'em," answered the old lady, who would have owned herself mistaken
if she could have looked forward to 1876, when the town
celebrated its centennial and proudly exhibited the little
scissors with which Mrs. Barrett cut paper for cartridges,
among other ancient trophies of that earlier day.

So the ancient cloth was carefully made into a boxful of
the finest lint and softest squares to lay on wounds and sent
to one of the Concord women who had gone as a nurse.

"Here's a treasure!" she said, as she came to it among
comforts newly arrived from home. "Just what I want for
my brave Rebel and poor little Johnny Bullard."

The "brave Rebel" was a Southern man who had fought
well and was badly wounded in many ways, yet never complained and in the midst of great suffering was always so
courteous, patient, and courageous, that the men called him
"our gentleman," and tried to show how much they respected
so gallant a foe. John Bullard was an English drummer boy,
who had been through several battles, stoutly drumming
away in spite of bullets and cannon balls, cheering many a
campfire with his voice, for he sang like a blackbird and was

always merry, always plucky, and so great a favorite in his regiment, that all mourned for "little Johnny" when his right arm was shot off at Gettysburg. It was thought he would die, but he pulled through the worst of it and was slowly struggling back to health, still trying to be gay, and beginning to chirp feebly now and then, like a convalescent bird.

"Here, Johnny, is some splendid lint for this poor arm, and some of the softest compresses for Carrol's wounds. He is asleep, so I'll begin with you, and while I work I'll amuse you with the story of the old tablecloth this lint came from," said Nurse Hunt, as she stood by the bed where the thin, white face smiled at her, though the boy dreaded the hard quarter of an hour he had to endure every day.

"Thanky, mum. We 'aven't 'ad a story for a good bit. I'm 'earty this mornin' and think I'll be hup by this day week, won't I?"

"I hope so. Now shut your eyes and listen; then you won't mind the twinges I give you, gentle as I try to be," answered the nurse, beginning her painful task.

Then she told the story of Tabby's tablecloth, and the boy enjoyed it immensely, laughing out at the slapping and the throwing water in the Ensign's face and openly rejoicing when the redcoats got the worst of it.

"As we've beaten all the rest of the world, I don't mind our 'aving bad luck that time. We har friends now, and I'll fight for you, mum, like a British bulldog, if I hever get the chance," said Johnny, when the tale and dressing were ended.

"So you shall. I like to turn a brave enemy into a faithful friend, as I hope we shall yet be able to do with our Southern brothers. I admire their courage and their loyalty to what they believe to be right, and we are all suffering the punishment we deserve for waiting till this sad war came, instead of settling the trouble years ago, as we might have done if we had loved honesty and honor more than money and power."

As she spoke, Miss Hunt turned to her other patient and saw by the expression of his face that he had heard both the tale and the talk. He smiled, and said, "Good morning," as usual, but when she stooped to lay a compress of the soft, wet damask on the angry wound in his breast, he whispered, with a grateful look, "You *have* changed one 'Southern brother' from an enemy into a friend. Whether I live or die, I never can forget how generous and kind you have all been to me."

"Thank you! It is worth months of anxiety and care to hear such words. Let us shake hands and do our best to make North and South as good friends as England and America now are," said the nurse, offering her hand.

"Me, too! I've got one 'and left, and I give it ye with all me 'art. God bless ye, sir, and a lively getting hup for the two of us!" cried Johnny, stretching across the narrow space that divided the beds, with a beaming face and true English readiness to forgive a fallen foe when he had proved a brave one.

The three hands met in a warm shake, and the act was a little lesson more eloquent than words to the lookers-on, for the spirit of brotherhood that should bind us all together worked the miracle of linking these three by the frail threads spun a century ago.

So Tabby's tablecloth did make a beautiful and useful end at last.

Lunch

"Sister Jerusha, it really does wear upon me to see those dear boys eat such bad pies and stuff day after day when they ought to have good wholesome things for lunch. I actually ache to go and give each one of 'em a nice piece of bread and butter or one of our big cookies," said kind Miss Mehitable Plummer, taking up her knitting after a long look at the

swarm of boys pouring out of the grammar school opposite,
to lark about the yard, sit on the posts, or dive into a dingy
little shop close by, where piles of greasy tarts and cakes lay
in the window. They would not have allured any but hungry
schoolboys and ought to have been labelled Dyspepsia and
Headache, so unwholesome were they.

Miss Jerusha looked up from her seventeenth patchwork
quilt and answered, with a sympathetic glance over the way,
"If we had enough to go round I'd do it myself and save these
poor deluded dears from the bilious turns that will surely
take them down before vacation comes. That fat boy is as
yellow as a lemon now, and no wonder, for I've seen him eat
half a dozen dreadful turnovers for one lunch."

Both old ladies shook their heads and sighed, for they led
a very quiet life in the narrow house that stood end to the
street, squeezed in between two stores, looking as out of
place as the good spinsters would have among the merry lads
opposite. Sitting at the front windows day after day, the
old ladies had learned to enjoy watching the boys, who came
and went, like bees to a hive, month by month. They had
their favorites and beguiled many a long hour speculating
on the looks, manners, and probable station of the lads. One
lame boy was Miss Jerusha's pet, though she never spoke
to him, and a tall bright-faced fellow, who rather lorded it
over the rest, quite won Miss Hetty's old heart by helping
her across the street on a slippery day. They longed to mend
some of the shabby clothes, to cheer up the dull discouraged
ones, advise the sickly, reprove the rude, and, most of all,
feed those who persisted in buying lunch at the dirty bake-
shop over the way.

The good souls were famous cooks and had many books
full of all manner of nice receipts, which they seldom used,

as they lived simply and saw little company. A certain kind of molasses cookie, made by their honored mother—a renowned housewife in her time—and eaten by the sisters as children, had a peculiar charm for them. A tin box was always kept full, though they only now and then nibbled one and preferred to give them away to poor children, as they trotted to market each day. Many a time had Miss Hetty felt sorely tempted to treat the boys but was a little timid, for they were rough fellows, and she regarded them much as a benevolent tabby would a party of frisky puppies.

Today the box was full of fresh cookies, crisp, brown, and sweet; their spicy odor pervaded the room, and the china-closet door stood suggestively open. Miss Hetty's spectacles turned that way, then went back to the busy scene in the street, as if trying to get courage for the deed. Something happened just then which decided her and sealed the doom of the bilious tarts and their maker.

Several of the younger lads were playing marbles on the sidewalk, for hopscotch, leapfrog, and friendly scuffles were going on in the yard, and no quiet spot could be found. The fat boy sat on a post nearby and, having eaten his last turnover, fell to teasing the small fellows peacefully playing at his feet. One was the shabby lame boy, who hopped to and fro with his crutch, munching a dry cracker, with now and then a trip to the pump to wash it down. He seldom brought any lunch, and seemed to enjoy this poor treat so much that the big bright-faced chap tossed him a red apple as he came out of the yard to get his hat, thrown there by the mate he had been playfully thrashing.

The lame child eyed the pretty apple lovingly and was preparing to take the first delicious bite, when the fat youth with a dexterous kick sent it flying into the middle of the street, where a passing wheel crushed it down into the mud.

"It's a shame! He *shall* have something good! The scamp!" And with this somewhat confused exclamation Miss Hetty threw down her work, ran to the closet, then darted to the front door, embracing the tin box, as if the house were on fire and that contained her dearest treasures.

"Sakes alive, what *is* the matter with sister?" ejaculated Miss Jerusha, going to the window just in time to see the fat boy tumble off the post as the tall lad came to the rescue, while the cripple went hopping across the street in answer to a kindly quavering voice that called out to him, "Come here, boy, and get a cookie—a dozen if you want 'em."

"Sister's done it at last!" And, inspired by this heroic example, Miss Jerusha threw up the window, saying, as she beckoned to the avenger, "You, too, because you stood by that poor little boy. Come right over and help yourself."

Charley Howe laughed at the indignant old ladies but, being a gentleman, took off his hat and ran across to thank them for their interest in the fray. Several other lads followed as irresistibly as flies to a honeypot, for the tin box was suggestive of cake, and they waited for no invitation.

Miss Hetty was truly a noble yet a droll sight as she stood there, a trim little old lady, with her cap strings flying in the wind, her rosy old face shining with good will, as she dealt out cookies with a lavish hand and a kind word to all.

"Here's a nice big one for you, my dear. I don't know your name, but I do, your face, and I like to see a big boy stand up for the little ones," she said, beaming at Charley as he came up.

"Thank you, ma'am. That's a splendid one. We don't get anything so nice over there." And Charley gratefully bolted the cake in three mouthfuls, having given away his own lunch.

"No indeed! One of these is worth a dozen of those nasty pies. I hate to see you eating them, and I don't believe your mothers know how bad they are," said Miss Hetty, diving for another handful into the depths of the box, which was half empty already.

"Wish you'd teach old Peck how you make 'em. We'd be glad enough to buy these and let the cockroach pies alone," said Charley, accepting another and enjoying the fun, for half the fellows were watching the scene from over the way.

"Cockroach pies! You don't mean to say?" cried Miss Hetty, nearly dropping her load in her horror at the idea, for she had heard of fricasseed frogs and roasted locusts and thought a new delicacy had been found.

"We find 'em in the applesauce sometimes, and nails and bits of barrel in the cakes, so some of us don't patronize Peck," replied Charley.

Little Briggs, the cripple, added eagerly, "I never do; my mother won't let me."

"He never has any money, that's why," bawled Dickson, the fat boy, dodging behind the fence as he spoke.

"Never you mind, sonny, you come here every day, and *I'll* see that you have a good lunch. Apples too, *red ones,* if you like them, with your cake," answered Miss Hetty, patting his head and sending an indignant glance across the street.

"Crybaby! Mollycoddle! Grandma's darling!" jeered Dickson and then fled, for Charley fired a ball at him with such good aim it narrowly escaped his nose.

"That boy will have the jaundice as sure as fate, and he deserves it," said Miss Hetty sternly, as she dropped the lid on the now empty box, for while she was talking the free-and-easy young gentlemen had been helping themselves.

"Thank you very much, ma'am, for my cookie. I won't forget to call tomorrow." And little Briggs shook hands with as innocent a face as if his jacket pocket were not bulging in a most suspicious manner.

"You'll get your death a cold, Hetty," called Miss Jerusha, and, taking the hint, Charley promptly ended the visit.

"Sheer off, fellows. We are no end obliged, ma'am, and I'll see that Briggs isn't put upon by sneaks."

Then the boys ran off, and the old lady retired to her parlor to sink into her easy chair, as much excited by this little feat as if she had led a forlorn hope to a storm a battery.

"I'll fill both those big tins tomorrow and treat every one of the small boys, if I'm spared," she panted, with a decided nod, as she settled her cap and composed her neat black skirts, with which the wind had taken liberties, as she stood on the steps.

"I'm not sure it isn't our duty to make and sell good, wholesome lunches to those boys. We can afford to do it cheap, and it wouldn't be much trouble. Just put the long table across the front entry for half an hour every day and let them come and get a bun, a cookie, or a buttered biscuit. It could be done, sister," said Miss Jerusha, longing to distinguish herself in some way also.

"It *shall* be done, sister!" And Miss Hetty made up her mind at that moment to devote some of her time and skill to rescuing those blessed boys from the unprincipled Peck and his cockroach pies.

It was pleasant, as well as droll, to see how heartily the good souls threw themselves into the new enterprise, how bravely they kept each other up when courage showed signs of failing, and how rapidly they became convinced that it was a duty to provide better food for the future defenders and rulers of their native land.

"You can't expect the dears to study with clear heads if they are not fed properly, and half the women in the world never think that what goes into children's stomachs affects their brains," declared Miss Hetty, as she rolled out vast sheets of dough next day, emphasizing her remarks with vigorous flourishes of the rolling pin.

"Our blessed mother understood how to feed a family.

Fourteen stout boys and girls, all alive and well, and you and I as smart at seventy-one and -two, as most folks at forty. Good, plain victuals and plenty of 'em is the secret of firm health," responded Miss Jerusha, rattling a pan of buns briskly into the oven.

"We'd better make some Brighton Rock. It is gone out of fashion, but our brothers used to be dreadful fond of it, and boys are about alike all the world over. Ma's *resate* never fails, and it will be a new treat for the little dears."

"S'pose we have an extra can of milk left and give 'em a good mugful? Some of those poor things look as if they never got a drop. Peck sells beer, aīd milk is a deal better. Shall we, sister?"

"We'll try it, Jerushy. In for a penny, in for a pound."

And upon that principle the old ladies did that thing handsomely, deferring the great event till Monday, that all might be in apple-pie order. They said nothing of it when the lads came on Friday morning, and all Saturday, which was a holiday at school, was a very busy one with them.

"Hullo! Miss Hetty *has* done it now, hasn't she? Look at that, old Peck, and tremble!" exclaimed Charley to his mates, as he came down the street on Monday morning, and espied a neat little sign on the sisters' door, setting forth the agreeable fact that certain delectable articles of food and drink could be had within at reasonable prices during recess.

No caps were at the windows, but behind the drawn curtains two beaming old faces were peeping out to see how the boys took the great announcement. Whoever remembers Hawthorne's half-comic, half-pathetic description of poor Hepzibah Pyncheon's hopes and fears, when arranging her gingerbread wares in the little shop, can understand something of the excitement of the sisters that day, as the time drew near when the first attempt was to be made.

"Who will set the door open?" said Miss Hetty when the fateful moment came, and boys began to pour out into the yard.

"I will!" And, nerving herself to the task, Miss Jerusha marched boldly around the table, set wide the door, and then, as the first joyful whoop from the boys told that the feast was in view, she whisked back into the parlor panic-stricken.

"There they come—hundreds of them, I should think by the sound!" she whispered, as the tramp of feet came nearer.

And the clamor of voices exclaimed, "What bully buns!" "Ain't those cookies rousers?" "New stuff too; looks first-rate." "I told you it wasn't a joke." "Wonder how Peck likes it?" "Dickson shan't come in." "You go first, Charley." "Here's a cent for you, Briggs; come on and trade like the rest of us."

"I'm so flurried I couldn't make change to save my life," gasped Miss Jerusha from behind the sofa, whither she had fled.

"It is *my* turn now. Be calm, and we shall soon get used to it."

Bracing herself to meet the merry chaff of the boys, as new and trying to the old lady as real danger would have been, Miss Hetty stepped forth into the hall to be greeted by a cheer, and then a chorus of demands for everything so temptingly set forth upon her table. Entrenched behind a barricade of buns, she dealt out her wares with rapidly increasing speed and skill, for as fast as one relay of lads was satisfied another came up, till the table was bare, the milk can ran dry, and nothing was left to tell the tale but an empty water pail and a pile of five-cent pieces.

"I hope I didn't cheat anyone, but I was flurried, sister; they were so very noisy and so hungry. Bless their dear hearts;

they are full now, I trust." And Miss Hetty looked over her glasses at the crumby countenances opposite, meeting many nods and smiles in return, as her late customers enthusiastically recommended her establishment to the patronage of those who had preferred Peck's questionable dainties.

"The Brighton Rock was a success; we must have a good store for tomorrow, and more milk. Briggs drank it like a baby, and your nice boy proposed my health like a little gentleman, as he is," replied Miss Jerusha, who had ventured out before it was too late and done the honors of the can with great dignity, in spite of some inward trepidation at the astonishing feats performed with the mug.

"Peck's nose is out of joint, if I may use so vulgar an expression, and *our* lunch a triumphant success. Boys know what is good, and we need not fear to lose their custom as long as we can supply them. I shall order a barrel of flour at once and heat up the big oven. We have put our hand to the work and must not turn back, for our honor is pledged now."

With which lofty remark Miss Hetty closed the door, trying to look utterly unconscious of the anxious Peck, who was flattening his nose against his dingy windowpane to survey his rivals over piles of unsold pastry.

The little venture *was* a success, and all that winter the old ladies did their part faithfully, finding the task more to their taste than everlasting patchwork and knitting, and receiving a fair profit on their outlay, being shrewd managers and rich in old-fashioned thrift, energy, and industry.

The boys revelled in wholesome fare and soon learned to love "the Aunties," as they were called, while such of the parents as took an interest in the matter showed their approval in many ways most gratifying to the old ladies.

The final triumph, however, was the closing of Peck's shop for want of custom, for few besides the boys patronized him. None mourned for him, and Dickson proved the truth of Miss Hetty's prophecy by actually having a bilious fever in the spring.

But a new surprise awaited the boys, for, when they came flocking back after the summer vacation, there stood the little shop, brave in new paint and fittings, full of all the old goodies, and over the door a smart sign, "Plummer & Co."

"By Jove, the Aunties are bound to cover themselves with glory. Let's go in and hear all about it. Behave now, you fellows, or I'll see about it afterward," commanded Charley, as he paused to peer in through the clean windows at the tempting display.

In they trooped, and, tapping on the counter, stood ready to greet the old ladies as usual, but to their great surprise a pretty young woman appeared and smilingly asked what they would have.

"We want the Aunties, if you please. Isn't this their shop?" said little Briggs, bitterly disappointed at not finding his good friends.

"You will find them over there at home as usual. Yes, this is their shop, and I'm their niece. My husband is the Co., and we run the shop for the aunts. I hope you'll patronize us, gentlemen."

"We will! We will! Three cheers for Plummer & Co.!" cried Charley, leading off three rousers that made the little shop ring again, and brought two caps to the opposite windows, as two cheery old faces smiled and nodded, full of satisfaction at the revolution so successfully planned and carried out.

How They Camped Out

"It looks so much like snow I think it would be wiser to put off your sleighing party, Gwen," said Mrs. Arnold, looking anxiously out at the heavy sky and streets still drifted by the last winter storm.

"Not before night, Mamma; we don't mind its being cloudy; we like it, because the sun makes the snow so dazzling when we get out of town. We can't give it up now, for here comes Patrick with the boys." And Gwen ran down to welcome the big sleigh, which just then drove up with four jolly lads skirmishing about inside.

"Come on!" called Mark, her brother, knocking his friends right and left, to make room for the four girls who were to complete the party.

"What do you think of the weather, Patrick?" asked Mrs. Arnold from the window, still undecided about the wisdom of letting her flock go out alone, papa having been called away after the plan was made.

"Faith, ma'am, it's an illigant day barring the wind, that's a thrifle could to the nose. I'll have me eye on the childer, ma'am, and there'll be no throuble at all, at all," replied the old coachman, lifting a round, red face out of his muffler and patting little Gus on the shoulder, as he sat proudly on the high seat holding the whip.

"Be careful, dears, and come home early."

With which parting caution mamma shut the window and watched the young folks drive away, little dreaming what would happen before they got back.

The wind was more than a "thrifle could," for when they got out of the city it blew across the open country in bitter blasts and made the eight little noses almost as red as old Pat's, who had been up all night at a wake and was still heavy-headed with too much whiskey, though no one suspected it.

The lads enjoyed themselves immensely snowballing one another, for the drifts were still fresh enough to furnish soft snow, and Mark, Bob, and Tony had many a friendly tussle in it as they went up hills or paused to breathe the horses after a swift trot along a level bit of road. Little Gus helped drive till his hands were benumbed in spite of the new red mittens, and he had to descend among the girls, who were cuddled cozily under the warm robes, telling secrets, eating candy, and laughing at the older boys' pranks.

Sixteen-year-old Gwendoline was matron of the party and kept excellent order among the girls, for Ruth and Alice were nearly her own age; and Rita, a most obedient younger sister.

"I say, Gwen, we are going to stop at the old house on the way home and get some nuts for this evening. Papa said we might, and some of the big Baldwins, too. I've got baskets, and while we fellows fill them you girls can look around the house," said Mark, when the exhausted young gentlemen returned to their seats.

"That will be nice. I want to get some books, and Rita has been very anxious about one of her dolls, which she is sure was left in the nursery closet. If we are going to stop, we ought to be turning back, Pat, for it is beginning to snow and will be dark early," answered Gwen, suddenly realizing that great flakes were fast whitening the roads and the wind had risen to a gale.

"Shure and I will, miss dear, as soon as iver I can, but it's round a good bit we must go, for I couldn't be turning here widout upsettin' the whole of yez, it's that drifted. Rest aisy, and I'll fetch up at the ould place in half an hour, plaze the powers," said Pat, who had lost his way and wouldn't own it, being stupid with a sup or two he had privately taken on the way, to keep the chill out of his bones, he said.

On they went again, with the wind at their backs, caring little for the snow that now fell fast or the gathering twilight, since they were going toward home, they thought. It was a very long half hour before Pat brought them to the country house, which was shut up for the winter. With difficulty they ploughed their way up to the steps and scrambled onto the piazza, where they danced about to warm their feet till Mark unlocked the door and let them in, leaving Pat to enjoy a doze on his seat.

"Make haste, boys; it is cold and dark here, and we must get home. Mamma will be so anxious, and it really is going to be a bad storm," said Gwen, whose spirits were dampened by the gloom of the old house and who felt her responsibility, having promised to be home early.

Off went the boys to attic and cellar, being obliged to light the lantern left here for the use of whoever came now and then to inspect the premises. The girls, having found books and doll, sat upon the rolled-up carpets or peeped about at the once gay and hospitable rooms, now looking very empty and desolate with piled-up furniture, shuttered windows, and fireless hearths.

"If we were going to stay long I'd have a fire in the library. Papa often does when he comes out, to keep the books from moulding," began Gwen, but was interrupted by a shout from without and, running to the door, saw Pat picking himself out of a drift while the horses were galloping down the avenue at full speed.

"Bejabbers, them villains give a jump when that fallin' branch struck 'em, and out I wint, bein' tuk unknownst, just thinkin' of me poor cousin Mike. May his bed above be aisy the day! Whist now, miss dear! I'll fetch 'em back in a jiffy. Stop still till I come, and kape them b'ys quiet."

With a blow to settle his hat, Patrick trotted gallantly away into the storm, and the girls went in to tell the exciting news to the lads, who came whooping back from their search, with baskets of nuts and apples.

"Here's a go!" cried Mark. "Old Pat will run halfway to town before he catches the horses, and we are in for an hour or two at least."

"Then do make a fire, for we shall die of cold if we have to wait long," begged Gwen, rubbing Rita's cold hands and looking anxiously at little Gus, who was about making up his mind to roar.

"So we will, and be jolly till the blunderbuss gets back. Camp down, girls, and you fellows come and hold the lantern while I get wood and stuff. It is so confoundedly dark, I shall break my neck down the shed steps." And Mark led the way to the library, where the carpet still remained, and comfortable chairs and sofas invited the chilly visitors to rest.

"How can you light your fire when you get the wood?" asked Ruth, a practical damsel, who looked well after her own creature comforts and was longing for a warm supper.

"Papa hides the matches in a tin box, so the rats won't get at them. Here they are, and two or three bits of candles for the sticks on the chimney piece, if he forgets to have the lantern trimmed. Now we will light up, and look cozy when the boys come back."

And producing the box from under a sofa cushion, Gwen cheered the hearts of all by lighting two candles, rolling up the chairs, and making ready to be comfortable. Thoughtful Alice went to see if Pat was returning and found a buffalo robe lying on the steps. Returning with this, she reported that there was no sign of the runaways and advised making ready for a long stay.

"How Mamma will worry!" thought Gwen but made light of the affair, because she saw Rita looked timid, and Gus shivered till his teeth chattered.

"We will have a nice time, and play we are shipwrecked people or Arctic explorers. Here come Dr. Kane and the sailors with supplies of wood, so we can thaw our pemmican and warm our feet. Gus shall be the little Eskimo boy, all dressed in fur, as he is in the picture we have at home," she said, wrapping the child in the robe and putting her own sealskin cap on his head to divert his mind.

"Here we are! Now for a jolly blaze, boys; and if Pat doesn't come back we can have our fun here instead of at home," cried Mark, well pleased with the adventure, as were his mates.

So they fell to work, and soon a bright fire was lighting up the room with its cheerful shine, and the children gathered about it, quite careless of the storm raging without and sure that Pat would come in time.

"I'm hungry," complained Gus as soon as he was warm.

"So am I," added Rita from the rug, where the two little ones sat toasting themselves.

"Eat an apple," said Mark.

"They are so hard and cold I don't like them," began Gus.

"Roast some!" cried Ruth.

"And crack nuts," suggested Alice.

"Pity we can't cook something in real camp style; it would be such fun," said Tony, who had spent weeks on Monadnock, living upon the supplies he and his party tugged up the mountain on their backs.

"We shall not have time for anything but what we have. Put down your apples and crack away, or we shall be obliged to leave them," advised Gwen, coming back from an observation at the front door with an anxious line on her forehead, for the storm was rapidly increasing, and there was no sign of Pat or the horses.

The rest were in high glee, and an hour or two slipped quickly away as they enjoyed the impromptu feast and played games. Gus recalled them to the discomforts of their situation by saying with a yawn and a whimper, "I'm so sleepy! I want my own bed and Mamma."

"So do I!" echoed Rita, who had been nodding for some

time and longed to lie down and sleep comfortably anywhere.
"Almost eight o'clock! By Jove, that old Pat *is* taking his
time, I think. Wonder if he has got into trouble? We can't do
anything and may as well keep quiet here," said Mark, looking at his watch and beginning to understand that the joke was
rather a serious one.

"Better make a night of it and all go to sleep. Pat can wake
us up when he comes. The cold makes a fellow *so* drowsy."
And Bob gave a stretch that nearly rent him asunder.

"I will let the children nap on the sofa. They are so tired
of waiting and may as well amuse themselves in that way as
in fretting. Come, Gus and Rita; each take a pillow, and I'll
cover you up with my shawl."

Gwen made the little ones comfortable, and they were off
in five minutes. The others kept up bravely till nine o'clock;
then the bits of candles were burnt out, the stories all told,
nuts and apples had lost their charm, and weariness and hunger caused spirits to fail perceptibly.

"I've eaten five Baldwins, and yet I want more—something
filling and good. Can't we catch a rat and roast him?" proposed Bob, who was a hearty lad and was ravenous by this
time.

"Isn't there anything in the house?" asked Ruth, who dared
not eat nuts for fear of indigestion.

"Not a thing that I know of except a few pickles in the
storeroom; we had so many, Mamma left some here," answered Gwen, resolving to provision the house before she left
it another autumn.

"Pickles alone are rather sour feed. If we only had a biscuit
now, they wouldn't be bad for a relish," said Tony, with the
air of a man who had known what it was to live on burnt
bean soup and rye flapjacks for a week.

"I saw a keg of soft soap in the shed. How would that go with the pickles?" suggested Bob, who felt equal to the biggest and acidest cucumber ever grown.

"Mamma knew an old lady who actually did eat soft soap and cream for her complexion," put in Alice, whose own fresh face looked as if she had tried the same distasteful remedy with success.

The boys laughed, and Mark, who felt that hospitality required him to do something for his guests, said briskly, "Let us go on a foraging expedition while the lamp holds out to burn, for the old lantern is almost gone, and then we are done for. Come on, Bob, your sharp nose will smell out food if there is any."

"Don't set the house afire, and bring more wood when you come, for we must have light of some kind in this poky place," called Gwen with a sigh, wishing every one of them were safely at home and abed.

A great tramping of boots, slamming of doors, and shouting of voices followed the departure of the boys, as well as a crash, a howl, and then a roar of laughter, as Bob fell down the cellar stairs, having opened the door in search of food and poked his nose in too far. Presently they came back, very dusty, cobwebby, and cold, but triumphantly bearing a droll collection of trophies. Mark had a piece of board and the lantern; Tony, a big wooden box and a tin pail; Bob fondly embraced a pickle jar and a tumbler of jelly which had been forgotten on a high shelf in the storeroom.

"Meal, pickles, jam, and boards. What a mess, and what are we to do with it all?" cried the girls, much amused at the result of the expedition.

"Can any of you make a hoecake?" demanded Mark.

"No, indeed! I can make caramels and coconut cakes," said Ruth proudly.

"I can make good toast and tea," added Alice.

"I can't cook anything," confessed Gwen, who was unusually accomplished in French, German, and music.

"Girls aren't worth much in the hour of need. Take hold, Tony; you are the chap for me." And Mark disrespectfully turned his back on the young ladies, who could only sit and watch the lads work.

"He can't do it without water," whispered Ruth.

"Or salt," answered Alice.

"Or a pan to bake it in," added Gwen; and then all smiled at the dilemma they foresaw.

But Tony was equal to the occasion and calmly went on with his task, while Mark arranged the fire and Bob opened the pickles. First the new cook filled the pail with snow till enough was melted to wet the meal; this mixture was stirred with a pine stick till thick enough, then spread on the board and set up before the bed of coals to brown.

"It never will bake in the world." "He can't turn it, so it won't be done on both sides." "Won't be fit to eat anyway!" And with these dark hints the girls consoled themselves for their want of skill.

But the cake did bake a nice brown; Tony did turn it neatly with his jackknife and the stick, and when it was done cut it into bits, added jelly, and passed it around on an old atlas; and everyone said, "It really does taste good!"

Two more were baked, and eaten with pickles for a change; then all were satisfied, and after a vote of thanks to Tony they began to think of sleep.

"Pat has gone home and told them we are all right, and

Mamma knows we can manage here well enough for one night, so don't worry, Gwen, but take a nap, and I'll lie on the rug and see to the fire."

Mark's happy-go-lucky way of taking things did not convince his sister, but, as she could do nothing, she submitted and made her friends as comfortable as she could.

All had plenty of wraps. So the girls nestled into the three large chairs; Bob and Tony rolled themselves up in the robe, with their feet to the fire, and were soon snoring like weary hunters. Mark pillowed his head on a log and was sound asleep in ten minutes in spite of his promise to be a sentinel.

Gwen's chair was the least easy of the three, and she could not forget herself like the rest but sat wide awake, watching the blaze, counting the hours, and wondering why no one came to them.

The wind blew fiercely, the snow beat against the blinds, rats scuttled about in the walls, and now and then a branch fell upon the roof with a crash. Weary, yet excited, the poor girl imagined all sorts of mishaps to Pat and the horses, recalled various ghost stories she had heard, and wondered if it was on such a night as this that a neighbor's house had been robbed. So nervous did she get at last that she covered up her face and resolutely began to count to a thousand, feeling that anything was better than having to wake Mark and own that she was frightened.

Before she knew it she fell into a drowse and dreamed that they were all cast away on an iceberg and a polar bear was coming up to devour Gus, who innocently called to the big white dog and waited to caress him.

"A bear! A bear! Oh, boys, save him!" murmured Gwen in her sleep, and the sound of her own distressed voice waked her.

The fire was nearly out, for she had slept longer than she knew; the room was full of shadows, and the storm seemed to have died away. In the silence which now reigned, unbroken even by a snore, Gwen heard a sound that made her start and tremble. Someone was coming softly up the back stairs. All the outer doors were locked, she was sure; all the boys lay in their places, for she could see and count the three long figures and little Gus in a bunch on the sofa. The girls had not stirred, and this was no rat's scamper, but a slow and careful tread, stealing nearer and nearer to the study door, left ajar when the last load of wood was brought in.

"Pat would knock or ring, and Papa would speak, so that we might not be scared. I want to scream, but I won't till I

see that it really is someone," thought Gwen, while her heart
beat fast and her eyes were fixed on the door, straining to see
through the gloom.

The steps drew nearer, paused on the threshold, and then
a head appeared as the door noiselessly swung wider open.
A man's head in a fur cap, but it was neither papa nor Pat
nor Uncle Ed. Poor Gwen would have called out then, but

her voice was gone, and she could only lie back, looking, mute and motionless. A tiny spire of flame sprang up and flickered for a moment on the tall dark figure in the doorway, a big man with a beard, and in his hand something that glittered. "Was it a pistol or a dagger or a dark lantern?" thought the girl, as the glimmer died away, and the shadows returned to terrify her.

The man seemed to look about him keenly for a moment, then vanished, and the steps went down the hall to the front door, which was opened from within, and someone admitted quietly. Whispers were heard, and then feet approached again, accompanied by a gleam of light.

"Now I must scream!" thought Gwen, and scream she did with all her might, as two men entered, one carrying a lantern, the other, a bright tin can.

"Boys! Robbers! Fire! Tramps! Oh, do wake up!" cried Gwen, frantically pulling Mark by the hair, and Bob and Tony by the legs, as the quickest way of rousing them.

Then there was a scene! The boys sprang up and rubbed their eyes, the girls hid theirs and began to shriek, while the burglars laughed aloud, and poor Gwen, quite worn out, fainted away on the rug. It was all over in a minute, however, for Mark had his wits about him, and his first glance at the man with the lantern allayed his fears.

"Hullo, Uncle Ed! We are all right. Got tired of waiting for you, so we went to sleep."

"Stop screaming, girls, and quiet those children! Poor little Gwen is badly frightened. Get some snow, Tom, while I pick her up," commanded the uncle, and order was soon established.

The boys were all right at once, and Ruth and Alice devoted themselves to the children, who were very cross and sleepy in spite of their fright. Gwen was herself in a moment and so ashamed of her scare that she was glad there was no more light to betray her pale cheeks.

"I should have known you, uncle, at once, but to see a strange man startled me, and he didn't speak, and I thought that can was a pistol," stammered Gwen, when she had collected her wits a little.

"Why, that's my old friend and captain, Tom May. Don't you remember him, child? He thought you were all asleep, so he crept out to tell me and let me in."

"How did he get in himself?" asked Gwen, glad to turn the conversation.

"Found the shed door open and surprised the camp by a flank movement. You wouldn't do for picket duty, boys," laughed Captain Tom, enjoying the dismay of the lads.

"Oh, thunder! I forgot to bolt it when we first went for the wood. Had to open it, the place was so plaguy dark," muttered Bob, much disgusted.

"Where's Pat?" asked Tony, with great presence of mind, feeling anxious to shift all blame to his broad shoulders.

Uncle Ed shook the snow from his hair and clothes, and, poking up the fire, leisurely sat down and took Gus on his knee before he replied, "Serve out the grog, Tom, while I spin my yarn."

Around went the can of hot coffee, and a few sips brightened up the young folks immensely, so that they listened with great interest to the tale of Pat's mishaps.

"The scamp was half-seas over when he started and deserves all he got. In the first place he lost his way, then tumbled overboard and let the horses go. He floundered after them a mile or two, then lost his bearings in the storm, pitched into a ditch, broke his head, and lay there till he was found. The fellows carried him to a house off the road, and there he is in a nice state, for, being his countrymen, they dosed him with whiskey till he was 'quiet and aisy,' and went to sleep, forgetting all about you, the horses, and his distracted mistress at home. The animals were stopped at the crossroads, and there we found them after a lively cruise around the country. Then we hunted up Pat, but what with the blow and too many drops of 'the crayther,' his head was in a muddle, and we could get nothing out of him. So we went home again, and then your mother remembered that you had mentioned stopping here, and we fitted out a new craft and set sail, prepared for a long voyage. Your father was away, so Tom volunteered, and here we are."

"A jolly lark! Now let us go home and go to bed," proposed Mark, with a gape.

"Isn't it 'most morning?" asked Tony, who had been sleeping like a dormouse.

"Just eleven. Now pack up, and let us be off. The storm is over, the moon is coming out, and we shall find a good supper waiting for the loved and lost. Bear a hand, Tom, and ship this little duffer, for he's off again."

Uncle Ed put Gus into the captain's arms, and, taking Rita himself, led the way to the sleigh which stood at the door. In they all bundled, and, after making the house safe, off they went, feeling that they had had a pretty good time on the whole.

"I will learn cooking and courage, before I try camping out again," resolved Gwen, as she went jingling homeward; and she kept her word.

The Hare and the Tortoise

Tramp, tramp, tramp! That was the boys going downstairs in a hurry.

Bump, bump! That was the bicycle being zigzagged through the hall.

Bang! That was the front door slamming behind both boys and bicycle, leaving the house quiet for a time, though the sound of voices outside suggested that a lively discussion was going on.

The bicycle fever had reached Perryville, and raged all summer. Now the town was very like a once tranquil pool infested with the long-legged water bugs that go skating over its surface in all directions, for wheels of every kind darted to and fro, startling horses, running over small children, and pitching their riders headlong in the liveliest manner.

Men left their business to see the lads try new wheels; women grew skillful in the binding of wounds and the mending of sorely rent garments; gay girls begged for rides, standing on the little step behind; and boys clamored for bicycles that they might join the army of martyrs to the last craze.

Sidney West was the proud possessor of the best wheel in town and displayed his treasure with immense satisfaction before the admiring eyes of his mates. He had learned to ride in a city rink, and flattered himself that he knew all there was to learn, except those feats which only professional gymnasts acquire. He mounted with skillful agility, rode with as much grace as the treadmill movement of the legs permit, and managed to guide his tall steed without much danger to himself or others. The occasional headers he took, and the bruises which kept his manly limbs in a chronic state of mourning, he did not mention, but concealed his stiffness heroically and bound his younger brother to eternal silence by the bribe of occasional rides on the old wheel.

Hugh was a loyal lad and regarded his big brother as the most remarkable fellow in the world; so he forgave Sid's domineering ways, as a willing slave, a devoted admirer, and a faithful imitator of all the masculine virtues, airs, and graces

of this elder brother. On one point only did they disagree, and
that was Sid's refusal to give Hugh the old wheel when the
new one came. Hugh had fondly hoped it would be his, hints
to that effect having been dropped when Sid wanted an errand done, and for weeks the younger boy had waited and
labored patiently, sure that his reward would be the small
bicycle on which he could proudly take his place as a member
of the newly formed club, with them to set forth, in the blue
uniform, with horns blowing, badges glittering, and legs flying, for a long spin—to return after dark, a mysterious line
of tall shadows, "with lanterns dimly burning" and warning
whistles sounding as they went.

Great, therefore, was his disappointment and wrath when
he discovered that Sid had agreed to sell the wheel to another
fellow, if it suited him, leaving poor Hugh the only boy of
his set without a machine. Much as he loved Sid, he could
not forgive him this underhand and mercenary transaction.
It seemed so unbrotherly to requite such long and willing
service, to dash such ardent hopes, to betray such blind confidence for filthy lucre; and, when the deed was done, to laugh,
and ride gaily away on the splendid British Challenge, the
desire of all hearts and eyes.

This morning Hugh had freely vented his outraged feelings, and Sid had tried to make light of the affair, though quite
conscious that he had been both unkind and unfair. A bicycle
tournament was to take place in the city, twenty miles away,
and the members of the club were going. Sid, wishing to distinguish himself, intended to ride thither and was preparing
for the long trip with great care. Hugh was wild to go, but,
having spent his pocket money and been forbidden to borrow,
he could not take the cars as the others had done; no horse
was to be had, and their own stud consisted of an old donkey,

who would have been hopeless even with the inducement
offered in the immortal ditty:

> If I had a donkey what wouldn't go,
> Do you think I'd whip him? Oh, no no!
> I'd take him to Jarley's Waxwork Show.

Therefore poor Hugh was in a desperate state of mind as
he sat on the gatepost watching Sid make his pet's toilet, till
every plated handle, rod, screw, and axle shone like silver.

"I know I could have ridden the Star if you hadn't let Joe
have it. I do think it was right down mean of you; so does
Aunt Ruth, and father, too, only he won't say so, because men
always stand by one another and snub boys."

This was strong language for gentle Hugh, but he felt that
he must vent his anguish in some way or cry like a girl—and
that disgrace must be avoided, even if he failed in respect to
his elders.

Sid was whistling softly as he oiled and rubbed, but he was
not feeling so easy as he looked and heartily wished that he
had not committed himself to Joe, for it would have been
pleasant to take "the little chap," as he called the fourteen-
year-older, along with him and do the honors of the rink on
this great occasion. Now it was too late, so he affected a careless air and added insult to injury by answering his brother's
reproaches in the joking spirit which is peculiarly exasperating at such moments.

"Children shouldn't play with matches, nor small boys with
bicycles. I don't want to commit murder and I certainly should
if I let you try to ride twenty miles when you can't go one
without nearly breaking your neck or your knees," and Sid
glanced with a smile at the neat darns which ornamented his
brother's trousers over those portions of his long legs.

"How's a fellow going to learn if he isn't allowed to try?

Might as well tell me to keep away from the water until I can swim. You give me a chance and see if I can't ride as well as some older fellows who have been pitched round pretty lively before *they* dared to try a twenty-mile spin," answered Hugh, clapping both hands on his knees to hide the telltale darns.

"If Joe doesn't want it, you can use the old wheel till I decide what to do with it. I suppose a man has a right to sell his own property if he likes," said Sid, rather nettled at the allusion to his own tribulations in times past.

"Of course he has, but if he's promised to give a thing he ought to do it and not sneak out of the bargain after he's got lots of work done to pay for it. That's what makes me mad, for I believed you and depended on it, and it hurts me more to have you deceive me than it would to lose ten bicycles." And Hugh choked a little at the thought, in spite of his attempt to look sternly indignant.

"You are welcome to your opinion, but I wouldn't cry about it. Play with chaps of your own size and don't hanker after men's property. Take the cars, if you want to go so much and stop bothering me," retorted Sid, getting cross because he was in the wrong and wouldn't own it.

"You know I can't! No money, and mustn't borrow. What's the use of twitting a fellow like that?" And Hugh with great difficulty refrained from knocking off the new helmet-hat which was close to his foot as Sid bent to inspect the shining hub of the cherished wheel.

"Take Sancho, then; you might arrive before the fun was over, if you carried whips and pins and crackers enough to keep the old boy going; you'd be a nice span."

This allusion to the useless donkey was cruel, but Hugh

held on to the last remnant of his temper and made a wild proposal in the despair of the moment.

"Don't be a donkey yourself. See here, why can't we ride and tie? I've tried this wheel, and got on tiptop. You'd be along to see to me, and we'd take turns. Do, Sid! I want to go awfully, and if you only will I won't say another word about Joe."

But Sid only burst out laughing at the plan, in the most heartless manner.

"No, thank you. I don't mean to walk a step when I can ride, or lend my new wheel to a chap who can hardly keep right side up on the old one. It looks like a jolly plan to you, I dare say, but *I* don't see it, young man."

"I hope *I* shan't be a selfish brute when I'm seventeen. I'll have a bicycle yet—A-No. 1—and then you'll see how I'll lend it, like a gentleman, and not insult other fellows because they happen to be two or three years younger."

"Keep cool, my son, and don't call names. If you are such a smart lad, why don't you walk, since wheels and horses and donkey fail. It's *only* twenty miles—nothing to speak of, you know."

"Well, I could do it if I liked. I've walked eighteen and wasn't half so tired as you were. Anyone can get over the ground on a bicycle, but it takes strength and courage to keep it up on foot."

"Better try it."

"I will, some day."

"Don't crow too loud, my little rooster; you are not cock of the walk yet."

"If I was, I wouldn't hit a fellow when he's down." And fearing he should kick over the tall bicycle that stood so temptingly near him, Hugh walked away, trying to whistle, though his lips were more inclined to tremble than to pucker.

"Just bring my lunch, will you? Auntie is putting it up; I must be off," called Sid, so used to giving orders that he did so even at this unpropitious moment.

"Get it yourself. I'm not going to slave for you any longer, old tyrant," growled Hugh, for the trodden worm turned at last, as worms will.

This was open revolt, and Sid felt that things were in a bad way but would not stop to mend them then.

"Whew! Here's a tempest in a teapot. Well, it is too bad, but I can't help it now. I'll make it all right tomorrow and bring him around with a nice account of the fun. Hullo, Bemis, going to town?" he called, as a neighbor came spinning noiselessly by.

"Part way, and take the cars at Lawton. It's hard riding over the hills and a bother to steer a wheel through the streets. Come on, if you're ready."

"All right," and, springing up, Sid was off, forgetting all about the lunch.

Hugh, dodging behind the lilac bushes, heard what passed and the moment they were gone ran to the gate to watch them out of sight with longing eyes, then turned away, listlessly wondering how he should spend the holiday his brother was going to enjoy so much.

At that moment Aunt Ruth hurried to the door, waving a leathern pouch well stored with cake and sandwiches, cold coffee, and pie.

"Sid's forgotten his bag. Run, call, stop him!" she cried, trotting down the walk with her cap strings waving wildly in the fresh October wind.

For an instant Hugh hesitated, thinking sullenly, "Serves

him right. I won't run after him." Then his kind heart got
the better of his bad humor, and, catching up the bag, he
raced down the road at his best pace, eager to heap coals of
fire on Sid's proud head—to say nothing of his own desire to
see more of the riders.

"They will have to go slowly up the long hill, and I'll catch
them then," he thought as he tore over the ground, for he was
a good runner and prided himself on his strong legs.

Unfortunately for his amiable intentions, the boys had
taken a short cut to avoid the hill and were out of sight down
a lane where Hugh never dreamed they would dare to go,
so mounted.

"Well, they have done well to get over the hill at this rate.
Guess they won't keep it up long," panted Hugh, stopping
short when he saw no signs of the riders.

The road stretched invitingly before him; the race had
restored his spirits, and curiosity to see what had become of
his friends lured him to the hilltop, where temptation sat
waiting for him. Up he trudged, finding the fresh air, the
sunny sky, the path strewn with red and yellow leaves, and
the sense of freedom so pleasant that when he reached the
highest point and saw the world all before him, as it were, a
daring project seemed to flash upon him, nearly taking his
breath away with its manifold delights.

"Sid said, 'Walk,' and why not?—at least to Lawton, and
take the cars from there, as Bemis means to do. Wouldn't the
old fellows be surprised to see me turn up at the rink? It's
quarter past eight now, and the fun begins at three; I could
get there easy enough, and, by Jupiter, I will! Got lunch all
here, and money enough to pay this carfare, I guess. If I
haven't, I'll go a little farther and take a horsecar. What a
lark! Here goes!" And with a whoop of boyish delight at

breaking bounds, away went Hugh down the long hill, like a colt escaped from its pasture.

The others were just ahead, but the windings of the road hid them from him; so all went on, unconscious of each other's proximity. Hugh's run gave him a good start, and he got over the ground famously for five or six miles; then he went more slowly, thinking he had plenty of time to catch a certain train. But he had no watch, and when he reached Lawton he had the pleasure of seeing the cars go out at one end of the station as he hurried in at the other.

"I won't give it up but just go on and do it afoot. That will be something to brag of when the other chaps tell big stories. I'll see how fast I can go, for I'm not tired, and can eat on the way. Much obliged to Sid for a nice lunch."

And chuckling over this piece of good luck, Hugh set out again, only pausing for a good drink at the town pump. The thirteen miles did not seem very long when he thought of them, but as he walked them they appeared to grow longer and longer, till he felt as if he must have travelled about fifty. He was in good practice, and fortunately had on easy shoes, but he was in such a hurry to make good time that he allowed himself no rest, and jogged on, up hill and down, with the resolute air of one walking for a wager. There we will leave him, and see what had befallen Sid, for his adventures were more exciting than Hugh's, though all seemed plain sailing when he started.

At Lawton he had parted from his friend and gone on alone, having laid in a store of gingerbread from a baker's cart and paused to eat, drink, and rest by a wayside brook. A few miles further he passed a party of girls playing lawn tennis, and, as he slowly rolled along regarding them from his lofty perch, one suddenly exclaimed, "Why, it's our neighbor, Sidney West! How did *he* come here?" and waving her racquet, Alice ran across the lawn to find out.

Very willing to stop and display his new uniform, which was extremely becoming, Sid dismounted, doffed his helmet, and smiled upon the damsels, leaning over the hedge like a knight of old.

"Come in and play a game, and have some lunch. You will have plenty of time, and some of us are going to the rink by and by. Do, we want a boy to help us, for Maurice is too lazy, and Jack has hurt his hand with that stupid baseball," said Alice, beckoning persuasively, while the other girls nodded and smiled hopefully.

Thus allured, the youthful Ulysses hearkened to the voice of the little Circe in a round hat and entered the enchanted grove, to forget the passage of time as he disported himself among the nymphs. He was not changed to a beast, as in the immortal story, though the three young gentlemen did lie about the lawn in somewhat grovelling attitudes, and Alice waved her racquet as if it were a wand, while her friends handed glasses of lemonade to the recumbent heroes during pauses in the game.

While thus blissfully engaged, time slipped away, and Hugh passed him in the race, quite unconscious that his brother was reposing in the tent that looked so inviting as the dusty, tired boy plodded by, counting every milestone with increasing satisfaction.

"If I get to Uncle Tim's by one o'clock, I shall have done very well. Four miles an hour is a fair pace, and only one stop. I'll telegraph to auntie as soon as I arrive, but she won't worry; she's used to having us turn up right when we get ready," thought Hugh, grateful that no overanxious mamma was fretting about his long absence. The boys had no mother, and Aunt Ruth was an easy old lady who let them do as they liked, to their great contentment.

As he neared his journey's end our traveller's spirits rose, and the blisters on his heels were forgotten in the dramatic scene his fancy painted, when Sid should discover him at Uncle Tim's, or calmly seated at the rink. Whistling gaily, he was passing through a wooded bit of road when the sound of voices made him look back to see a carriage full of girls approaching, escorted by a bicycle rider, whose long blue legs looked strangely familiar.

Anxious to keep his secret till the last moment, also conscious that he was not in company trim, Hugh dived into the wood, out of sight, while the gay party went by, returning to the road as soon as they were hidden by a bend.

"If Sid hadn't been so mean, I should have been with him, and had some of the fun. I don't feel like forgiving him in a hurry for making me foot it, like a tramp, while he is having such a splendid time."

If Hugh could have known what was to happen very soon after he muttered these words to himself, as he wiped his hot face, and took the last sip of the coffee to quench his thirst, he would have been sorry he uttered them, and have forgiven his brother everything.

While he was slowly toiling up the last long hill, Sid was coasting down on the other side, eager to display his courage and skill before the girls, being of an age when boys begin to wish to please and astonish the gentler creatures whom they have hitherto treated with indifference or contempt. It was a foolish thing to do, for the road was rough, with steep banks on either side and a sharp turn at the end; but Sid rolled gaily along, with an occasional bump, till a snake ran across the road, making the horse shy, the girls scream, the rider turn to

see what was the matter, and in doing so lose his balance, just
when a large stone needed to be avoided. Over went Sid,
down rattled the wheel, up rose a cloud of dust, and sudden
silence fell upon the girls at sight of this disaster. They expected their gallant escort would spring up and laugh over
his accident, but, when he remained flat upon his back, where
he had alighted after a somersault, with the bicycle spread
over him like a pall, they were alarmed and flew to the rescue.

A cut on the forehead was bleeding, and the blow had
evidently stunned him for a moment. Luckily, a house was
near, and a man seeing the accident hastened to offer more

efficient help than any the girls had wit enough to give in the
first flurry, as all four only flapped wildly at Sid with their
handkerchiefs and exclaimed excitedly, "What shall we do?
Is he dead? Run for water. Call somebody, quick."

"Don't be scat, gals; it takes a sight of thumpin' to break
a boy's head. He ain't hurt much, kinder dazed for a minute.
I'll hist up this pesky *mash*ine and set him on his legs, if he
ain't damaged 'em."

With these cheering words, the farmer cleared away the
ruins and propped the fallen rider against a tree, which treat-
ment had such a good effect that Sid was himself in a moment
and much disgusted to find what a scrape he was in.

"This is nothing, a mere bump; quite right, thanks. Let us
go on at once; so sorry to alarm you, ladies." He began his
polite speech bravely but ended with a feeble smile and a
clutch at the tree, suddenly turning sick and dizzy again.

"You come along a me. I'll tinker you and your whirligig
up, young man. No use sayin' go ahead, for the thing is broke,
and you want to keep quiet for a spell. Drive along, gals. I'll
see to him, and my old woman can nuss him better'n a dozen
flutterin' young things scat half to death."

Taking matters into his own hands, the farmer had boy and
bicycle under his roof in five minutes, and, with vain offers
of help, many regrets, and promises to let his Uncle Tim
know where he was, in case he did not arrive, the girls reluctantly drove away, leaving no sign of the catastrophe except the trampled road, and a dead snake.

Peace was hardly restored when Hugh came down the hill,
little dreaming what had happened, and for the second time
passed his brother, who just then was lying on a sofa in
the farmhouse, while a kind old woman adorned his brow
with a large black plaster, suggesting brown paper steeped

in vinegar for the various bruises on his arms and legs. "Someone killed the snake and made a great fuss about it, I should say," thought Hugh, observing the signs of disorder in the dust, but, resisting a boy's interest in such affairs, he stoutly tramped on, sniffing the whiffs of sea air that now and then saluted his nose, telling him that he was nearing his much-desired goal.

Presently the spires of the city came in sight, to his great satisfaction, and only the long bridge and a street or two lay between him and Uncle Tim's easy chair, into which he soon hoped to cast himself.

Halfway across the bridge a farm wagon passed, with a bicycle laid carefully on the barrels of vegetables going to market. Hugh gazed affectionately at it, longing to borrow it for one brief, delicious spin to the bridge end. Had he known that it was Sid's broken wheel, going to be repaired without loss of time, thanks to the good farmer's trip to town, he would have paused to have a hearty laugh, in spite of his vow not to stop till his journey was over.

Just as Hugh turned into the side street where Uncle Tim lived, a horsecar went by, in one corner of which sat a pale youth, with a battered hat drawn low over his eyes, who handed out his ticket with the left hand and frowned when the car jolted, as if the jar hurt him. Had he looked out the window, he would have seen a very dusty boy, with a pouch over his shoulder, walking smartly down the street where his relation lived. But Sid carefully turned his head aside, fearing to be recognized, for he was on his way to a certain club to which Bemis belonged, preferring his sympathy and hospitality to the humiliation of having his mishap told at home by Uncle Tim, who would be sure to take Hugh's part and exult over the downfall of the proud. Well for him that he avoided that comfortable mansion, for on the doorstep stood Hugh, beaming with satisfaction as the clock struck one, proclaiming that he had done his twenty miles in a little less than five hours.

"Not bad for a 'little chap,' even though he is 'a donkey,' " chuckled the boy, dusting his shoes, wiping his red face, and touching himself up as well as he could, in order to present as fresh and unwearied an aspect as possible, when he burst upon his astonished brother's sight.

In he marched when the door opened, to find his uncle and two rosy cousins just sitting down to dinner. Always glad to see the lads, they gave him a cordial welcome and asked for his brother.

"Hasn't he come yet?" cried Hugh, surprised, yet glad to be the first on the field.

Nothing had been seen of him, and Hugh at once told his tale, to the great delight of his jolly uncle and the admiring wonder of Meg and May, the rosy young cousins. They all enjoyed the exploit immensely and at once insisted that the pedestrian should be refreshed by a bath, a copious meal, and a good rest in the big chair, where he repeated his story by particular request.

"You deserve a bicycle, and you shall have one, as sure as my name is Timothy West. I like pluck and perseverance, and you've got both; so come on, my boy, and name the wheel you like best. Sid needs a little taking down, as you lads say, and this will give it to him, I fancy. I'm a younger brother myself, and I know what their trials are."

As his uncle made these agreeable remarks, Hugh looked as if *his* trials were all over, for his face shone with soap and satisfaction, his hunger was quenched by a splendid dinner, his tired feet luxuriated in a pair of vast slippers, and the blissful certainty of owning a first-class bicycle filled his cup to overflowing. Words could hardly express his gratitude, and nothing but the hope of meeting Sid with this glorious news would have torn him from the reposeful paradise where he longed to linger. Pluck and perseverance, with cold cream on the blistered heels, got him into his shoes again, and he rode away in a horsecar, as in a triumphal chariot, to find his brother.

"I won't brag, but I do feel immensely tickled at this day's work. Wonder how he got on. Did it in two or three hours, I suppose, and is parading around with those swell club fellows at the rink. I'll slip in and let him find me, as if I wasn't a bit proud of what I've done, and didn't care two pins for anybody's praise."

With this plan in his head, Hugh enjoyed the afternoon very much, keeping a sharp lookout for Sid, even while astonishing feats were being performed before his admiring eyes. But nowhere did he see his brother, for he was searching for a blue uniform and a helmet with a certain badge on it, while Sid in a borrowed hat and coat sat in a corner looking on, whenever a splitting headache and the pain in his bones allowed him to see and enjoy the exploits in which he had hoped to join.

Not until it was over did the brothers meet, as they went out, and then the expression on Sid's face was so comical that Hugh laughed till the crowd about them stared, wondering what the joke could be.

"How in the world did *you* get here?" asked the elder boy, giving his hat a sudden pull to hide the plaster.

"Walked, as you advised me to."

Words cannot express the pleasure that answer gave Hugh, or the exultation he vainly tried to repress, as his eyes twinkled and a grin of real boyish fun shone upon his sunburnt countenance.

"You expect me to believe that, do you?"

"Just as you please. I started to catch you with your bag, and when I missed you, thought I might as well keep on. Got in about one, had dinner at uncle's, and been enjoying these high jinks ever since."

"Very well, for a beginning. Keep it up and you'll be a Rowell [1] by and by. What do you suppose father will say to you, small boy?"

"Not much. Uncle will make that all right. *He* thought it was a plucky thing to do, and so did the girls. When did you get in?" asked Hugh, rather nettled at Sid's want of enthusiasm, though it was evident he was much impressed by the "small boy's" prank.

"I took it easy after Bemis left me. Had a game of tennis at the Blanchards' as I came along, dinner at the club, and strolled up here with the fellows. Got a headache and don't feel up to much."

As Sid spoke and Hugh's keen eye took in the various signs of distress which betrayed a hint of the truth, the grin changed to a hearty "Ha! Ha!" as he smote his knees exclaiming gleefully, "You've come to grief! I know it, I see it. Own up, and don't shirk, for I'll find it out somehow, as sure as you live."

"Don't make such a row in the street. Get aboard this car, and I'll tell you, for you'll give me no peace till I do," answered Sid, well knowing that Alice would never keep the secret.

To say that it was "nuts" to Hugh faintly expressed the interest he took in the story which was extracted bit by bit from the reluctant sufferer, but, after a very pardonable crow over

[1] A champion bicyclist. *Ed.*

the mishaps of his oppressor, he yielded to the sympathy he felt for his brother and was very good to him.

This touched Sid and filled him with remorse for past unkindness, for one sees one's faults very plainly and is not ashamed to own it, when one is walking through the Valley of Humiliation.

"Look here, I'll tell you what I'll do," he said, as they left the car, and Hugh offered an arm, with a friendly air pleasant to see. "I'll give you the old wheel and let Joe get another where he can. It's small for him, and I doubt if he wants it, anyway. I do think you were a plucky fellow to tramp your twenty miles in good time and not bear malice either, so let's say 'Done,' and forgive and forget."

"Much obliged, but uncle is going to give me a new one, so Joe needn't be disappointed. I know how hard that is and am glad to keep him from it, for he's poor and can't afford a new one."

That answer was Hugh's only revenge for his own trials, and Sid felt it, though he merely said, with a hearty slap on the shoulder, "Glad to hear it. Uncle is a trump, and so are you. We'll take the last train home, and I'll pay your fare."

"Thank you. Poor old man, you did get a bump, didn't you?" exclaimed Hugh, as they took off their hats in the hall, and the patch appeared in all its gloomy length and breadth.

"Head will be all right in a day or two, but I stove in my helmet and ground a hole in both knees of my new shorts. Had to borrow a fit-out of Bemis and leave my rags behind. We needn't mention any more than is necessary to the girls; I hate to be fussed over," answered Sid, trying to speak carelessly.

Hugh had to stop and have another laugh, remembering the taunts his own mishaps had called forth, but he did not retaliate, and Sid never forgot it. Their stay was a short one, and Hugh was the hero of the hour, quite eclipsing his brother, who usually took the first place but now very meekly played second fiddle, conscious that he was not an imposing figure, in a coat much too big for him, with a patch on his forehead, a purple bruise on one cheek, and a general air of dilapidation very trying to the usually spruce youth.

When they left, Uncle Tim patted Hugh on the head—a liberty the boy would have resented if the delightful old gentleman had not followed it up by saying, with a reckless generosity worthy of record, "Choose your bicycle, my boy, and send the bill to me." Then turning to Sid he added, in a tone that made the pale face redden suddenly, "And do you remember that the tortoise beat the hare in the old fable we all know?"

Jerseys, or the Girls' Ghost

"Well, what do you think of her? She has only been here a day, but it doesn't take *us* long to make up our minds," said Nelly Blake, the leader of the school, as a party of girls stood chatting around the register one cold November morning.

"I like her; she looks so fresh and pleasant, and so strong. I just wanted to go and lean up against her when my back ached yesterday," answered Maud, a pale girl wrapped in a shawl.

"I'm afraid she's very energetic, and I do hate to be hurried," sighed plump Cordelia, lounging in an easy chair.

"I know she is, for Biddy says she asked for a pail of cold water at six this morning, and she's out walking now. Just think; how horrid," cried Kitty with a shiver.

"I wonder what she does for her complexion. Never saw such a lovely color. Real roses and cream," said Julia, shutting one eye to survey the freckles on her nose, with a gloomy frown.

"I longed to ask what sort of braces she wears, to keep her so straight. I mean to by and by; she looks as if she wouldn't snub a body." And Sally vainly tried to square her own round shoulders, bent with much poring over books, for she was the bright girl of the school.

"She wears French corsets, of course. Nothing else gives one such a fine figure," answered Maud, dropping the shawl to look with pride at her own wasplike waist and stiff back.

"Couldn't move about so easily and gracefully if she wore a straitjacket like you. She's not a bit of a fashion plate, but a splendid woman, just natural and hearty and sweet. I feel as if I shouldn't slouch and poke so much if I had her to brace me up," cried Sally, in her enthusiastic way.

"I know one thing, girls, and that is, *she* can wear a jersey and have it set elegantly, and *we* can't," said Kitty, laboring with her own, which would wrinkle and twist, in spite of many hidden pins.

"Yes, I looked at it all breakfast time and forgot my second cup of coffee, so my head aches as if it would split. Never saw anything fit so splendidly in my life," answered Nelly, turning to the mirror, which reflected a fine assortment of many-colored jerseys; for all the girls were out in their fall suits, and not one of the new jackets set like Miss Orne's, the teacher who had arrived to take Madame's place while that excellent old lady was laid up with a rheumatic fever.

"They are pretty and convenient, but I'm afraid they will be a trial to some of us. Maud and Nelly look the best, but they have to keep stiff and still, or the wrinkles come. Kit has no peace in hers, and poor Cordy looks more like a meal bag than ever, while I am a perfect spectacle, with my round shoulders and long thin arms. 'A jersey on a bean-pole' describes me; but let us be in the fashion or die," laughed Sally, exaggerating her own defects by poking her head forward and blinking through her glasses in a funny way.

There was a laugh and then a pause, broken in a moment by Maud, who said, in a tone of apprehension, "I do hope Miss Orne isn't full of the new notions about clothes and food and exercise and rights and rubbish of that sort. Mamma hates such ideas, and so do I."

"I hope she *is* full of good, wise notions about health and work and study. It is just what we need in this school. Madame is old and lets things go, and the other teachers only care to get through and have an easy time. We ought to be a great deal better, brisker, and wiser than we are, and I'm ready for a good stirring up if anyone will give it to us," declared Sally, who was a very independent girl and had read as well as studied much.

"You Massachusetts girls are always raving about self-culture and ready for queer new ways. I'm contented with the old

ones and want to be let alone and finished off easily," said
Nelly, the pretty New Yorker.

"Well, I go with Sally and want to get all I can in the way
of health, learning, and manners while I'm here; and I'm
real glad Miss Orne has come, for Madame's old-fashioned,
niminy priminy ways did fret me dreadfully. Miss Orne is
more like our folks out West—spry and strong and smart, see
if she isn't," said Julia, with a decided nod of her auburn
head.

"There she is now! Girls, she's running! Actually trotting
up the avenue—not like a hen, but a boy—with her elbows
down and her head up. Do come and see!" cried Kitty, dancing
about at the window as if she longed to go and do likewise.

All ran in time to see a tall young lady come up the wide
path at a good pace, looking fresh and blithe as the goddess of
health, as she smiled and nodded at them, so like a girl that
all returned her salute with equal cordiality.

"She gives a new sort of interest to the old treadmill, doesn't
she?" said Nelly, as they scattered to their places at the stroke
of nine, feeling unusually anxious to appear well before the
new teacher.

While they pull down their jerseys and take up their books,
we will briefly state that Madame Stein's select boarding
school had for many years received six girls at a time and
finished them off in the old style. Plenty of French, German,
music, painting, dancing, and deportment turned out well-
bred, accomplished, and amiable young ladies, ready for fashionable society, easy lives, and entire dependence on other
people. Dainty and delicate creatures usually, for, as in most
schools of this sort, minds and manners were much cultivated,
but bodies rather neglected. Heads and backs ached, dyspepsia
was a common ailment, and poorlies of all sorts afflicted the

dear girls, who ought not to have known what "nerves" meant and should have had no bottles in their closets holding wine-and-iron, cough mixtures, soothing drops and cod-liver oil for weak lungs. Gymnastics had once flourished, but the fashion had gone by, and a short walk each day was all the exercise they took, though they might have had glorious romps in the old coach house and bowling alley in bad weather and lovely rambles about the spacious grounds, for the house was in the suburbs and had once been a fine country mansion. Some of the liveliest girls did race down the avenue now and then, when Madame was away, and one irrepressible creature had actually slid down the wide balusters, to the horror of the entire household.

In cold weather all grew lazy and cuddled under blankets and around registers, like so many warmth-loving pussies— poor Madame's rheumatism making her enjoy a hothouse temperature and indulge the girls in luxurious habits. Now she had been obliged to give up entirely and take to her bed, saying, with the resignation of an indolent nature, "If Anna Orne takes charge of the school I shall feel no anxiety. *She* is equal to anything."

She certainly looked so as she came into the schoolroom ready for her day's work, with lungs full of fresh air, brain stimulated by sound sleep, wholesome exercise, and a simple breakfast, and a mind much interested in the task before her. The girls' eyes followed her as she took her place, involuntarily attracted by the unusual spectacle of a robust woman. Everything about her seemed so fresh, harmonious, and happy, that it was a pleasure to see the brilliant color in her cheeks, the thick coils of glossy hair on her spirited head, the flash of white teeth as she spoke, and the clear, bright glance of eyes both keen and kind. But the most admiring glances

were on the dark-blue jersey that showed such fine curves of
the broad shoulders, round waist, and plump arms, without a
wrinkle to mar its smooth perfection.

Girls are quick to see what is genuine, to respect what
is strong, and to love what is beautiful; so before that day
was over, Miss Orne had charmed them all, for they felt
that she was not only able to teach but to help and amuse
them.

After the other teachers went to their rooms, glad to be free
from the chatter of half a dozen lively tongues, Miss Orne
remained in the drawing room and set the girls to dancing
till they were tired, then gathered them round the long table
to do what they liked till prayer time. Some had novels, others
did fancywork or lounged, and all wondered what the new
teacher would do next.

Six pairs of curious eyes were fixed upon her, as she sat
sewing on some queer bits of crash, and six lively fancies
vainly tried to guess what the articles were, for no one was
rude enough to ask. Presently she tried on a pair of mittens,
and surveyed them with satisfaction, saying as she caught
Kitty staring with uncontrollable interest, "These are my
beautifiers; I never like to be without them."

"Are they to keep your hands white?" asked Maud, who
spent a good deal of time caring for her own. "I wear old kid
gloves at night after cold-creaming mine."

"I wear these for five minutes night and morning, for a good
rub, after dipping them in cold water. Thanks to these rough
friends, I seldom feel the cold, get a good color, and keep
well," answered Miss Orne, polishing up her smooth cheek
till it looked like a rosy apple.

"I'd like the color, but not the crash. Must it be so rough,
and with *cold* water?" asked Maud, who often privately

rubbed her pale face with a bit of red flannel, rouge being forbidden except for theatricals.

"Best so; but there are other ways to get a color. Run up and down the avenue three or four times a day, eat no pastry, and go to bed early," said Miss Orne, whose sharp eye had spied out the little weaknesses of the girls and whose kind heart longed to help them at once.

"It makes my back ache to run, and Madame says we are too old now."

"Never too old to care for one's health, my dear. Better run now than lie on a sofa by and by, with a back that never stops aching."

"Do you cure your headaches in that way?" asked Nelly, rubbing her forehead wearily.

"I never have them," and Miss Orne's bright eyes were full of pity for all pain.

"What do you do to help it?" cried Nelly, who firmly believed that it was inevitable.

"I give my brain plenty of rest, air, and good food. I never know I have any nerves, except in the enjoyment they give me, for I have learned how to use them. I was not brought up to believe that I was born an invalid and was taught to understand the beautiful machinery God gave me and to keep it religiously in order."

Miss Orne spoke so seriously that there was a brief pause in which the girls were wishing that someone had taught them this lesson and made them as strong and lovely as their new teacher.

"If crash mittens would make my jersey set like yours I'd have a pair at once," said Cordy, sadly eyeing the buttons on her own, which seemed in danger of flying off if their plump wearer moved too quickly.

"Brisk runs are what you want, and less confectionary, sleep, and lounging in easy chairs," began Miss Orne, all ready to prescribe for these poor girls, the most important part of whose education had been so neglected.

"Why, how did you know?" said Cordy, blushing, as she bounced out of her luxurious seat and whisked into her pocket the paper of chocolate creams she was seldom without.

Her round eyes and artless surprise set the others to laughing and gave Sally courage to ask what she wanted, then and there.

"Miss Orne, I wish you would show us how to be strong and hearty, for I do think girls are a feeble set nowadays. We certainly need stirring up, and I hope you will kindly do it. Please begin with me; then the others will see that I mean what I say."

Miss Orne looked up at the tall, overgrown girl who stood before her, with broad forehead, nearsighted eyes, and narrow chest of a student—not at all what a girl of seventeen should be, physically, though a clear mind and a brave spirit shone in her clever face and sounded in her resolute voice.

"I shall very gladly do what I can for you, my dear. It is very simple, and I am sure that a few months of my sort of training will help you much, for you are just the kind of girl who should have a strong body, to keep pace with a very active brain," answered Miss Orne, taking Sally's thin, inky fingers in her own, with a friendly pressure that showed her good will.

"Madame says violent exercise is not good for girls, so we gave up gymnastics long ago," said Maud, in her languid voice, wishing that Sally would not suggest disagreeable things.

"One does not need clubs, dumbbells, and bars for my style of exercise. Let me show you," and, rising, Miss Orne went through a series of energetic but graceful evolutions, which put every muscle in play without great exertion.

"That looks easy enough," began Nelly.

"Try it," answered Miss Orne, with a sparkle of fun in her blue eyes.

They did try—to the great astonishment of the solemn portraits on the wall, unused to seeing such antics in that dignified apartment. But some of the girls were out of breath in five minutes; others could not lift their arms over their heads; Maud and Nelly broke several bones in their corsets, trying to stoop; and Kitty tumbled down, in her efforts to touch her toes without bending her knees. Sally got on the best of all, being long of limb, easy in her clothes, and full of enthusiasm.

"Pretty well for beginners," said Miss Orne, as they paused at last, flushed and merry. "Do that regularly every day, and you will soon gain a few inches across the chest and fill out the new jerseys with firm, elastic figures."

"Like yours," added Sally, with a face full of such honest admiration that it could not offend.

Seeing that she had made one convert and knowing that girls, like sheep, are sure to follow a leader, Miss Orne said no more then, but waited for the leaven to work. The others called it one of Sally's notions but were interested to see how she would get on and had great fun, when they went to bed, watching her faithful efforts to imitate her teacher's rapid and effective motions.

"The windmill is going!" cried Kitty, as several of them sat on the bed, laughing at the long arms swinging about.

"That is the hygienic elbow-exercise, and that the Orne Quickstep, a mixture of the grasshopper's skip and the water bug's slide," added Julia, humming a tune in time to the stamp of the other's foot.

"We will call these the Jersey Jymnastics, and spell the last with a J, my dear," said Nelly; and the name was received with as much applause as the young ladies dared to give it at that hour.

"Laugh on, but see if you don't all follow my example sooner or later, when I become a model of grace, strength, and beauty," retorted Sally, as she turned them out and went to bed tingling all over with a delicious glow that sent the blood from her hot head to warm her cold feet and bring her the sound, refreshing sleep she so much needed.

This was the beginning of a new order of things, for Miss Orne carried her energy into other matters besides gymnastics, and no one dared oppose her when Madame shut her ears to all complaints, saying, "Obey her in everything, and don't trouble me."

Pitchers of fresh milk took the place of tea and coffee; cake and pie were rarely seen, but better bread, plain puddings, and plenty of fruit.

Rooms were cooled off, feather beds sent up to the garret, and thick curtains abolished. Sun and air streamed in, and great cans of water appeared suggestively at doors in the morning. Earlier hours were kept, and brisk walks taken by nearly all the girls, for Miss Orne baited her hook cleverly and always had some pleasant project to make the wintry expeditions inviting. There were games in the parlor instead of novels and fancywork in the evening, shorter lessons, and longer talks on the many useful subjects that are best learned from the lips of a true teacher. A cooking class was started, not to make fancy dishes, but the plain, substantial ones all housewives should understand. Several girls swept their own rooms, and liked it after they saw Miss Orne do hers in a becoming dustcap; and these same pioneers, headed by Sally, boldly coasted on the hill, swung clubs in the coach house, and played tag in the bowling alley rainy days.

It took time to work these much-needed changes, but young people like novelty; the old routine had grown tiresome, and Miss Orne made things so lively and pleasant it was impossible to resist her wishes. Sally did begin to straighten up, after a month or two of regular training; Maud outgrew both corsets and backache; Nelly got a fresh color; Kitty found her thin arms developing visible muscles; and Julia considered herself a Von Hillern,[1] after walking ten miles without fatigue.

But dear, fat Cordy was the most successful of all and rejoiced greatly over the loss of a few pounds when she gave up overeating, long naps, and lazy habits. Exercise became a sort of mania with her, and she was continually trudging off for a constitutional or trotting up and down the halls when bad weather prevented the daily tramp. It was the desire of her soul to grow thin, and such was her ardor that Miss Orne had to check her sometimes, lest she should overdo the matter.

"All this is easy and pleasant now, because it is new," she said, "and there is no one to criticize our simple, sensible way, but when you go away I am afraid you will undo the good I have tried to do you. People will ridicule you, fashion will condemn, and frivolous pleasures make our wholesome ones seem hard. Can you be steadfast, and keep on?"

"We will!" cried all the girls, but the older ones looked a little anxious, as they thought of going home to introduce the new ways alone.

Miss Orne shook her head, earnestly wishing that she could impress the important lesson indelibly upon them, and very soon something happened which had that effect.

[1] A champion cross-country hiker. *Ed.*

April came, and the snowdrops and crocuses were up in the garden beds. Madame was able to sit at her window, peering out like a dormouse waking from its winter sleep; and much did the good lady wonder at the blooming faces turned up to nod and smile at her, the lively steps that tripped about the house, and the amazing spectacle of *her* young ladies racing round the lawn as if they liked it. No one knew how Miss Orne reconciled her to this new style of deportment, but she made no complaint—only shook her impressive cap when the girls came beaming in to pay little visits, full of happy chat about their affairs. They seemed to take a real interest in their studies now, to be very happy, and all looked so well that the wise old lady said to herself, "Looks are everything with women, and I have never been able to show such a bouquet of blooming creatures at my breaking up as I shall this year. I will let well enough alone, and, if fault is found, dear Anna's shoulders are broad enough to bear it."

Things were in this promising state, and all were busily preparing for the May fete, at which time this class of girls would graduate, when the mysterious events occurred to which we have alluded.

They were gathered—the girls, not the events—round the table one night, discussing, with the deep interest befitting such an important topic, what they should wear on examination day.

"*I* think white silk jerseys and pink or blue skirts would be lovely—so pretty and so appropriate for the J. J. Club, and so nice for us to do our exercises in. Miss Orne wants us to show how well we go together, and, of course, we want to please her," said Nelly, taking the lead as usual in matters of taste.

"Of course!" cried all the girls, with an alacrity which

plainly showed how entirely the new friend had won their hearts.

"I wouldn't have believed that six months could make such a difference in one's figure and feelings," said Maud, surveying her waist with calm satisfaction, though it was no longer slender but in perfect proportion to the rest of her youthful shape.

"I've had to let out every dress, and it's a mercy I'm going home, for I shouldn't be decent if I kept on at this rate." And Julia took a long breath, proud of her broad chest, expanded by plenty of exercise, and loose clothing.

"I take mine in and don't have to worry about my buttons flying off, *à la* Clara Peggotty. I'm so pleased I want to be training all the time, for I'm not half thin enough yet," said Cordy, jumping up for a trot around the room, that not a moment might be lost.

"Come, Sally, you ought to join in the jubilee, for you have done wonders and will be as straight as a ramrod in a little while. Why so sober tonight? Is it because our dear Miss Orne leaves us to sit with Madame?" asked Nelly, missing the gayest voice of the six, and observing her friend's troubled face.

"I'm making up my mind whether I'd better tell you something or not. I don't want to scare the servants, trouble Madame, or vex Miss Orne, for I know *she* wouldn't believe a word of it, though I saw it with my own eyes," answered Sally, in such a mysterious tone that the girls with one voice cried, "Tell us, this minute!"

"I will, and perhaps some of you can explain the matter."

As she spoke, Sally rose and stood on the rug with her hands behind her, looking rather wild and queer, for her short hair was in a toss, her eyes shone large behind her round glasses, and her voice sank to a whisper as she made this startling announcement:

"I've seen a ghost!"

A general shiver pervaded the listeners, and Cordy poked her head under the sofa pillows with a faint cry, while the rest involuntarily drew nearer to one another.

"Where?" demanded Julia, the bravest of the party.

"On top of the house."

"Good gracious! When, Sally?" "What did it look like?" "Don't scare us for fun," cried the girls, undecided whether to take this startling story in jest or earnest.

"Listen, and I'll tell you all about it," answered Sally, holding up her finger impressively.

"Night before last I sat till eleven, studying. Against the rules, I know, but I forgot, and when I was through I opened my window to air the room. It was bright moonlight, so I took a stroll along the top of the piazza, and coming back with my eyes on the sky I naturally saw the roof of the main house from my wing. I couldn't have been asleep, could I? Yet, I solemnly declare I saw a white figure with a veil over its head roaming to and fro quietly as a shadow. I looked and looked; then I called softly, but it never answered, and suddenly it was gone."

"What did you do?" quavered Cordy, in a smothered voice from under the pillow.

"Went straight in, took my lamp, and marched up to the cupola. Not a sign of anyone, all locked and the floor dusty, for we never go there now, you know. I didn't like it but just said, 'Sally, go to bed; it's an optical illusion and serves you right for studying against the rule.' That was the first time."

"Mercy on us! Did you see it again?" cried Maud, getting hold of Julia's strong arm for protection.

"Yes, in the bowling alley at midnight," whispered Sally.

"Do shut the door, Kit, and don't keep clutching at me in that scary way; it's very unpleasant," said Nelly, glancing nervously over her shoulder as the six pairs of wide-opened eyes were fixed on Sally.

"I got up to shut my window last night and saw a light in the alley—a dim one, but bright enough to show me the same white thing going up and down, with the veil as before. I'll confess I was nervous then, for you know there *is* a story that in old times the man who lived here wouldn't let his daughter marry the lover she wanted, and she pined away and died and said she'd haunt the cruel father, and she did. Old Mrs. Foster told me all about it when I first came, and Madame asked me not to repeat it, so I never did. I don't believe in ghosts, mind you, but what on earth is it, trailing about in that ridiculous way?"

Sally spoke nervously and looked excited, for in spite of courage and common sense she *was* worried to account for the apparition.

"How long did it stay?" asked Julia, with her arm round Maud, who was trembling and pale.

"A good fifteen minutes by my watch, then vanished, light and all, as suddenly as before. I didn't go to look after it that time, but if I see it again I'll hunt till I find out what it is. Who will go with me?"

No one volunteered, and Cordy emerged long enough to say imploringly, "Do tell Miss Orne, or get the police," then dived out of sight again and lay quaking like an ostrich with its head in the sand.

"I won't! Miss Orne would think I was a fool, and the police don't arrest ghosts. I'll do it myself, and Julia will help me, I know. She is the bravest of you and hasn't developed her biceps for nothing," said Sally, bent on keeping all the glory of the capture to themselves if possible.

Flattered by the compliment to her arms, Julia did not decline the invitation but made a very sensible suggestion, which was a great relief to the timid, till Sally added a new fancy to haunt them.

"Perhaps it is one of the servants moon-struck or lovelorn. Myra looks sentimental, and is always singing,

"I'm waiting, waiting, darling,
Morning, night, and noon;
Oh, meet me by the river
When softly shines the moon."

"It's not Myra; I asked her, and she turned pale at the mere idea of going anywhere alone after dark and said cook had seen a banshee gliding down the Lady's Walk one night, when she got up for camphor, having the face-ache. I said no more, not wanting to scare them; ignorant people are so super-stitious."

Sally paused, and the girls all tried not to look "scared" or "superstitious," but did not succeed very well.

"What are you going to do?" asked Nelly, in a respectful tone, as Julia and Sally stood side by side, like Horatius and Herminius waiting for Spurius Lartius [1] to join them.

"Watch, like cats for a mouse, and pounce as soon as pos-sible. All promise to say nothing; then we can't be laughed at if it turns out some silly thing, as it probably will," an-swered Sally.

"We promise!" solemnly answered the girls, feeling deeply impressed with the thrilling interest of the moment.

[1] These are characters in Lord Macauly's *Lays of Ancient Rome*—very ex-citing reading! *Ed.*

"Very well; now don't talk about it or think about it till we report, or no one will sleep a wink," said Sally, walking off with her ally as coolly as if, after frightening them out of their wits, they could forget the matter at word of command.

The oath of silence was well kept but lessons suffered and so did sleep, for the excitement was great, especially in the morning, when the watchers reported the events of the night, and in the evening, when they took turns to go on guard. There was much whisking of dressing gowns up and down the corridor of the west wing, where our six roomed, as the girls flew to ask questions early each day, or scurried to bed, glancing behind them for the banshee as they went.

Miss Orne observed the whispers, nods, and eager confabulations but said nothing, for Madame had confided to her that the young ladies were planning a farewell gift for her. So she was blind and deaf and smiled at the important airs of her girlish admirers.

Three or four days passed, and no sign of the ghost appeared. The boldest openly scoffed at the false alarm, and the most timid began to recover from their fright.

Sally and Julia looked rather foolish as they answered, "no news," morning after morning, to the inquiries which were rapidly losing the breathless eagerness so flattering to the watchers.

"You dreamed it, Sally. Go to sleep, and don't do it again," said Nelly, on the fifth day, as she made her evening call and found the girls yawning and cross for want of rest.

"She has exercised too much and produced a morbid state of the brain," laughed Maud.

"I just wish she wouldn't scare me out of my senses for nothing," grumbled Cordy; "I used to sleep like a dormouse, and now I dream dreadfully and wake up tired out. Come along, Kit, and let the old ghosts carry off these silly creatures."

"My regards to the Woman in White *when* you see her again, dear," added Kitty, as the four went off to laugh at the whole thing, though they carefully locked their doors and took a peep out of window before going to sleep.

"We may as well give it up and have a good rest. I'm worn out, and so are you, if you'd own it," said Julia, throwing herself down for a nap before midnight.

"I shall *not* give it up till I'm satisfied. Sleep away, I'll read awhile and call you if anything comes," answered Sally, bound to prove the truth of her story if she waited all summer.

Julia was soon off, and the lonely watcher sat reading till past eleven, then put out her light and went to take a turn on the flat roof of the piazza that ran round the house, for the night was mild and the stars companionable. As she turned to come back, her sharp eye caught sight of something moving on the house top as before, and soon, clear against the soft gloom of the sky, appeared the white figure flitting to and fro.

A long look, and then Sally made a rush at Julia, shaking her violently as she said in an excited whisper, "Come! She is there. Quick! Upstairs to the cupola; I have the candle and the key."

Carried away by the other's vehemence Julia mutely obeyed, trembling, but afraid to resist; and noiseless as two shadows, they crept up the stairs, arriving just in time to see the ghost vanish over the edge of the roof, as if it had dissolved into thin air. Julia dropped down in a heap, desperately frightened, but Sally pulled her up and led her back to their room, saying, when she got there, with grim satisfaction,

"Did I dream it all? Now I hope they will believe me."

"What was it? Oh, what could it be?" whimpered Julia,
quite demoralized by the spectacle.

"I begin to believe in ghosts, for no human being could fly off in that way, with nothing to walk on. I shall speak to Miss Orne tomorrow; I've had enough of this sort of fun," said Sally, going to the window, with a strong desire to shut and lock it.

But she paused with her hand raised, as if turned to stone, for as she spoke the white figure went slowly by. Julia dived into the closet, with one spring. Sally, however, was on her mettle now, and, holding her breath, leaned out to watch. With soundless steps the veiled thing went along the roof, and paused at the further end.

Never waiting for her comrade, Sally quietly stepped out and followed, leaving Julia to quake with fear and listen for an alarm.

None came, and in a few minutes, that seemed like hours, Sally returned, looking much excited but was sternly silent, and to all the other's eager questions she would only give this mysterious reply, "I know all but cannot tell till morning. Go to sleep."

Believing her friend offended at her base desertion at the crisis of the affair, Julia curbed her curiosity and soon forgot it in sleep. Sally slept also, feeling like a hero reposing after a hard-won battle.

She was up betimes and ready to receive her early visitors with an air of triumph, which silenced every jeer and convinced the most skeptical that she had something sensational to tell at last.

When the girls had perched themselves on any available article of furniture, they waited with respectful eagerness, while Sally retired to the hall for a moment, and Julia rolled her eyes, with her finger on her lips, looking as if she could tell much if she dared.

Sally returned somewhat flushed, but very sober, and in a few dramatic words related the adventures of the night, up to the point where she left Julia quivering ignominiously in the closet, and, like Horatius, faced the foe alone.

"I followed till the ghost entered a window."

"Which?" demanded five awestruck voices at once.

"The last."

"Ours?" whispered Kitty, pale as her collar, while Cordy, her roommate, sat aghast.

"As it turned to shut the window the veil fell back, and I saw the face." Sally spoke in a whisper and added, with a sudden start, "I see it now!"

Every girl sprang or tumbled off her perch as if an electric shock had moved them, and stared about them as Nelly cried wildly, "Where? Oh, where?"

"There!" and Sally pointed at the palest face in the room, while her own reddened with the mirth she was vainly trying to suppress.

"Cordy?"

A general shriek of amazement and incredulity followed the question, while Sally laughed till the tears ran down her cheeks at the dumb dismay of the innocent ghost.

As soon as she could be heard she quickly explained, "Yes, it was Cordy, walking in her sleep. She wore her white flannel wrapper, and a cloud [1] round her head, and took her exercise over the roofs at midnight, so that no time might be lost. I don't wonder she is tired in the morning, after such dangerous gymnastics as these."

"But she couldn't vanish in that strange way off the house-top without breaking her neck," said Julia, much relieved but still mystified.

[1] A loose-knit woolen scarf. *Ed.*

"She didn't fly or fall, but went down the ladder left by the painters. Look at the soles of her felt slippers, if you doubt me, and see the red paint from the roof. We couldn't open the cupola windows, you remember, but this morning I took a stroll and looked up and saw how she did it asleep, though she never would dare do it awake. Somnambulists do dreadfully dangerous things, you know," said Sally, as if her experience of those peculiar people had been vast and varied.

"How could I? It's horrid to think of. Why did you let me, Kit?" cried Cordy, uncertain whether to be proud or ashamed of her exploit.

"Never dreamed of *your* doing such a silly thing and never waked up. Sleepwalkers are always quiet, and if I had seen you I'd have been too scared to know you. I'll tie you to the bedpost after this and not let you scare the whole house," answered Kitty, regarding it all as a fine joke.

"What did I do when I got in?" asked Cordy, curiously.

"Took off your things and went to bed as if you were glad to get back. I didn't dare to wake you and kept the fun all to myself till this morning. Thought I ought to have a good laugh for my pains since I did all the work," answered Sally, in high glee at the success of her efforts.

"I did want to get as thin as I could before I went home; the boys plague me so, and I suppose it wore upon me and set me to walking at night. I'm very sorry, and I never will again if I can help it. Please forgive me, and don't tell anyone but Miss Orne; it was so silly," begged poor Cordy tearfully.

All promised and comforted her, and praised Sally, and plagued Julia, and had a delightfully noisy and exciting half hour before the breakfast bell rang.

Miss Orne wondered what made the young faces so gay and

the laughter so frequent, as mysterious hints and significant nods went on around the table, but as soon as possible she was borne into the schoolroom and told the thrilling tale.

Her interest and surprise were very flattering, and when the subject had been well discussed she promised to prevent any further escapades of this sort and advised Cordy to try the Banting method [1] for the few remaining weeks of her stay.

"I'll try anything that will keep me from acting ghost and making everyone afraid of me," said Cordy, secretly wondering why she had not broken her neck in her nocturnal gymnastics.

"Do you believe in ghosts, Miss Orne?" asked Maud, who did, in spite of the comic explanation of this one.

"Not the old-fashioned sort, but there is a modern kind that we are all afraid of more or less," answered Miss Orne, with a half-playful, half-serious look at the girls around her.

"Do tell about them, please," begged Kitty, while the rest looked both surprised and interested.

"There is one which I am very anxious to keep you from fearing. Women are especially haunted by it, and it prevents them from doing, being, and thinking all that they might and ought. 'What will people say?' is the name of this formidable ghost; and it does much harm, for few of us have the courage to live up to what we know to be right in all things. You are soon to go away to begin your lives in earnest, and I do hope that whatever I have been able to teach you about the care of minds and bodies will not be forgotten or neglected because it may not be the fashion outside our little world."

"*I* never will forget or be afraid of that ghost, Miss Orne,"

[1] William Banting wrote about a dietetic method of reducing corpulence. *Ed.*

cried Sally, quick to understand and accept the warning so opportunely given.

"I have great faith in *you*, dear, because you have proved yourself so brave in facing phantoms more easily laid. But this is a hard one to meet and vanquish; so watch well, stand firm, and let these jerseys that you are so fond of cover not only healthy young bodies but happy hearts, both helping you to be sweet, wise, and useful women in the years to come. Dear girls, promise me this, and I shall feel that our winter has not been wasted, and that our spring is full of lovely promise for a splendid summer."

As she spoke, with her own beautiful face bright with hope and tenderness, Miss Orne opened her arms and gathered them all in, to seal their promise with grateful kisses more eloquent than words.

Long after their school days were over, the six girls kept the white jerseys they wore at the breaking-up festival, as relics of the J. J.; and long after they were scattered far apart, they remembered the lessons which helped them to be what their good friend hoped—healthy, happy, and useful women.

The Cooking Class

A young girl in a little cap and a big apron sat poring over a cookbook, with a face full of the deepest anxiety. She had the kitchen to herself, for mamma was out for the day, cook was off duty, and Edith could mess to her heart's content. She belonged to a cooking class, the members of which were to have a lunch at two o'clock with the girl next door, and now the all-absorbing question was, what to make. Turning the pages of the well-used book, she talked to herself as the various receipts met her eye.

"Lobster salad and chicken croquettes I've had, and neither was very good. Now I want to distinguish myself by something very nice. I'd try a meat-porcupine or a mutton-duck if there was time, but they are fussy and ought to be rehearsed before given to the class. Bavarian cream needs berries and whipped cream, and I *won't* tire my arms beating eggs. Apricots *à la Neige* is an easy thing and wholesome, but the girls won't like it, I know, as well as some rich thing that will make them ill, as Carrie's plum pudding did. A little meat dish is best for lunch. I'd try sweetbreads and bacon, if I didn't hate to burn my face and scent my clothes, frying. Birds are elegant; let me see if I can do larded grouse. No, I don't like to touch that cold, fat stuff. How mortified Ella was, when she had birds on toast and forgot to draw them. Potted pigeons—the very thing! Had that in our last lesson, but the girls are all crazy about puff paste, so they won't try pigeons. Why didn't I think of it at once? For we've got them in the house and don't want them today, Mamma being called away. All ready too—so nice! I do detest to pick and clean birds. 'Simmer from one to three hours.' Plenty of time. I'll do it! I'll do it! La, la, la!"

And away skipped Edith in high spirits, for she did not love to cook, yet wished to stand well with the class, some members of which were very ambitious and now and then succeeded with an elaborate dish, more by good luck than skill.

Six plump birds were laid out on a platter, with their legs folded in the most pathetic manner; these Edith bore away in triumph to the kitchen, and, opening the book before her, went to work energetically, resigning herself to frying the pork and cutting up the onion, which she had overlooked when hastily reading the recipe. In time they were stuffed, the legs tied down to the tails, the birds browned in the stew-pan and put to simmer with a pinch of herbs.

"Now I can clean up and rest a bit. If I ever have to work for a living, I *won't* be a cook," said Edith, with a sigh of weariness as she washed her dishes, wondering how there could be so many, for no careless Irish girl would have made a greater clutter over this small job than the young lady who had not yet learned one of the most important things that a cook should know.

The bell rang just as she got done and was planning to lie and rest on the dining room sofa till it was time to take up her pigeons.

"Tell whoever it is that I'm engaged," she whispered, as the maid passed, on her way to the door.

"It's your cousin, miss, from the country, and she has a trunk with her. Of course she's to come in?" asked Maria, coming back in a moment.

"Oh, dear me! I forgot all about Patty. Mamma said any day this week, and this is the most inconvenient one of the seven. Of course, she must come in. Go and tell her I'll be there in a minute," answered Edith, too well-bred not to give even an unwelcome guest a kindly greeting.

Whisking off cap and apron and taking a last look at the birds, just beginning to send forth a savory steam, she went to meet her cousin.

Patty was a rosy, country lass of sixteen, plainly dressed and rather shy but a sweet, sensible little body, with a fresh, rustic air which marked her for a field flower at once.

"How do you do, dear? So sorry Mamma is away, called to a sick friend in a hurry. But I'm here and glad to see you. I've an engagement at two, and you shall go with me. It's only a lunch close by, just a party of girls; I'll tell you about it up-stairs."

Chatting away, Edith led Patty up to the pretty room ready

for her, and soon both were laughing over a lively account of the exploits of the cooking class. Suddenly, in the midst of the cream pie which had been her great success, and nearly the death of all who partook thereof, Edith paused, sniffed the air like a hound and, crying tragically, "They are burning! They are burning!" rushed downstairs as if the house was on fire.

Much alarmed, Patty hurried after her, guided to the kitchen by the sound of lamentation. There she found Edith hanging over a stewpan, with anguish in her face and despair in her voice, as she breathlessly explained the cause of her flight.

"My pigeons! Are they burnt? Do smell and tell me? After all my trouble I shall be heartbroken if they are spoilt."

Both pretty noses sniffed and sniffed again as the girls bent over the pan, regardless of the steam which was ruining their crimps and reddening their noses. Reluctantly, Patty owned that a slight flavor of scorch *did* pervade the air but suggested that a touch more seasoning would conceal the sad fact.

"I'll try it. Did you ever do any? Do you love to cook? Don't you want to make something to carry? If would please the girls and make up for my burnt mess," said Edith, as she skimmed the broth and added pepper and salt with a lavish hand.

"I don't know anything about pigeons, except to feed and pet them. We don't eat ours. I can cook plain dishes and make all kinds of bread. Would biscuit or teacake do?"

Patty looked so pleased at the idea of contributing to the feast that Edith could not bear to tell her that hot biscuit and teacake were not just the thing for a city lunch. She accepted the offer, and Patty fell to work so neatly and skillfully that, by the time the pigeons were done, two pans full of delicious little biscuits were baked, and, folded in a nice napkin, lay ready to carry off in the porcelain plate with a wreath of roses painted on it.

In spite of all her flavoring, the burnt odor and taste still lingered around Edith's dish, but, fondly hoping no one would perceive it, she dressed hastily, gave Patty a touch here and there and set forth at the appointed time to Augusta's lunch.

Six girls belonged to this class, and the rule was for each to bring her contribution and set it on the table prepared to receive them all; then, when the number was complete, the covers were raised, the dishes examined, eaten (if possible), and pronounced upon, the prize being awarded to the best. The girl at whose house the lunch was given provided the prize, and they were often both pretty and valuable.

On this occasion a splendid bouquet of Jaqueminot roses in a lovely vase ornamented the middle of the table, and the eyes of all rested admiringly on it, as the seven girls gathered around, after depositing their dishes.

Patty had been kindly welcomed, and soon forgot her shyness in wonder at the handsome dresses, graceful manners, and lively gossip of the girls. A pleasant, merry set, all wearing the uniform of the class, dainty white aprons and coquettish caps with many-colored ribbons, like stage maidservants. At the sound of a silver bell, each took her place before the covered dish which bore her name, and, when Augusta said, "Ladies, we will begin," off went napkins, silver covers, white paper, or whatever hid the contribution from longing eyes. A moment of deep silence, while quick glances took in the prospect, and then a unanimous explosion of laughter followed, for six platters of potted pigeons stood upon the board, with nothing but the flowers to break the ludicrous monotony of the scene.

How they laughed! For a time they could do nothing else, because if one tried to explain she broke down and joined in the gale of merriment again quite helplessly. One or two got hysterical and cried as well as laughed, and all made such a noise that Augusta's mamma peeped in to see what was the matter. Six agitated hands pointed to the comical sight on the table, which looked as if a flight of potted pigeons had alighted there, and six breathless voices cried in a chorus, "Isn't it funny? Don't tell!"

Much amused, the good lady retired to enjoy the joke alone, while the exhausted girls wiped their eyes and began to talk, all at once. Such a clatter! But out of it all Patty evolved the fact that each meant to surprise the rest—and they certainly had.

"I tried puff paste," said Augusta, fanning her hot face.

"So did I," cried the others.

"And it was a dead failure."

"So was mine," echoed the voices.

"Then I thought I'd do the other dish we had that day—"

"Just what I did."

"Feeling sure you would all try the pastry, and perhaps get on better than I."

"Exactly our case," and a fresh laugh ended this general confession.

"Now we must eat our pigeons, as we have nothing else, and it is against the rule to add from outside stores. I propose that we each pass our dish around; then we can all criticize it and so get some good out of this very funny lunch."

Augusta's plan was carried out, and, all being hungry after

their unusual exertions, the girls fell upon the unfortunate birds like so many famished creatures. The first one went very well, but when the dishes were passed again, each taster looked at it anxiously, for none was very good; there was nothing to fall back upon, and variety is the spice of life, as everyone knows.

"Oh, for a slice of bread," sighed one damsel.

"Why didn't we think of it?" asked another.

"I did, but we always have so much cake I thought it was foolish to lay in rolls," exclaimed Augusta, rather mortified at the neglect.

"I expected to have to taste six pies, and one doesn't want bread with pastry, you know."

As Edith spoke she suddenly remembered Patty's biscuits, which had been left on the side table by their modest maker, as there seemed to be no room for them.

Rejoicing now over the rather despised dish, Edith ran to get it, saying as she set it in the middle, with a flourish, "My cousin's contribution. She came so late we only had time for that. So glad I took the liberty of bringing her and them."

A murmur of welcome greeted the much-desired addition to the feast, which would have been a decided failure, without it, and the pretty plate went briskly around, till nothing was left but the painted roses in it. With this help the best of the potted pigeons were eaten, while a lively discussion went on about what they would have next time.

"Let us each tell our dish and not change. We shall never learn if we don't keep to one thing till we do it well. I will choose mince pie, and bring a good one, if it takes me all the week to do it," said Edith, heroically taking the hardest thing she could think of, to encourage the others.

Fired by this noble example, each girl pledged herself to

do or die, and a fine list of rich dishes was made out by these ambitious young cooks. Then a vote of thanks to Patty was passed, her biscuit unanimously pronounced the most successful contribution, and the vase presented to the delighted girl, whose blushes were nearly as deep as the color of the flowers behind which she tried to hide them.

Soon after this ceremony the party broke up, and Edith went home to tell the merry story, proudly adding that the country cousin had won the prize.

"You rash child, to undertake mince pie. It is one of the hardest things to make, and about the most unwholesome when eaten. Read the receipt and see what you have pledged yourself to do, my dear," said her mother, much amused at the haps and mishaps of the cooking class.

Edith opened her book and started bravely off at "puff paste"; but by the time she had come to the end of the three pages devoted to directions for the making of that indigestible delicacy, her face was very sober, and, when she read aloud the following receipt for the mincemeat, despair slowly settled upon her like a cloud.

One cup chopped meat; 1½ cups raisins; 1½ cups currants; 1½ cups brown sugar; 1⅓ cups molasses; 3 cups chopped apples; 1 cup meat liquor; 2 teaspoonfuls salt; 2 teaspoonfuls cinnamon ½ teaspoonful mace; ½ teaspoonful powdered cloves; 1 lemon, grated; ¼ piece citron, sliced; ½ cup brandy; ¼ cup wine; 3 teaspoonfuls rosewater.

"Oh me, what a job! I shall have to work at it every day till next Saturday, for the paste alone will take all the wits I've got. I *was* rash, but I spoke without thinking and wanted to do something really fine. We can't be shown about things, so I must blunder along as well as I can," groaned Edith.

"I can help about the measuring, and weighing, and chopping. I always help Mother at Thanksgiving time, and she makes splendid pies. We only have mince then, as she thinks it's bad for us," said Patty, full of sympathy and good will.

"What are you to take to the lunch?" asked Edith's mother, smiling at her daughter's mournful face, bent over the fatal book full of dainty messes, that tempted the unwary learner to her doom.

"Only coffee. I can't make fancy things, but my coffee is always good. They said they wanted it, so I offered."

"I will have my pills and powders ready, for if you all go on at this rate you will need a dose of some sort after your lunch. Give your orders, Edith, and devote your mind to the task. I wish you good luck and good digestion, my dears."

With that the mamma left the girls to cheer each another and lay plans for a daily lesson till the perfect pie was made.

They certainly did their best, for they began on Monday, and each morning through the week went to the mighty task with daily increasing courage and skill. They certainly needed the former, for even good-natured Nancy got tired of having "the young ladies messing around so much," and looked cross as the girls appeared in the kitchen.

Edith's brothers laughed at the various failures which appeared at table, and dear Mamma was tired of tasting pastry and mincemeat in all stages of progression. But the undaunted damsels kept on till Saturday came, and a very superior pie stood ready to be offered for the inspection of the class.

"I never want to see another," said Edith, as the girls dressed together, weary, but well satisfied with their labor, for the pie had been praised by all beholders, and the fragrance of Patty's coffee filled the house, as it stood ready to be poured, hot and clear, into the best silver pot, at the last moment.

"Well, I feel as if I'd lived in a spice mill this week, or a pastry cook's kitchen, and I am glad we are done. Your brothers won't get any pie for a long while I guess, if it depends on you," laughed Patty, putting on the new ribbons her cousin had given her.

"When Florence's brothers were here last night, I heard those rascals making all sorts of fun of us, and Alf said we ought to let them come to lunch. I scorned the idea and made their mouths water telling about the good things we were going to have," said Edith, exulting over the severe remarks she had made to these gluttonous young men, who adored pie, yet jeered at unfortunate cooks.

Florence, the lunch-giver of the week, had made her table pretty with a posy at each place, put the necessary roll in each artistically folded napkin, and hung the prize from the gas burner—a large blue satin bag full of the most delicious bonbons money could buy. There was some delay about beginning, as one distracted cook sent word that her potato puffs *wouldn't* brown and begged them to wait for her. So they adjourned to the parlor and talked till the flushed, but triumphant Ella arrived with the puffs in fine order.

When all was ready and the covers raised, another surprise awaited them—not a merry one, like the last, but a very serious affair, which produced domestic warfare in two houses at least. On each dish lay a card bearing a new name for these carefully prepared delicacies. The mince pie was re-christened "Nightmare," veal cutlets "Dyspepsia," escalloped lobster "Fits," lemon sherbet "Colic," coffee "Palpitation," and so on, even to the pretty sack of confectionary which was labelled "Toothache."

Great was the indignation of the insulted cooks, and a general cry of "Who did it?" arose. The poor maid who waited on them declared with tears that not a soul had been in, and she herself only absent five minutes getting the ice water. Florence felt that her guests had been outraged and promised to find out the wretch and punish him or her in the most terrible manner. So the irate young ladies ate their lunch before it cooled but forgot to criticize the dishes so full were they of wonder at this daring deed. They were just beginning to calm down, when a loud sneeze caused a general rush toward the sofa that stood in a recess of the dining room. A small boy, nearly suffocated with suppressed laughter and dust, was dragged forth and put on trial without a moment's delay. Florence was judge, the others jury, and the unhappy youth, being penned in a corner, was ordered to tell the truth, the whole truth, and nothing but the truth, on penalty of a sound whipping with the big Japanese war fan that hung on the wall over his head.

Vainly trying to suppress his giggles, Phil faced the seven ladies like a man, and told as little as possible, delighting to torment them, like a true boy.

"Do you know who put those cards there?"

"Don't you wish *you* did?"

"Phil Gordon, answer at once."

"Yes, I do."

"Was it Alf? He's at home Saturdays, and it's just like a horrid Harvard Soph to plague us so."

"It was—not."

"Did you see it done?"

"I did."

"Man, or woman? Mary fibs and may have been bribed."

"Man," with a chuckle of great glee.

"Do I know him?"

"Oh, don't you!"

"Edith's brother Rex?"

"No, ma'am."

"Do be a good boy, and tell us. We won't scold, though it was a very, very rude thing to do."

"What will you give me?"

"Do you need to be bribed to do your duty?"

"Well, I guess it's no fun to hide in that stuffy place, and smell nice grub, and see you tuck away without offering a fellow a taste. Give me a good go at the lunch, and I'll see what I can do for you."

"Boys are such pigs! Shall we, girls?"

"Yes, we *must* know."

"Then go and stuff, you bad boy, but we shall stand guard over you till you tell us who wrote and put those insulting cards here."

Florence let out the prisoner and stood by him while he ate, in a surprisingly short time, the best of everything on the table, well knowing that such a rare chance would not soon be his again.

"Now give me some of that candy, and I'll tell," demanded the young Shylock, bound to make the best of his power while it lasted.

"Did you ever see such a little torment! I can't give the nice bonbons, because we haven't decided who is to have them."

"Never mind. Pick out a few and get rid of him," cried the girls, hovering around their prey and longing to shake the truth out of him.

A handful of sweeties was reluctantly bestowed, and then all waited for the name of the evildoer with breathless interest.

"Well," began Phil, with exasperating slowness, "Alf wrote the cards and gave me half a dollar to put 'em around. Made a nice thing of it, haven't I?" and before one of the girls could catch him he had bolted from the room, with one hand full of candy, the other of mince pie, and his face shining with the triumphant glee of a small boy who has teased seven big girls and got the better of them.

What went on just after that is not recorded, though Phil

peeped in at the windows, hooted through the slide, and beat a tattoo on the various doors. The opportune arrival of his mother sent him whooping down the street, and the distressed damsels finished their lunch with what appetite they could.

Edith got the prize, for her pie was pronounced a grand success, and partaken of so copiously that several young ladies had reason to think it well named "Nightmare" by the derisive Alfred. Emboldened by her success, Edith invited them all to her house on the next Saturday, and suggested that she and her cousin provide the lunch, as they had some new dishes to offer, not down in the receipt book they had been studying all winter.

As the ardor of the young cooks was somewhat damped by various failures and the discovery that good cooking is an art not easily learned, anything in the way of novelty was welcome; and the girls gladly accepted the invitation, feeling a sense of relief at the thought of not having any dish to worry about, though not one of them owned that she was tired of "messing," as the disrespectful boys called it.

It was unanimously decided to wither with silent scorn the audacious Alfred and his ally, Rex, while Phil was to be snubbed by his sister till he had begged pardon for his share of the evil deed. Then, having sweetened their tongues and tempers with the delicious bonbons, the girls departed, feeling that the next lunch would be an event of unusual interest.

The idea of it originated in a dinner which Patty got one day, when Nancy, who wanted a holiday, was unexpectedly called away to the funeral of a cousin—the fifth relative who had died in a year, such was the mortality in the jovial old creature's family. Edith's mother was very busy with a dressmaker, and gladly accepted the offer the girls made to get dinner alone.

"No fancy dishes, if you please; the boys come in as hungry as hunters and want a good solid meal; so get something wholesome and plain, and plenty of it," was the much-relieved lady's only suggestion, as she retired to the sewing room and left the girls to keep house in their own way.

"Now, Edie, you be the mistress and give your orders, and I'll be cook. Only have things that go well together—not all baked or all boiled, because there isn't room enough on the range, you know," said Patty, putting on a big apron with an air of great satisfaction, for she loved to cook, and was tired of doing nothing.

"I'll watch all you do and learn, so that the next time Nancy goes off in a hurry, I can take her place and not have to give the boys what they hate—a picked-up dinner," answered Edith, pleased with her part, yet a little mortified to find how few plain thing she could make well.

"What do the boys like?" asked Patty, longing to please them, for they all were very kind to her.

"Roast beef, and custard pudding, with two or three kinds of vegetables. Can we do all that?"

"Yes, indeed. I'll make the pudding right away and have it baked before the meat goes in. I can cook as many vegetables as you please, and soup too."

So the order was given and all went well, if one might judge by the sounds of merriment in the kitchen. Patty made her best gingerbread and cooked some apples with sugar and spice for tea, and at the stroke of two had a nice dinner smoking on the table, to the great contentment of the hungry boys, who did eat like hunters and advised Mamma to send old Nancy away and keep Patty for cook, which complimentary but rash proposal pleased their cousin very much.

"Now this is useful cookery and well done, though it looks

so simple. Any girl can learn how and be independent of servants, if need be. Drop your class, Edith, and take a few lessons of Patty. That would suit me better than French affairs, that are neither economical nor wholesome."

"I will, Mamma, for I'm tired of creaming butter, larding things, and beating eggs. These dishes are not so elegant, but we must have them; so I may as well learn, if Pat will teach me."

"With pleasure—all I know. Mother thinks it a very important part of a girl's education, for if you can't keep servants you can do your own work well, and if you are rich you are not so dependent as an ignorant lady is. All kinds of useful sewing and housework come first with us, and the accomplishments afterward, as time and money allow."

"That sort of thing turns out the kind of girl I like, and so does every sensible fellow. Good luck to you, cousin, and my best thanks for a capital dinner and a wise little lecture for dessert."

Rex made his best bow as he left the table, and Patty colored high with pleasure at the praise of the tall collegian. Out of this, and the talk the ladies had afterward, grew the lunch which Edith proposed, and to the preparation of which went much thought and care, for the girls meant to have many samples of country fare, so that various tastes might be pleased. The plan gradually grew as they worked, and a little surprise was added, which was a great success.

When Saturday came the younger boys were all packed off for a holiday in the country, that the coast might be clear.

"No hiding under sofas in my house, no meddling with my dinner, if you please, gentlemen," said Edith, as she saw the small brothers safely off, and fell to work with Patty and the maid to arrange the dining room to suit the feast about to be spread there.

As antique furniture is the fashion nowadays, it was easy to collect all the old tables, chairs, china, and ornaments in the house and make a pleasant place of the sunny room where a tall clock always stood, and damask hangings a century old added much to the effect. A massive mahogany table was set forth with ancient silver, glass, china, and all sorts of queer old saltcellars, pepperpots, pickle dishes, knives, and spoons. High-backed chairs stood around it, and the guests were received by a very pretty old lady in plum-colored satin, with a muslin pelerine, and a large lace cap most becoming to the rosy face it surrounded. A fat watch ticked in the wide belt, mitts covered the plump hands, and a reticule hung at the side. Madam's daughter, in a very short-waisted pink silk gown, muslin apron, and frill, was even prettier than her mother, for her dark, curly hair hung on her shoulders, and a little cap was stuck on the top, with long pink streamers. Her mitts went to the elbow, and a pink sash was tied in a large bow behind.

Great was the pleasure this little surprise gave the girls, and gay was the chatter that went on as they were welcomed by the hostesses, who constantly forgot their parts. Madam frisked now and then, and "Pretty Peggy" was so anxious about dinner that she was not as devoted to her company as a well-bred young lady should be. But no one minded, and, when the bell rang, all gathered about the table eager to see what the feast was to be.

"Ladies, we have endeavored to give you a taste of some of the good old dishes rather out of fashion now," said Madam, standing at her place, with a napkin pinned over the purple dress and a twinkle in the blue eyes under the wide cap frills. "We thought it would be well to introduce some of them to the class and to our family cooks, who either scorn the plain dishes, or don't know how to cook them *well*. There is variety, and we hope all will find something to enjoy. Peggy, uncover, and let us begin."

At first the girls looked a little disappointed, for the dishes were not very new to them, but when they tasted a real "boiled dinner" and found how good it was—also baked beans, neither hard, greasy, nor burnt; beefsteak, tender, juicy, and well flavored; potatoes, mealy in spite of the season; Indian pudding, made as few modern cooks know how to do it; brown bread, with homemade butter; and pumpkin pie that cut like wedges of vegetable gold—they changed their minds and began to eat with appetites that would have destroyed their reputations as delicate young ladies, if they had been seen. Tea in eggshell cups, election cake, and cream cheese with fruit ended the dinner; and, as they sat admiring the tiny old spoons, the crisp cake, and the little cheeses like snowballs, Edith said, in reply to various compliments paid her, "Let us give honor where honor is due. Patty suggested this and did most of the cooking; so thank her and borrow her receipt book. It's very funny, ever so old, copied and tried by her grandmother, and full of directions for making quantities of nice things, from pie like this to a safe, sure wash for the complexion. May dew, rose leaves, and lavender—doesn't that sound lovely?"

"Let me copy it," cried several girls afflicted with freckles or sallow with too much coffee and confectionary.

"Yes, indeed. But I was going to say, as we have no prize today, we have prepared a little souvenir of our old-fashioned dinner for each of you. Bring them, daughter; I hope the ladies will pardon the homeliness of the offering and make use of the hint that accompanies each."

As Edith spoke, with a comical mingling of the merry girl and the stately old lady she was trying to personate, Patty brought from the sideboard, where it had stood covered up, a silver salver on which lay five dainty little loaves of bread; on the top of each appeared a receipt for making the same, nicely written on colored cards, and held in place by a silver scarf pin.

"How cunning!" "What lovely pins!" "I'll take the hint and learn to make a good bread at once." "It smells as sweet as a nut, and isn't hard or heavy a bit." "Such a pretty idea, and so clever of you to carry it out so well."

These remarks went on as the little loaves went around, each girl finding her pin well suited to her pet fancy or foible, for all were different, and all very pretty, whether the design was a palette, a skate, a pen, a racquet, a fan, a feather, a bar of music, or a daisy.

Seeing that her dinner was a success in spite of its homeliness, Edith added the last surprise, which had also been one to Patty and herself when it arrived, just in time to be carried out. She forgot to be Madam now and said, with a face full of mingled merriment and satisfaction, as she pushed her cap askew and pulled off her mitts. "Girls, the best joke of all is that Rex and Alf sent the pins and made Phil bring them with a most humble apology for their impertinence last week. A meeker boy I never saw, and for that we may thank Floy, but I think the dinner Pat and I got the other day won Rex's heart, so that he made Alf eat humble pie in this agreeable manner. We won't say anything about it but all wear our pins and show the boys that we can forgive and forget as 'sweet girls' should, though we do cook and have ideas of our own beyond looking pretty and minding our older brothers."

"We will!" cried the chorus with one voice.

And Florence added, "I also propose that when we have learned to make something beside 'kickshaws,' as the boys call our fancy dishes, we have a dinner like this and invite those rascals to it, which will be heaping coals of fire on their heads and stopping their mouths forevermore from making jokes about our cooking class."

Music and Macaroni

Among the pretty villages that lie along the wonderful Corniche Road which runs from Nice to Genoa, none was more beautiful than Valrose. It deserved its name, for it was indeed a "valley of roses." The little town with its old church nestled among the olive and orange trees that clothed the hillside, sloping up to purple mountains towering behind. Lower down stretched the vineyards, and the valley was a bed of flowers all the year around. There were acres of violets, verbenas, mignonette, and every sweet-scented blossom that grows, while hedges of roses, and alleys of lemon trees with their white stars made the air heavy with perfume. Across the plain, one saw the blue sea rolling to meet the bluer sky, sending fresh airs and soft rains to keep Valrose green and beautiful even through the summer heat. Only one ugly thing marred the lovely landscape, and that was the factory, with its tall chimneys, its red walls, and ceaseless bustle. But old ilex trees tried to conceal its ugliness; the smoke curled gracefully from its chimney tops; and the brown men talked in their musical language as they ran about the busy courtyard, or did strange things below in the stillroom. Handsome black-eyed girls sang at the open windows at their pretty work, and delicious odors filled the place, for here the flowers that bloomed outside were changed to all kinds of delicate perfumes to scent the hair of great ladies and the handkerchiefs of dainty gentlemen all the world over.

The poor roses, violets, mignonette, orange-flowers, and their sisters were brought here in great baskets to yield up their sweet souls in hot rooms where fires burned and great vats boiled; then they were sent up to be imprisoned in pretty flasks of all imaginable shapes and colors by the girls, who put gilded labels on them, packed them in delicate boxes, and sent them away to comfort the sick, please the rich, and put money in the pockets of the merchants.

Many children were employed in the light work of weeding beds, gathering flowers, and running errands; among these none were busier, happier, or more beloved than Florentino and his sister Stella. They were orphans, but they lived with old Mariuccia in her little stone house near the church, contented with the small wages they earned, though their clothes were poor; their food, salad, macaroni, rye bread, and thin wine, with now and then a taste of meat when Stella's lover or some richer friend gave them a treat on gala days.

They worked hard and had their dreams of what they would do when they had saved up a little store. Stella would marry her Beppo and settle in a home of her own, but Tino was more ambitious, for he possessed a sweet boyish voice and sang so well in the choir, at the merrymakings, and about his work, that he was called the "little nightingale," and was much praised and petted not only by his mates but by the good priest who taught him his music and the travellers who often came to the factory and were not allowed to go till Tino had sung to them.

All this made the lad vain, and he hoped one day to go away as Baptista had gone, who now sang in a fine church at Genoa and sent home gold napoleons to his old parents. How this was to come about Tino had not the least idea, but he cheered his work with all manner of wild plans and sang his best at Mass, hoping some stranger would hear and take him away as Signor Pulci had taken big Tista, whose voice was not half so wonderful as his own, all had said. No one came, however, and Tino at thirteen was still at work in the valley —a happy little lad, singing all day long as he carried his fragrant loads to and fro, ate his dinner of bread and beans fried in oil, with a crust, under the ilex trees, and slept like a dormouse at night on his clean straw in the loft at Mariuccia's, with the moon for his candle and the summer warmth for his coverlet.

One day in September, as he stood winnowing mignonette seed in a quiet corner of the vast garden, he was thinking deeply over his hopes and plans, and practicing the last chant Father Angelo had taught him, while he shook and held the sieve high, to let the wind blow away the dead husks, leaving the brown seeds behind.

Suddenly, as he ended his lesson with a clear high note that seemed to rise and die softly away like the voice of an angel in the air, the sound of applause startled him, and, turning, he saw a gentleman sitting on the rude bench behind him, a well-dressed, handsome, smiling gentleman, who clapped his white hands and nodded and said gaily, "Bravo, my boy; that was well done! You have a wonderful voice; sing again."

But Tino was too abashed for the moment and could only stand and stare at the stranger, a pretty picture of boyish confusion, pleasure, and shyness.

"Come, tell me all about it, my friend. Who taught you so well? Why are you here and not where you should be, learning to use this fine pipe of yours, and make fame and money by it?" said the gentleman, still smiling as he leaned easily in his seat and swung his gloves.

Tino's heart began to beat fast as he thought, "Perhaps my chance has come at last! I must make the most of it." So, taking courage, he told his little story.

When he ended, the stranger gave a nod, saying, "Yes, you are the 'little nightingale' they spoke of up at the inn. I came to find you. Now sing me something gay, some of your folk songs. That sort will suit you best."

Anxious to make the most of his chance, Tino took courage and sang away as easily as a bird on a bough, pouring out one after another the barcaroles, serenades, ballads, and drinking songs he had learned from the people about him.

The gentleman listened, laughed, and applauded as if well pleased, and when Tino stopped to take breath, he gave another nod more decided than the first, and said with his engaging smile, "You are indeed a wonder, and quite wasted here. If *I* had you I should make a man of you and put money in your pocket as fast as you opened your mouth."

Tino's eyes sparkled at the word "money," for sweet as was the praise, the idea of having full pockets bewitched him, and he asked eagerly, "How, signor?"

"Well," answered the gentleman, idly tapping his nose with a rosebud which he had pulled as he came along, "I should take you to my hotel in Nice; wash, brush, and trim you up a little; put you into a velvet suit with a lace collar, silk stockings, and buckled shoes; teach you music; feed you well; and when I thought you fit, carry you with me to the salons of the great people, where I give concerts. There you would sing these gay songs of yours and be petted, praised, and pelted with bonbons, francs, and kisses perhaps—for you are a pretty lad, and these fine ladies and idle gentlemen are always ready to welcome a new favorite. Would you fancy that sort of life better than this? You can have it if you like."

Tino's black eyes shone; the color deepened in his brown cheeks; and he showed all his white teeth as he laughed and exclaimed with a gesture of delight, *"Mio Dio!* But I *would,* signor! I'm tired of this work; I long to sing, to see the world, to be my own master, and let Stella and the old woman know that I am big enough to have my own way. Do you really mean it? When can I go? I'm ready now, only I had better run and put on my holiday suit and get my guitar."

"Good! There's a lad of spirit. I like that well. A guitar, too? Bravo, my little troubadour, we shall make a sensation in the drawing rooms, and fill our pockets shortly. But there is no haste, and it would be well to ask these friends of yours, or there might be trouble. I don't *steal* nightingales, I buy them; and I will give the old woman, whoever she may be, more than you would earn in a month. See, I, too, am a singer, and this I made at Genoa in a week." As he spoke, Signor Mario pulled a well-filled purse from one pocket, a handful of gold and silver coin from the other, and chinked them before the boy's admiring eyes.

"Let us go!" cried Tino, flinging down the sieve as if done with work forever. "Stella is at home today; come at once to Mariuccia—it is not far; and when they hear these fine plans, they will be glad to let me go, I am sure."

Away he went across the field of flowers, through the court-yard, up the steep street, straight into the kitchen where his pretty sister sat eating artichokes and bread while the old woman twirled her distaff in the sun. Both were used to strangers, for the cottage was a picturesque place, half hidden, like a bird's nest, in vines and fig trees, with a gay little plot of flowers before it; travellers often came to taste Mariuccia's honey, for her bees fared well, and their combs were running over with the sweetness of violets and roses, put up in dainty little waxen boxes made by better workmen than any found at the factory.

The two women listened respectfully while Signor Mario told his plan in his delightfully gracious way, and Stella was much impressed by the splendor of the prospect before her brother. But the wise old woman shook her head and declared decidedly that the boy was too young to leave home yet. Father Angelo was teaching him well; he was safe and happy where he was; and there he should remain, for she had sworn by all the saints to his dying mother that she would guard him as "the apple of her eye" till he was old enough to take care of himself.

In vain Mario shook his purse before her eyes, Stella

pleaded, and Tino stormed; the faithful soul would not give up, much as she needed money, loved Stella, and hated to cross the boy who was in truth the apple of her eye and the darling of her heart. There was a lively scene in the little room, for everyone talked at once, gesticulated wildly, and grew much excited in the discussion; but nothing came of it, and Signor Mario departed wrathfully, leaving Mariuccia looking as stern as fate with her distaff, Stella in tears, and Tino in such a rage he could only dash up to the loft and throw himself on his rude bed, there to kick and sob and tear his hair and wish there might be ten thousand earthquakes to swallow that cruel old woman up in the twinkling of an eye.

Stella came to beg him to be comforted and eat his supper, but he drew the wooden bolt and would not let her in saying sternly, "I *never* will come down till Mariuccia says I may go; I will starve first. I am not a child to be so treated. Go away, and let me alone; I hate you both!"

Poor Stella retired, heartbroken, and when all her entreaties failed to change their guardian's decision, she went to consult Father Angelo. He agreed with the old woman that it was best to keep the boy safe at home, as they knew nothing of the strange gentleman or what might befall Tino if he left the shelter of his own humble home and friends.

Much disappointed, Stella went to pray devoutly in the church, and, then, meeting her Beppo, soon forgot all about the poor little lad who had sobbed himself to sleep upon his straw.

The house was quiet when he awoke; no lights shone from any neighbor's windows, and all was still except the nightingales singing in the valley. The moon was up, and her friendly face looked in at the little window so brightly that the boy felt comforted and lay staring at the soft light while his mind worked busily. Some evil spirit, some naughty Puck bent on mischief must have been abroad that night, for into Tino's head there suddenly popped a splendid idea; at least *he* thought it so, and in his rebellious state found it all the more tempting because danger and disobedience and defiance all had a part in it.

Why not run away? Signor Mario was not to leave till next morning. Tino could easily slip out early and join the kind gentleman beyond the town. This would show the women that he, Tino, had a will of his own and was not to be treated like a child any more. It would give them a good fright, make a fine stir in the place, and add to his glory when he returned with plenty of money to display himself in the velvet suit and silk stockings—a famous fellow who knew what he was about and did not mean to be insulted or tied to an old woman's apron strings forever.

The longer he thought, the more delightful the idea became, and he resolved to carry it out, for the fine tales he had heard made him more discontented than ever with his present simple, carefree life. Up he got, and by the light of the moon took from the old chest his best suit. Moving very softly, he put on the breeches and jacket of rough blue cloth, the coarse linen shirt, the red sash, and the sandals of russet leather that laced about his legs to the knee. A few clothes, with his rosary, he tied up in a handkerchief, and laid the little bundle ready with his Sunday hat, a broadbrimmed, pointed-crown affair with a red band and a cock's feather to adorn it.

Then he sat at the window waiting for dawn to come, fearing to sleep lest he be too late. It seemed an almost endless night, the first he had ever spent awake, but red streaks came in the east at last, and he stole to the door, meaning to creep noiselessly downstairs, take a good hunch of bread and a gourd full of wine, and slip off while the women slept. To his dismay he found the door barred on the outside. His courage had ebbed a little as the time for action came, but at this new insult he got angry again, and every dutiful impulse flew away in a minute.

"Ah, they think to keep me, do they? Behold, then, how I cheat the silly things! They have never seen me climb down the fig tree and thought me safe. Now I will vanish and leave them to tear their hair and weep for me in vain."

Flinging out his bundle and carefully lowering his old guitar, Tino leaned from the little window, caught the nearest branch of the tree that bent toward the wall, and swung himself down as nimbly as a squirrel. Pausing only to pick several bunches of ripe grapes from the vine about the door, he went softly through the garden and ran away along the road toward Nice as fast as his legs could carry him.

Not till he reached the top of the long hill a mile away, did he slacken his lively pace; then, climbing a bank, he lay down to rest under some olive trees and ate his grapes as he watched the sunrise. Travellers always left the Falcone Inn early to enjoy the morning freshness, so Tino knew that Signor Mario would soon appear; and when the horses paused to rest on the hilltop, the "little nightingale" would present himself as unexpectedly as if he had fallen from heaven.

But Signor Mario was a lazy man, and Tino had time to work himself into a fever of expectation, doubt, and fear before the roll of wheels greeted his longing ears. Yes, it was the delightful stranger, reading papers and smoking as he rode, quite blind to the beauty all around him, blind also to the sudden appearance of a picturesque little figure by the roadside as the carriage stopped. Even when he looked, he did not recognize shabby Tino in the well-dressed beggar, as he thought him, who stood bareheaded and smiling, with hat in one hand, bundle in the other, and guitar slung on his back. He waved his hand as if to say, "I have nothing for you," and was about to bid the man drive on, but Tino cried out boldly, "Behold me, signor! I am Tino, the singing boy of Valrose. I have run away to join you if you will have me. Ah, please do! I wish so much to go with you."

"Bravo!" cried Mario, well pleased. "That is a lad of spirit, and I am glad to have you. I don't steal nightingales, as I told you down yonder, but if they get out of their cages and perch on my finger, I keep them. In with you, boy! There is no time to lose."

In scrambled happy Tino, and, settling himself and his property on the seat opposite, amused his new master with a lively account of his escape. Mario laughed and praised him; Luigi, the servant, grinned as he listened from the coach box; and the driver resolved to tell the tale at the Falcone, when he stopped there on his return to Genoa, so the lad's friends might know what had become of him.

After a little chat Signor Mario returned to his newspapers, and Tino, tired with his long vigil and brisk run, curling himself up on the seat, pillowed his head on his bundle and fell fast asleep, rocked by the motion of the carriage as it rolled along the smooth road.

When he waked, the sun was high; the carriage stood before a wayside inn; the man and horses were gone to their dinners; and the signor lay under some mulberry trees in the garden while Luigi set forth upon the grass the contents of a well-filled hamper which they had brought with them, his master being one who looked well after his own comfort. The sight of food drew Tino toward it as straight as a honey jar draws flies, and he presented himself with his most engaging

air. Being in a good humor, the new master bade the hungry
lad sit down and eat, which he did—so heartily that larded
fowl, melon, wine, and bread vanished as if by magic. Never
had food tasted so good to Tino, and, rejoicing with true
boyish delight in the prospect of plenty to eat, he went off
to play Morso with the driver, while the horses rested and
Mario took a siesta on the grass.

When they set forth again, Tino received his first music
lesson from the new teacher, who was well pleased to find
how quickly the boy caught the air of a Venetian boat-song
and how sweetly he sang it. Then Tino strummed on his
guitar and amused his hearers with all the melodies he knew,
from church chants to drinking songs. Mario taught him how
to handle his instrument gracefully, speak a few polite phrases,
and sit properly instead of sprawling awkwardly or lounging
idly.

So the afternoon wore away; and at dusk they reached Nice.
To Tino it looked like an enchanted city as they drove down
to it from the soft gloom and stillness of the country. The
sea broke gently on the curving shore, sparkling with the
lights of the *Promenade des Anglais* which overlooks it. A
half circle of brilliant hotels came next; behind these the
glimmer of villas scattered along the hillside shone like fire-
flies among gardens and orange groves; and higher still the
stars burned in the violet sky. Soon the moon would be up,
to hang like a great lamp from that splendid dome, turning
sea and shore to a magic world by her light. Tino clapped his
hands and looked about him with all the pleasure of his
beauty-loving race as they rattled through the gay streets and
stopped at one of the fine hotels.

Here Mario put on his grand air and was shown to the
apartment he had ordered from Genoa. Tino meekly fol-

lowed, and Luigi brought up the rear with the luggage. Tino felt as if he had got into a fairy tale when he found himself in a fine parlor where he could only sit and stare about him, while his master refreshed in the chamber beyond, and the man ordered dinner. A large closet was given the boy to sleep in, with a mattress and blanket, a basin and pitcher, and a few pegs to hang his clothes on. But it seemed very nice after the loft; and when he had washed his face, shaken the dust off, and smoothed his curly head as well as he could, he returned to the parlor to gloat over such a dinner as he had never eaten before.

Mario was in a good humor and anxious to keep the lad so; therefore, he plied him with good things to eat, fine promises, and the praise in which that vain little soul delighted. Tino went to bed early, feeling that his fortune was made, and his master went off to amuse himself at a gaming table, for that was his favorite pastime.

Next day the new life began. After a late breakfast, a music lesson was given which both interested and dismayed Tino, for his master was far less patient than good old Father Angelo and swore at him when he failed to catch a new air as quickly as he expected. Both were tired and rather cross when it ended, but Tino soon forgot the tweaking of his ear and the scolding, when he was sent away with Luigi to buy the velvet suit and sundry necessary articles for the young troubadour.

It was a lovely day, and the gay city was all alive with the picturesque bustle which always fills it when the season begins. Red-capped fishermen were launching their boats from the beach, flower girls hastening from the gardens with their fragant loads to sell on the *Promenade*, where invalids sunned themselves, nurses led their rosy troops to play, fine ladies strolled, and men of all nations paced to and fro at certain hours. In the older part of the city, work of all sorts went on —coral carvers filled their windows with pretty ornaments, pastry cooks tempted with dainty dishes; milliners showed hats fresh from Paris, and Turkish merchants hung out rich rugs and carpets at their doors. Church bells chimed; priests with incense and banners went through the streets on holy errands; the *Pifferoni* piped gaily; orange women and chestnut sellers called their wares in musical voices; even the little scullions who go about scouring saucepans at back doors made a song of their cry, *"Casseròla!"*

Tino had a charming time and could hardly believe his senses when one fine thing after another was bought for him and ordered home. Not only the suit, but two ruffled shirts, a crimson tie for the lace collar, a broad new ribbon for the guitar, handkerchiefs, hose, and delicate shoes, as if he were a gentleman's son. When Luigi added a little mantle and a hat such as other well-dressed lads of his age wore, Tino exclaimed, "This also! *Mio Dio,* never have I known so kind a man as Signor Mario. I shall serve him well and love him even better than you do."

Luigi shrugged his shoulders and answered with a disagreeable laugh, "Long may you think so, *poverino;* I serve for money, not love, and look to it that I get my wages, else it would go ill with both of us. Keep all you can get, boy; our master is apt to forget his servants."

Tino did not like the look, half scornful, half pitiful, which Luigi gave him, and wondered why he did not love the good signor. Later he found out, but all was pleasant now, and lunch at a cafe completed the delights of that long morning.

The rooms were empty when they returned, and, bidding him keep out of mischief, Luigi left Tino alone for several hours. But he found plenty of amusement in examining all the wonders the apartment contained, receiving the precious parcels as they arrived, practicing his new bow before the long mirror, and eating the nuts that he had bought of a jolly old woman at a street corner.

Then he went to lounge on the balcony that ran along the front of the hotel and watched the lively scene below, till sunset sent the promenaders home to dress for dinner. Feeling a sudden pang of homesickness as he thought of Stella, Tino got his guitar and sang the old songs to comfort his loneliness.

The first was hardly ended before one after the other five little heads popped out of a window farther down the balcony, and presently a group of pretty children were listening and smiling as the nice boy played and sang to them. A gentleman looked out, and a lady evidently listened, for the end of a lace flounce lay on the threshold of the long window, and a pair of white hands clapped when he finished a gay air in his best style.

This was his first taste of applause, and he liked it and twanged away merrily till his master's voice called him in just as he was beginning to answer the questions the eager children asked him.

"Go and dress! I shall take you down to dinner with me presently. But mind this; *I* will answer questions; *you* keep quiet and leave me to tell what I think best. Remember, or I pack you home at once."

Tino promised and was soon absorbed in getting into his new clothes; Luigi came to help him, and, when he was finished off, a very handsome lad emerged from the closet to make his best bow to his master, who, also in fine array, surveyed him with entire approval.

"Very good! I thought you would make a passable butterfly when you shed your grub's skin. Stand up and keep your hands out of your pockets. Mind what I told you about supping soup noisily, and don't handle your fork like a shovel. See what others do, smile, and hold your tongue. There is the gong. Let us go."

Tino's heart beat fast as he followed Mario down the long hall to the great *salle à manger* with its glittering *table d'hôte* and many guests. But the consciousness of new clothes sustained him, so he held up his head, turned out his toes, and took his place, trying to look as if everything was not very new and dazzling to him.

Two elderly ladies sat opposite, and he heard one say to the other in bad Italian, "Behold the lovely boy, Maria; I should like to paint him."

And the other answered, "We will be amiable to him, and perhaps we may get him for a model. Just what I want for a little Saint John."

Tino smiled at them till his black eyes sparkled and his white teeth shone, for he understood and enjoyed their praise. The artistic ladies smiled back and watched him with interest long after he had forgotten them, for that dinner was a serious affair to the boy, with a heavy silver spoon and fork to manage, a napkin to unfold, and three glasses to steer clear of for fear of a general upset, so awkward did he feel.

Everyone else was too busy to mind his mistakes, and the ladies set them down to bashfulness, as he got red in the face and dared not look up after spilling his soup and dropping a roll.

Presently, while waiting for dessert, he forgot himself in something Mario was saying to his neighbor on the other side: "A poor little fellow whom I found starving in the streets at Genoa. He has a voice; I have a heart, and I adore music. I took him to myself and shall do my best for him. Ah, yes! In this selfish world one must not forget the helpless and the poor."

Tino stared, wondering what other boy the good signor had befriended and was still more bewildered when Mario turned to him with a paternal air, to add in that pious tone so new to the boy, "This is my little friend, and he will gladly come and sing to your young ladies after dinner. Many thanks for the honor; I shall bring him out at my parlor concerts and so fit him for his place by and by. Bow and smile, quick!"

The last words were in a sharp whisper; and Tino obeyed with a sudden bob of the head that sent his curls over his eyes and then laughed such a boyish laugh as he shook them back that the gentleman leaning forward to look at him joined in it, and the ladies smiled sympathetically as they pushed a dish of bonbons nearer to him. Mario gave him an indulgent look and went on in the same benevolent tone telling all he meant to do, till the kindly gentleman from Rome was much interested, having lads of his own and being fond of music.

Tino listened to the fine tales told of him and hoped no one would ask him about Genoa, for he would surely betray that he had never been there and could not lie as glibly as Mario did. He felt rather like the little old woman who did not know whether she was herself or not, but consoled himself by smiling at the ladies and eating a whole plateful of little cakes standing near him.

When they rose, Tino made his bow, and Mario walked down the long hall with his hand on the boy's shoulder and a friendly air very impressive to the spectators, who began at once to gossip about the pretty lad and his kind protector, just as the cunning gentleman planned to have them.

As soon as they were out ot sight, Mario's manner changed; and telling Tino to sit down and digest his dinner, or he wouldn't be able to sing a note, he went to the balcony to smoke till the servant came to conduct them to Conte Alborghetti's salon.

"Now mind, boy; do exactly as I tell you, or I'll drop you like a hot chestnut and leave you to get home as you can," said Mario, in a sharp whisper, as they paused on the threshold of the door.

"I will, signor, indeed I will!" murmured Tino, scared by the flash of his master's black eye and the grip of his hand, as he pulled the bashful boy forward.

In they went, and for a moment Tino only perceived a large light room full of people, who all looked at him as he stood beside Mario with his guitar slung over his shoulder, red cheeks, and such a flutter at his heart that he felt sure he could never sing there. The amiable host came to meet and present them to a group of ladies, while a flock of children drew near to look at and listen to the "nice singing boy from Genoa."

Mario, having paid his thanks and compliments in his best manner, opened the little concert by a grand piece upon the piano, proving that he was a fine musician, though Tino already began to fancy he was not quite so good a man as he wished to appear. Then he sang several airs from operas, and Tino forgot himself in listening delightedly to the mellow voice of his master, for the lad loved music and had never heard any like this before.

When Tino's turn came, he had lost his first shyness, and, though his lips were dry and breath short, and he gave the guitar an awkward bang against the piano as he pulled it around ready to play upon, the curiosity in the faces of the children and the kindly interest of the ladies gave him courage to start bravely off with *"Bella Monica"*—the easiest as well as gayest of his songs. It went well, and with each verse his voice grew clearer, his hand firmer, and his eyes fuller of boyish pleasure in his own power to please.

For please he did, and, when he ended with a loud twang

and kissed his hand to the audience as he always used to do to the girls at home, everyone clapped heartily, and the gentlemen cried, *"Bravo, piccolo!* He sings in truth like a little nightingale; encore, encore!"

These were sweet sounds to Tino, and he needed no urging to sing *"Lucia"* in his softest tones, "looking like one of Murillo's angels!" as a young lady said, while he sang away with his eyes piously lifted in the manner Mario had taught him.

Then followed a grand march from the master while the boy rested, after which Tino gave more folk songs and ended with a national air in which all joined like patriotic and enthusiastic Italians, shouting the musical chorus, *"Viva Italia!"* till the room rang.

Tino quite lost his head at that and began to prance as if the music had got into his heels. Before Mario could stop him, he was showing one of the little girls how to dance the Saltarello as the peasants dance it during Carnival; and all the children were capering gaily about the wide polished floor with Tino strumming and skipping like a young faun from the woods.

The elder people laughed and enjoyed the pretty sight till trays of ices and bonbons came in; and the little party ended in a general enjoyment of the good things children most delight in. Tino heard his master receiving the compliments of the company and saw the host slip a paper into his hand, but, boylike, he contented himself with a pocketful of sweetmeats and the entreaties of his little patrons to come again soon, and so backed out of the room, after bowing till he was dizzy and bumping against a marble table in a very painful manner.

"Well, how do you like, the life I promised you? Is it all I said? Do we begin to fill our pockets and enjoy ourselves even sooner than I expected?" asked Mario, with a good-natured slap of the shoulder, as they reached his apartment again.

"It is splendid! I like it much, very much! And I thank you with all my heart," cried Tino, gratefully kissing the hand that could tweak sharply, as well as caress when things suited its owner.

"You did well, even better than I hoped, but in some things we must improve. Those legs must be taught to keep still, and you must not forget that you are a peasant when among your betters. It passed very well tonight with those little persons, but in some places it would have put me in a fine scrape. Capers! But I feared at one moment you would have embraced the young contessa, when she danced with you."

Mario laughed as poor Tino blushed and stammered, "But, signor, she was so little, only ten years old, and I thought no harm to hold her up on that slippery floor. See, she gave me all these and bade me come again. I would gladly have kissed her, she was so like little Annina at home."

"Well, well, no harm is done; but I see the pretty brown girls down yonder have spoiled you, and I shall have to keep an eye on my gallant young troubadour. Now to bed, and don't make yourself ill with all those confections. *Felice nòtte,* Don Giovanni!" and away went Mario to lose at play every franc of the money the generous count had given him "for the poor lad."

That was the beginning of a new and charming life for Tino, and for two months he was a busy and a happy boy, with only a homesick fit now and then when Mario was out of temper or Luigi put more than his fair share of work on his shoulders. The parlor concerts went well, and the nightingale was soon a favorite toy in many salons. Night after night

Tino sang and played, was petted and praised, and then trotted home to dream feverishly of new delights, for this exciting life was fast spoiling the simple lad who used to be so merry and busy at Valrose. The more he had, the more he wanted, and soon grew discontented, jealous, and peevish. He had cause to complain of some things, for none of the money earned ever came to him, and, when he plucked up courage to ask for his promised share, Mario told him he had only earned his food and clothes as yet. Then Tino rebelled and got a beating, which made him outwardly as meek as a lamb but inwardly a very resentful, unhappy boy, and spoiled all his pleasure in music and success.

He was neglected all day and left to do what he liked till needed at night, so he amused himself by lounging about the hotel or wandering on the beach to watch the fishermen cast their nets. Lazy Luigi kept him doing errands when he could, but for hours the boy saw neither master nor man and wondered where they were. At last he found out, and his dream of fame and fortune ended in smoke.

Christmas week was a gay one for everybody, and Tino thought good times had come again, for he sang at several children's fetes, received some pretty gifts from the kind Alborghettis, and even Mario was amiable enough to give him a golden napoleon after a run of good luck at the cards. Eager to show his people that he *was* getting on, Tino begged Antoine, the friendly waiter who had already written one letter to Stella for him, to write another and send by a friend going that way a little parcel containing the money for Mariuccia, a fine Roman sash for Stella, and many affectionate messages to all his old friends.

It was well he had that little satisfaction, for it was his last chance to send good news or exult over his grand success.

Troubles came with the new year, and in one week our poor little jay found himself stripped of all his borrowed plumes and left a very forlorn bird indeed.

Trotting about late at night in silk stockings and getting wet more than once in the winter rains gave Tino a bad cold. No one cared for it, and he was soon as hoarse as a crow. His master forced him to sing several times in spite of the pain he suffered, and when at the last concert he broke down completely Mario swore at him for "a useless brat," and began to talk of going to Milan to find a new set of singers and patrons. Had Tino been older, he would have discovered some time sooner that Signor Mario was losing favor in Nice, as he seldom paid a bill and led a very gay, extravagant life. But, boylike, Tino saw only his own small troubles and suspected nothing when Luigi one day packed up the velvet suit and took it away "to be repaired," he said. It *was* shabby, and Tino, lying on the sofa with a headache and sharp cough, was glad no one ordered him to go with it, for the Tramontana [1] was blowing, and he longed for old Mariuccia's herb tea and Stella's cosseting, being quite ill by this time.

That night as he lay awake in his closet coughing, feverish, and restless, he heard his master and Luigi moving about till very late, evidently packing for Paris or Milan, and Tino wondered if he would like either place better than Nice and wished they were not so far from Valrose. In the midst of his meditations he fell asleep, and, when he woke, it was morning. He hurried up and went out to see what the order of the day was to be, rather pleased at the idea of travelling about the world.

To his surprise no breakfast appeared; the room was in confusion; every sign of Mario had vanished but empty bottles

[1] A violent northerly wind, especially of the Adriatic. *Ed.*

and a long hotel bill lying upaid upon the table. Before Tino could collect his wits, Antoine came flying in to say with wild gesticulations and much French wrath that "the rascal Mario had gone in the night, leaving immense debts behind him, and the landlord in an apoplexy of rage."

Poor Tino was so dismayed he could only sit and let the storm pelt about his ears; for not only did the waiter appear, but the chambermaid, the coachman, and at last the indignant host himself, all scolding at once as they rummaged the rooms, questioned the bewildered boy, and wrung their hands over the escape of these dishonest wretches.

"You also, little beast, have grown fat upon my good fare! And who is to pay me for all you have eaten, not to mention the fine bed, the washing, the candles, and the coaches you have had? Ah, great heavens! What is to become of us when such things occur?" And the poor landlord tore his hair with one hand while he shook his other fist at Tino.

"Dear sir, take all I have; it is only an old guitar and a few clothes. Not a centime do I own, but I will work for you. I can clean saucepans and run errands. Speak for me, Antoine; you are my only friend now."

The lad looked so honest and ill and pathetic, as he spoke with his poor hoarse voice and looked beseechingly about him, that Antoine's kind heart was melted, and he advised the boy to slip away home as soon as possible and so escape all further violence and trouble. He slipped two francs into Tino's empty pocket, and, as soon as the room was cleared, helped him tie up the few old clothes that remained. The host carried off the guitar as the only thing he could seize, so Tino had less to take away than he brought, when Antoine led him out by the back way, with a good sandwich of bread and meat for his breakfast, and bade him go to the square and try to beg a ride to Valrose on some of the carriages often going thither on the way to Genoa.

With many thanks Tino left the great hotel, feeling too miserable to care much what became of him, for all his fine dreams were spoiled, like the basket of china the man kicked over in the *Arabian Nights,* while dreaming he was a king. How could he go home, sick, poor, and forsaken, after all the grand tales he had lately told in his letter? How they would laugh at him, the men and girls at the factory! How Mariuccia would wag her old head and say, *"Ecco!* Is it not as I foretold?"* Even Stella would weep over him and be sorry to see her dear boy in such a sad plight, yet what could he do? His voice was gone and his guitar, or he might sing about the streets, as Mario described his doing at Genoa, and so earn his daily bread till something turned up. Now he was quite helpless, and, much against his will, he went to see if any chance of getting home appeared.

The day was showery, and no party was setting off for the famous drive along the Corniche Road. Tino was glad of it and went to lie on a bench at the café where he had often been with Luigi. His head ached, and his cough left him no peace, so he spent some of his money in syrup and water to quell the trouble and with the rest paid for a good dinner and supper.

He told his sad tale to the cook and was allowed to sleep in the kitchen after scrubbing saucepans to pay for it. But no one wanted him, and, in the morning, after a cup of coffee and a roll, he found himself cast upon the world again. He would not beg, and, as dinnertime approached, hunger reminded him of a humble friend whom he had forgotten in his own days of plenty.

He loved to stroll along the beach and read the names on

the boats drawn up there, for all were the names of saints, and it was almost as good as going to church to read the long list of Saint Brunos, Saint Francises, and Saint Ursulas. Among the fishermen was one who had always a kind word for the lad, who enjoyed a sail or a chat with Marco whenever nothing better turned up to amuse his leisure hours. Now in his trouble Tino remembered him and went to the beach to ask help, for he felt ill as well as sad and hungry.

Yes, there sat the good fellow eating the bread and macaroni his little daughter had brought for his dinner, and a smile welcomed poor Tino as he sat down beside this only friend to tell his story.

Marco growled in his black beard and shook his knife with an awful frown when he heard how the lad had been deserted. Then he smiled, patted Tino's back, thrust the copper basin of food into one hand and a big lump of the brown bread into the other, inviting him to eat in such a cordial way that the poor meal tasted better than the dainty fare at the hotel.

A draught of red wine from the gourd cheered Tino up, as did the good and kind words, and when Marco bade him go home with little Manuela to the good wife he gladly went, feeling that he must lie down somewhere, his head was so giddy and the pain in the breast so sharp.

Buxom Teresa received him kindly, put him straight to bed in her own boy's little room, laid a cool cloth on his hot head, a warm one on his aching chest, and left him to sleep, much comforted by her motherly care. It was well the good soul befriended him, for he needed help sorely and would have fared ill if those humble folk had not taken him in.

For a week or two he lay in Beppo's bed burning with fever, and when he could sit up again was too feeble to do anything but smile gratefully and try to help Manuela mend nets. Marco would hear of no thanks, saying, "Good deeds bring good luck. Behold my haul of fish each day thou hast been here, *poverino!* I am well paid, and Saint Peter will bless my boat for thy sake."

Tino was very happy in the little dark, shabby house that smelt of onions, fish, and tar, that was full of brown children and the constant clack of Teresa's lively tongue as she gossiped with her neighbors or fried polenta for the hungry mouths that never seemed filled.

But the time came when Tino could go about, and then he begged for work, anxious to be independent and earn a little so that in the spring he could go home without empty pockets.

"I have taken thought for thee, my son, and work warm and easy is ready if thou wilt do it. My friend Tommaso Neri, makes the good macaroni nearby. He needs a boy to mind the fire and see to the donkey who grinds below there. Food, shelter, and such wages as thou art able to earn, he will give thee. Shall it be?"

Tino gratefully accepted, and with hearty embraces all around went off one day to see his new place. It was in the old part of Nice, a narrow, dirty street, a little shop with one window full of the cheaper sorts of this favorite food of all Italians, and behind the shop, a room where an old woman sat spinning while two little boys played with pine cones and pretty bits of marble at her feet.

A fat, jolly man, with a shining face and loud voice, greeted Marco and the lad, saying he "was worn to a thread with much work, since that bad imp of a donkey boy had run away leaving the blessed macaroni to spoil, and poor Carmelita to perish for want of care. Come below at once, and behold the desolation of the place."

With that he led the way to the cellar, where a small furnace fire burned, and an old gray donkey went around and around, turning a wheel which set some unseen machinery in motion with a dismal creaking sound. Down through many holes in one part of the wooden floor overhead came long pipes of macaroni, hardening as they hung quivering in the hot air till stiff enough to be cut off in handfuls and laid to dry on wire trays over the furnace.

Tino had never seen the good macaroni made before and was much interested in the process, though it was of the rudest kind. In a room upstairs a great vat of flour and water was kept stirring around and around and forced down to the place below by the creaking wheel which patient Carmelita turned all day. The cellar was dark but warm, and Tino felt that it would be comfortable there with the old donkey for a comrade, jolly Tommaso for a master, and enough to eat— for it was evident the family lived well, so plump and shining were all the faces, so cheery the tempers of the old women and little lads.

There Marco left him, well satisfied that he had done his best for the poor boy, and there Tino lived for three months, busy, well fed, and contented, till spring sunshine made him long for the sweet air, the green fields, and dear faces at Valrose. Tommaso was lazy but kind and, if the day's work was done in time, let Tino out to see Marco's children or to run on the beach with little Jacopo and Seppi. The grandmother gave him plenty of rye bread, thin wine, and macaroni fried in oil; old Carmelita learned to love him and to lean her gray head on his shoulder with joyful waggings of her long ears as he caressed her, and each week increased the little hoard in an old shoe hidden behind a beam.

But it was a dull life for a boy who loved music, flowers,

light, and freedom, and he soon grew tired of seeing only a procession of legs go by the low window level with the street; the creak of the wheel was not half so welcome as the brisk rattle of the mill at home, and the fat little lads always climbing over him could not be so dear as sister Stella and pretty Annina, the wine-maker's daughter, at Valrose. Even the kind old woman who often saved an orange for him, and gave him a gay red cotton handkerchief on his birthday, was less to his taste than Mariuccia, who adored him in spite of her scolding and stern ways.

So he looked about for travellers going to Genoa, and one happy day, as he returned from church, he saw, sitting under two red umbrellas before two easels beside the road, the two elderly ladies of the hotel. Both wore brown hats like mushrooms; both had gray curls bobbing in the wind; and both were painting away for dear life, trying to get a good sketch of the ruined gateway, where passion flowers climbed and roses nodded through the bars.

Tino stopped to look, as many another passer-by had done, and, glancing up to see if he admired their work, the good ladies recognized their "Saint John," as they called the pretty boy who had vanished before they could finish the pictures they had begun of him.

They were so glad to see him that he opened his heart to them and found to his great joy that in a week they were to drive to Genoa and would gladly take him along if he would sit to them meantime. Of course, he agreed, and ran home to tell his master that he must go. Tommaso bewailed his loss but would not keep him; and, as Marco's son Beppo was willing to take his place till another lad could be found, Tino was free to sit in a sheepskin for the Misses Blair as often as they liked.

It was a very happy week, and when the long desired day came at last Tino was so gay he danced and sang till the dingy cellar seemed to be full of birds in high spirits. Poor Carmelita gratefully ate the cabbage he gave her as a farewell offering; the old woman found her box full of her favorite snuff; and each small boy grew more shiny than ever over a new toy presented by Tino. Tommaso wept as he held him in his fat arms and gave him a bundle of half-baked macaroni as a reward for his faithful service, while Marco and all his family stood at the hotel door to see the carriage depart.

"Really quite like a wedding, with all those orange-flowers and roses," said Miss Priscilla, as Teresa and Manuela threw great bunches of flowers into their laps and kissed their hands to the departing travellers.

Sitting proudly aloft, Tino waved his old hat to these good friends till he could see them no more; then having, with some difficulty, bestowed his long bundle from Tommaso, his basket of fish from Marco, his small parcel of clothes, and the immense bouquet the children had made for him, he gave himself up to the rapture of that lovely April day.

The kind ladies had given him a new suit of clothes like the old ones and paid him well besides, so he felt quite content with the picturesque peasant garments he wore, having had enough of fine feathers, and gaily jingled the money in his pocket, though it was not the fortune he had foolishly hoped to make so easily. He was a wiser boy than the one who went over that road six months before and decided that even if his voice did come back in time, he would be in no hurry to leave home till he was sure it was the wisest thing to do. He had some very serious thoughts and sensible plans in his young head, and for a time was silent and sober. But soon the delicious air, the lovely scenery, and the many questions of the ladies raised his spirits, and he chattered away till they stopped for dinner.

All that long bright day they drove along the wonderful road, and as night fell saw Valrose lying green and peaceful in the valley as they paused on the hilltop to enjoy its beauty. Then they went slowly down to the Falcone, and the moment the luggage was taken in, rooms secured, and dinner ordered, Tino, who had been quivering with impatience, said eagerly, "Dear signoras, now I go to my own people to embrace them, but in the morning we come to thank you for your great kindness to me."

Miss Priscilla opened her mouth to send some message, but Tino was off like an arrow and never stopped till he burst into the little kitchen where Mariuccia sat shelling dry beans, and Stella was packing mandarins in dainty baskets for market. Like an affectionate little bear did the boy fall upon and embrace the two astonished women, while Stella laughed and cried and Mariuccia called on all the saints to behold how tall and fat and beautiful her angel had become, and to thank them for restoring him to their arms. The neighbors rushed in, and till late that night there was the sound of many voices in the stone cottage under the old fig tree.

Tino's adventures were listened to with the deepest interest, and a very hearty welcome was given him. All were impressed with the splendors he had seen, afflicted by his trials, and grateful for his return. No one laughed or reproached, but regarded him as a very remarkable fellow and predicted that whether his voice came back or not, he was born for good luck and would prosper. So at last he got to bed in the old loft and fell asleep with the same friendly moon looking in at him as it did before, only now it saw a quiet face, a very happy heart, and a contented boy, glad to be safe again under the humble roof that was his home.

Early next morning a little procession of three went to the Falcone bearing grateful offerings to the dear signoras who sat on the portico enjoying the balmy air that blew up from the acres of flowers below. First came Tino, bearing a great basket of the delicious little oranges which one never tastes in their perfection unless one eats them fresh from the tree; then, Stella with two pretty boxes of perfume; and bringing up the rear, old Mariuccia with a blue jar of her best honey, which like all that of Valrose was famous.

The ladies were much delighted with these gifts, and promised to stop and see the givers of them on their return from Genoa, if they came that way. Tino took a grateful farewell of the good souls, Stella kissed their hands, with her dark eyes full of tender thanks, and Mariuccia begged the saints to have them in their special keeping by land and by sea, for their kindness to her boy.

An hour later, as the travellers drove down the steep road from the village, they were startled by a sudden shower of violets and roses which rained upon them from a high bank beside the path. Looking up, they saw Tino and his sister laughing, waving their hands and tossing flowers as they called in their musical language, *"Arrivederla, signore! Grazie, grazie!"* till the carriage rolled around the corner looking as if it were Carnival time, so full was it of fragrant violets and lovely roses.

"Nice creatures! How prettily they do things! I hope we *shall* see them again, and I wonder if the boy will ever be famous. Such a pity to lose that sweet voice of his!" said Miss Maria, the younger of the sisters, as they drove along in a nest of sweet and pretty gifts.

"I hope not, for he will be much safer and happier in this

charming place than wandering about the world and getting into trouble as these singers always do. *I* hope he will be wise enough to be contented with the place in which his lot is cast," answered Miss Priscilla, who knew the world and had a good old-fashioned love for home and all it gives us.

She was right; Tino *was* wise, and though his voice did come back in time, it was no longer wonderful; and he was contented to live on at Valrose, a busy, happy, humble gardener all his life, saying with a laugh when asked about his runaway adventures, "Ah, I have had enough of music and macaroni; I prefer my flowers and my freedom."

The Banner of Beaumanoir

Larks were singing in the clear sky over Dinan, the hill-
sides were white with hosts of blooming cherry trees, and the
valley golden with willow blossoms. The gray tower of the

good Duchess Anne was hung with garlands of ivy and gay with tufts of fragrant wallflowers, and along the fosse the shadows deepened daily as the young leaves thickened on the interlacing branches overhead. Women sang while they beat their clothes by the pool; wooden shoes clattered to and fro as the girls brought water from the fountain in Place St. Louis; men, with their long hair, embroidered jackets, and baggy breeches drank cider at the inn doors; and the great Breton horses shook their high collars till the bells rang again, as they passed along the roads that wound between wide fields of colza, buckwheat, and clover.

Up at the château, which stood near the ruins of the ancient castle, the great banner streamed in the wind, showing, as its folds blew out, the device and motto of the Beaumanoirs —two clasped hands and the legend, *"En tout chemin loyauté."* In the courtyard, hounds brayed, horses pranced, and servants hurried about, for the count was going to hunt the wild boar. Presently, away they went, with the merry music of horns, the clatter of hoofs, and the blithe ring of voices, till the pleasant clamor died away in the distant woods, where mistletoe clung to the great oaks, and menhirs and dolmens, mysterious relics of the Druids, were to be seen.

From one of the windows of the château tower a boy's face looked out, full of eager longing—a fine, strong face, but sullen now, with black brows, dark, restless eyes, and lips set, as if rebellious thoughts were stirring in his mind. He watched the gay cavalcade disappear, until a sunny silence settled over the landscape, broken only by the larks and the sound of a girl's voice singing. As he listened, the frown smoothed itself from his brow, and his eye brightened when it rested on a blue-gowned, white-capped figure, sprinkling webs of linen spread to bleach in the green meadow by the River Rance.

"If I may not hunt, I'll away to Yvonne and take a holiday. She can tell better tales than any in this weary book, the bane of my life!"

As he spoke, the boy struck a volume that lay on the wide ledge, with a petulant energy that sent it fluttering down into the courtyard below. Half-ashamed and half-amused, young Gaston peeped to see if this random shot had hit anyone. But all was quiet and deserted now; so, with a boyish laugh and daring glance at the dangerous descent, he said to the doves cooing on the roof overhead, "Here's a fine pretext for escape. Being locked in, how can I get my lesson unless I fetch the book? Tell no tales of the time I linger, and you shall be well fed, my pretty birds."

Then swinging himself out as if it were no new feat, he climbed boldly down through the ivy that half hid the carved flowers and figures which made a ladder for his agile feet.

The moment he touched ground, he raced away like a hound in full scent to the meadow, where he was welcomed by a rosy, brown-eyed lass, whose white teeth shone as she laughed to see him leap the moat, dodge behind the wall, and come bounding toward her, his hair streaming in the wind and his face full of boyish satisfaction in this escapade.

"The old tale," he panted, as he threw himself down upon the grass and flung the recovered book beside him. "This dreary Latin drives me mad, and I will *not* waste such days as this poring over dull pages like a priest, when I should be hunting like a knight and gentleman."

"Nay, dear Gaston, but you ought, for obedience is the first duty of the knight, and honor of the gentleman," answered the girl, in a soft, reproachful tone, which seemed to touch the lad, as the voice of a master tames a high-mettled horse.

"Had Father Nevin trusted to my honor, I would not have run away, but he locked me in, like a monk in a cell, and that I will not bear. Just one hour, Yvonne—one little hour of freedom—then I will go back, else there will be no sport for me tomorrow," said the lad, recklessly pulling up the bluets that starred the grass about him.

"Ah, if I were set to such a task, I would so gladly learn it, that I might be a fitter friend for you," said the girl, reverently turning the pages of the book she could not read.

"No need of that; I like you as you are, and, by my faith, I doubt your great willingness, for when I last played tutor and left you to spell out the pretty legend of St. Coventin and his little fish, I found you fast asleep with the blessed book upon the floor," said Gaston and laughed, turning the tables on his mentor, with great satisfaction.

The girl laughed also as she retored, "My tutor should not have left me to play with his dogs. I bore my penance better than you and did not run away. Come now, we'll be merry. Will you talk, or shall I sing, while you rest this hot head and dream of horse and hound and spearing the wild boar?" added Yvonne, smoothing the locks of hair scattered on the grass, with a touch as gentle as if the hand were that of a lady and not that of a peasant, rough with hard work.

"Since I may not play a man's part yet, amuse me like a boy with the old tales your mother used to tell, when we watched the fagots blaze in the winter nights. It is long since I have heard one, and I am never tired hearing of the deeds I mean to match, if not outdo, someday."

"Let me think a bit till I remember your favorites, and do you listen to the bees above there in the willow, setting you a good example, idle boy," said Yvonne, spreading a coarse apron for his head, while she sat beside him racking her brain for tales to beguile this truant hour.

Her father was the count's forester, and when the countess had died some sixteen years before, leaving a month-old boy, good Dame Gillian had taken the motherless baby and nursed and reared him with her little girl, so faithfully and tenderly that the count never could forget the loyal service. As babies, the two slept in one cradle; as children, they played and quarreled together; and as boy and girl, they defended, comforted, and amused each other. But time brought inevitable changes, and both felt that the hour of separation was near, for, while Yvonne went on leading the peasant life to which she was born, Gaston was receiving the education befitting a young count. The chaplain taught him to read and write, with lessons in sacred history, and a little Latin; of the forester he learned woodcraft; and his father taught him horsemanship and the use of arms, accomplishments considered all-important in those days.

Gaston cared nothing for books, except such as told tales of chivalry, but dearly loved athletic sports and at sixteen rode the most fiery horse without a fall, handled a sword admirably, could kill a boar at the first shot, and longed ardently for war, that he might prove himself a man. A brave, high-spirited, generous boy, he had a very tender spot in his heart for the good woman who had been a mother to him and his little foster sister, whose idol he was. For days he seemed to forget these humble friends and led the gay, active life of his age and rank, but if wounded in the chase, worried by the chaplain, disappointed in any plan, or in disgrace for any prank, he turned instinctively to Dame Gillian and Yvonne, sure of help and comfort for mind and body.

Companionship with him had refined the girl and given her glimpses of a world into which she could never enter, yet where she could follow with eager eyes and high hopes the fortunes of this dear Gaston, who was both her prince and brother. Her influence over him was great, for she was of a calm and patient nature, as well as brave and prudent beyond her years. His will was law; yet in seeming to obey, she often led him, and he thanked her for the courage with which she helped him to control his fiery temper and strong will. Now, as she glanced at him she saw that he was already more tranquil, under the soothing influence of the murmuring river, the soft flicker of the sunshine, and a blessed sense of freedom.

So, while she twisted her distaff, she told the stirring tales of warriors, saints, and fairies, whom all Breton peasants honor, love, and fear. But best of all was the tale of Gaston's own ancestor, Jean de Beaumanoir, "the hero of Ploërmel, where, when sorely wounded and parched with thirst, he cried for water, and Geoffrey du Bois answered, like a grim old warrior as he was, 'Drink thy blood, Beaumanoir, and the thirst will pass,' and he drank, and the battle madness seized him, and he slew ten men, winning the fight against great odds, to his everlasting glory."

"Ah, those were the times to live in! If they could only come again, I would be a second Jean!"

Gaston sprang to his feet as he spoke, all aglow with the warlike ardor of his race, and Yvonne looked up at him, sure that he would prove himself a worthy descendant of the great baron and his wife, the daughter of the brave Du Guesclin.

"But you shall not be treacherously killed, as he was, for I will save you, as the peasant woman saved poor Giles de Bretagne when starving in the tower, or fight for you, as Jeanne d'Arc fought for her lord," answered Yvonne, dropping her distaff to stretch out her hand to him, for she, too, was on her feet.

Gaston took the faithful hand and, pointing to the white banner floating over the ruins of the old castle, said heartily, "We will always stand by each other and be true to the motto of our house till death."

"We will!" answered the girl, and both kept the promise loyally, as we shall see.

Just at that moment the sound of hoofs made the young enthusiasts start and look toward the road that wound through the valley to the hill. An old man on a slowly pacing mule was all they saw, but the change that came over both was comical in its suddenness, for the gallant knight turned to a truant schoolboy, daunted by the sight of his tutor, while the rival of the Maid of Orleans grew pale with dismay.

"I am lost if he spy me, for my father vowed I should not hunt again unless I did my task. He will see me if I run, and where can I hide till he has passed?" whispered Gaston, ashamed of his panic, yet unwilling to pay the penalty of his prank.

But quick-witted Yvonne saved him, for, lifting one end of the long web of linen, she showed a hollow whence some great stone had been removed, and Gaston slipped into the green nest over which the linen lay smoothly when replaced.

On came the chaplain, glancing sharply about him, being of an austere and suspicious nature. He saw nothing, however, but the peasant girl in her quaint cap and wooden sabots, singing to herself as she leaned against a tree, with her earthen jug in her hand. The mule paused in the light shadow of the willows, to crop a mouthful of grass before climbing the hill, and the chaplain seemed glad to rest a moment, for the day was warm and the road dusty.

"Come hither, child, and give me draught of water," he called, and the girl ran to fill her pitcher, offering it with a low reverence.

"Thanks, daughter! A fine day for the bleaching, but over-warm for much travel. Go to your work, child: I will tarry a moment in the shade before I return to my hard task of sharpening a dull youth's wit," said the old man when he had drunk, and, with a frowning glance at the room where he had left his prisoner, he drew a breviary from his pocket and began to read, while the mule browsed along the roadside.

Yvonne went to sprinkling the neglected linen, wondering with mingled anxiety and girlish merriment how Gaston fared. The sun shone hotly on the dry cloth, and, as she approached the boy's hiding place, a stir would have betrayed him had the chaplain's eyes been lifted.

"Sprinkle me quickly; I am stifling in this hole," whispered an imploring voice.

"Drink thy blood, Beaumanoir, and the thirst will pass," quoted Yvonne, taking a naughty satisfaction in the igno-minious captivity of the wilful boy. A long sigh was the only answer he gave, and, taking pity on him, she made a little hollow in the linen where she knew his head lay and poured in water till a choking sound assured her Gaston had enough. The chaplain looked up, but the girl coughed loudly, as she went to refill her jug, with such a demure face that he suspected nothing and presently ambled away to seek his re-fractory pupil.

The moment he disappeared, a small earthquake seemed to take place under the linen, for it flew up violently, and a pair of long legs waved joyfully in the air as Gaston burst into a ringing laugh, which Yvonne echoed heartily. Then, springing up, he said, throwing back his wet hair and shaking his finger at her, "You dared not betray me, but you nearly drowned me, wicked girl. I cannot stop for vengeance now, but I'll toss you into the river some day and leave you to get out as you can."

Then he was off as quickly as he came, eager to reach his prison again before the chaplain came to hear the unlearned lesson. Yvonne watched him till he climbed safely in at the high window and disappeared with a wave of the hand, when she, too, went back to her work, little dreaming what brave parts both were to play in dangers and captivities of which these youthful pranks and perils were but a foreshadowing.

Two years later, in the month of March 1793, the insurrection broke out in Vendée, and Gaston had his wish, for the old count had been an officer of the king's household and hastened to prove his loyalty. Yvonne's heart beat high with pride as she saw her foster brother ride gallantly away beside his father, with a hundred armed vassals behind them, and the white banner fluttering above their heads in the fresh wind.

She longed to go with him, but her part was to watch and wait, to hope and pray, till the hour came when she, like many another woman in those days, could prove herself as brave as a man and freely risk her life for those she loved.

Four months later the heavy tidings reached them that the old count was killed and Gaston taken prisoner. Great was the lamentation among the old men, women, and children left behind, but they had little time for sorrow, for a band of marauding Vendeans burned the château, and laid waste the abbey.

"Now, mother, I must up and away to find and rescue Gaston. I promised, and if he lives, it shall be done. Let me go; you are safe now, and there is no rest for me till I know how he fares," said Yvonne, when the raid was over and the frightened peasants ventured to return from the neighboring forests, whither they had hastily fled for protection.

"Go, my girl, and bring me news of our young lord. May you lead him safely home again to rule over us," answered Dame Gillian, devoted still, for her husband was reported dead with his master; yet she let her daughter go without a murmur, feeling that no sacrifice was too great.

So Yvonne set out, taking with her Gaston's pet dove and the little sum of money carefully hoarded for her marriage portion. The pretty winged creature, frightened by the destruction of its home, had flown to her for refuge, and she had cherished it for its master's sake. Now, when it would not leave her but came circling around her head a league away from Dinan, she accepted the good omen and made the bird the companion of her perilous journey.

There is no room to tell all the dangers, disappointments, and fatigues endured before she found Gaston, but, after being often misled by false rumors, she at last discovered that he was a prisoner in Fort Penthièvre. His own reckless courage had brought him there, for in one of the many skirmishes in which he had taken part, he ventured too far away from his men and was captured after fighting desperately to cut his way out. Now, alone in his cell, he raged like a caged eagle, feeling that there was no hope of escape, for the fort stood on a plateau of precipitous rock washed on two sides by the sea. He had heard of the massacre of the royalist emigrants who landed there and tried to prepare himself for a like fate, hoping to die as bravely as young Sombreuil, who was shot with twenty others on what was afterward named the *"Champ des Martyrs."* His last words, when ordered by the executioner to kneel, were, "I do it, but one knee I bend for my God; the other, for my king."

Day after day Gaston looked down from his narrow window, past which the gulls flew screaming, and watched the fishers at their work, the women gathering seaweed on the shore, and the white sails flitting across the Bay of Quiberon. Bitterly did he regret the wilfulness which brought him there, well knowing that if he had obeyed orders he would now be free to find his father's body and avenge his death.

"Oh, for one day of liberty, one hope of escape, one friend to cheer this dreadful solitude!" he cried, when weeks had passed and he seemed utterly forgotten.

As he spoke, he shook the heavy bars with impotent strength, then bent his head as if to hide even from himself the few hot tears wrung from him by captivity and despair.

Standing so, with eyes too dim for seeing, he felt something brush against his hair, and a bird lit on the narrow ledge. He thought it was a gull, and paid no heed, but in a moment a soft coo startled him, and, looking up, he saw a white dove struggling to get in.

"Blanchette!" he cried, and the pretty creature flew to his hand, pecking at his lips in the old caressing way he knew so well.

"My faithful bird, God bless thee!" exclaimed the poor lad, holding the dove close against his cheek to hide the trembling of his lip, so touched, so glad was he to find in his dreary prison even a dumb friend and comforter.

But Blanchette had her part to play and presently fluttered back to the window ledge, cooing loudly as she pecked at something underneath her wing.

Then Gaston remembered how he used to send messages to Yvonne by this carrier dove and with a thrill of joy looked for the token, hardly daring to hope that any would be found. Yes! There, tied carefully among the white feathers, was a tiny roll of paper with these words rudely written on it: "Be ready; help will come. Y."

"The brave girl! The loyal heart! I might have known she would keep her promise and come to save me," and Gaston dropped on his knees in gratitude.

Blanchette meantime tripped about the cell on her little rosy feet, ate a few crumbs of the hard bread, dipped her beak in the jug of water, dressed her feathers daintily, then flew to the bars and called him. He had nothing to send back by this sure messenger but a lock of hair, and this he tied with the same thread, in place of the note. Then kissing the bird he bade it go, watching the silver wings flash in the sunshine as it flew away, carrying joy with it and leaving hope behind.

After that the little courier came often, unperceived, carrying letters to and fro, for Yvonne sent bits of paper, and Gaston wrote his answers with his blood and a quill from Blanchette's wing. He thus learned how Yvonne was living in a fisher's hut on the beach and working for his rescue as well as she dared. Every day she might be seen gathering seaweed on the rocks or twirling her distaff at the door of the dilapidated hut, not as a young girl, but as an old woman, for she had stained her fair skin, put on ragged clothes, and hidden her fresh face under the penthouse cap worn by the women of Quiberon. Her neighbors thought her a poor soul left desolate by the war and let her live unmolested. So she worked on secretly and steadily, playing her part well and biding her time till the long hempen rope was made, the sharp file procured unsuspected, and a boat ready to receive the fugitives.

Her plan was perilously simple, but the only one possible, for Gaston was well guarded, and out of that lofty cell it seemed that no prisoner could escape without wings. A bird and a woman lent him those wings, and his daring flight was a nine days' wonder at the fort. Only a youth accustomed to feats of agility and strength could have safely made that dangerous escape along the face of the cliff that rose straight up from the shore. But Gaston was well trained, and the boyish pranks that used to bring him into dire disgrace now helped to save his life.

Thus, when the order came, written in the rude hand he had taught Yvonne long ago, "Pull up the thread which Blanchette will bring at midnight. Watch for a light in the bay. Then come down, and St. Barbe protect you," he was ready; the tiny file of watch spring, brought by the bird, had secretly done its work, and several bars were loose. He knew that the attempt might cost him his life but was willing to gain liberty even at that price, for imprisonment seemed worse than death to his impatient spirit. The jailer went his last round, the great bell struck the appointed hour, and Gaston stood at the window, straining his eyes to catch the first ray of the promised light, when the soft whir of wings gladdened his ear, and Blanchette arrived, looking scared and wet and weary, for rain fell, the wind blew fitfully, and the poor bird was un-used to such wild work as this. But obedient to its training, it flew to its master; and no angel could have been more wel-come than the storm-beaten little creature as it nestled in his bosom, while he untangled the lengths of strong thread wound about one of its feet.

He knew what to do, and, tying a bit of the broken bar to one end as a weight, he let it down, praying that no cruel gust would break or blow it away. In a moment a quick jerk at the thread bade him pull again. A cord came up, and, when that was firmly secured, a second jerk was the signal for the last and most important haul. Up came the stout rope, knotted here and there to add safety and strength to the hands and feet that were to climb down that frail ladder, unless some cruel fate dashed the poor boy dead upon the rocks below. The rope was made fast to an iron staple inside, the bars were torn away, and Gaston crept through the narrow opening to perch on the ledge without, while Blanchette flew down to tell Yvonne he was coming.

The moment the distant spark appeared, he bestirred himself, set his teeth, and boldly began the dangerous descent.

Rain blinded him, the wind beat him against the rock, bruising hands and knees, and the way seemed endless, as he climbed slowly down, clinging with the clutch of a drowning man and blessing Yvonne for the knots that kept him from slipping when the gusts blew him to and fro. More than once he thought it was all over, but the good rope held fast, and strength and courage upheld him, and he dropped at last breathless and bleeding, beside the faithful Yvonne.

There was no time for words, only a grasp of the hand, a sigh of gratitude, and they were away to the boat that tossed on the wild water with a single rower in his place.

"It is our Hoël. I found him looking for you. He is true as steel. In, in, and off, or you are lost!" whispered Yvonne, flinging a cloak about Gaston, thrusting a purse, a sword, and a flask into his hand, and holding the boat while he leaped in.

"But you?" he cried, "I cannot leave you in peril, after all you have dared and done for me."

"No one suspects me; I am safe. Go to my mother; she will hide you, and I will follow soon."

Waiting for no further speech, she pushed the boat off and watched it vanish in the darkness, then went away to give thanks, and rest after her long work and excitement.

Gaston reached home safely, and Dame Gillian concealed him in the ruins of the abbey, till anxiety for Yvonne drove him out to seek and rescue in his turn. For she did not come, and, when a returning soldier brought word she had been arrested in her flight and sent to Nantes, Gaston could not rest but, disguising himself as a peasant, went to find her, accompanied by faithful Hoël, who loved Yvonne and would gladly die for her and his young master. Their hearts sank when they discovered that she was in the Boufflay, an old fortress, once a royal residence, now a prison, crowded with unfortunate and innocent creatures, arrested on the slightest pretexts and guillotined or drowned by the infamous Carrier. Hundreds of men and women were there, suffering terribly, and among them was Yvonne, brave still, but with no hope of escape, for few were saved and then only by some lucky accident. Like a sister of mercy she went among the poor souls crowded together in the great halls—hungry, cold, sick, and despairing—and they clung to her as if she were some strong, sweet saint who could deliver them or teach them how to die.

After some weeks of this terrible life, her name was called one morning on the list for that day's execution, and she rose to join the sad procession setting forth.

"Which is it to be?" she asked, as she passed one of the men who guarded them, a rough fellow, whose face was half hidden by a shaggy beard.

"You will be drowned; we have no time to waste on women," was the brutal answer, but as the words passed his lips, a slip of paper was pressed into her hand, and these words breathed into her ear by a familiar voice, "I am here!"

It was Gaston, in the midst of enemies, bent on saving her at the risk of his life, remembering all he owed her and the motto of his race. The shock of this discovery nearly betrayed them both and turned her so white that the woman next her put her arm about her, saying sweetly, "Courage, my sister; it is soon over."

"I fear nothing now!" cried Yvonne and went on to take her place in the cart, looking so serene and happy that those about her thought her already fit for heaven.

No need to repeat the dreadful history of the Noyades; it is enough to say that in the confusion of the moment Yvonne found opportunity to read and destroy the little paper, which said briefly, "When you are flung into the river, call my name and float. I shall be near."

She understood and, being placed with a crowd of wretched women on the old vessel which lay in the River Loire, she employed every moment in loosening the rope that tied her hands and keeping her eye on the tall, bearded man who moved about seeming to do his work, while his blood boiled with suppressed wrath and his heart ached with unavailing pity. It was dusk before the end came for Yvonne, and she was all unnerved by the sad sights she had been forced to see, but when rude hands seized her, she made ready for the plunge, sure that Gaston would "be near." He was, for in the darkness and uproar, he could leap after her unseen, and while she floated he cut the rope, then swam down the river with her hand upon his shoulder till they dared to land. Both were nearly spent with the excitement and exertion of that dreadful hour, but Hoël waited for them on the shore and helped Gaston carry poor Yvonne into a deserted house, where they gave her fire, food, dry garments, and the gladdest welcome one human creature ever gave to another.

Being a robust peasant, the girl came safely through hardships that would have killed or crazed a frailer creature, and she was soon able to rejoice with the brave fellows over this escape, so audaciously planned and so boldly carried out. They dared stay but a few hours and before dawn were hastening through the least frequented state of the country, which made fugitives no unusual sight and refugees plentiful. One more adventure, and that a happy one, completed their joy and turned their flight into a triumphant march.

Pausing in the depths of the great forest of Hunaudaye to rest, the two young men went to find food, leaving Yvonne to tend the fire and make ready to cook the venison they hoped to bring. It was nightfall, and another day would see them in Dinan, they hoped, but the lads had consented to pause for the girl's sake, for she was worn out with their rapid flight. They were talking of their adventures in high spirits, when Gaston laid his hand on Hoël's mouth and pointed to a green slope before them. An early moon gave light enough to show them a dark form moving quickly into the coppice, and something like the antlers of a stag showed above the tall brakes before they vanished. "Slip around and drive him this way. I never miss my aim, and we will sup royally tonight," whispered Gaston, glad to use the arms with which they had provided themselves.

Hoël slipped away, and presently a rustle in the wood betrayed the cautious approach of the deer. But he was off before a shot could be fired, and the disappointed hunters followed long and far, resolved not to go back empty-handed. They had to give it up, however, and were partially consoled by a rabbit, which Hoël flung over his shoulder, while Gaston, forgetting caution, began to sing an old song the women of Brittany love so well.

> "*Quand vous étiez captif, Bertrand, fils de Bretagne,*
> *Tous les fuseaux tournaient aussi dans la campagne.*"

He got no further, for the stanza was finished by a voice that had often joined in the ballad, when Dame Gillian sang it to the children, as she spun,

> "*Chaque femme apporte son écheveau de lin;*
> *Ce fut votre rançon, Messire du Guesclin.*"

Both paused, thinking that some spirit of the wood mocked them, but a loud laugh, and a familiar "Holà! Holà!" made Hoël cry, "The forester!" while Gaston dashed headlong into the thicket whence the sound came, there to find the jolly forester, indeed, with a slain deer by his side, waiting to receive them with open arms.

"I taught you to stalk the deer and spear the boar, not to hunt your fellow creatures, my lord. But I forgive you, for it was well done, and I had a hard run to escape," he said, still laughing.

"But how came you here?" cried both the youths in great excitement, for the good man was supposed to be dead, with his old master.

"A long tale, for which I have a short and happy answer. Come home to supper with me, and I'll show you a sight that will gladden hearts and eyes," he answered, shouldering his load and leading the way to a deserted hermitage, which had served many a fugitive for a shelter. As they went, Gaston poured out his story and told how Yvonne was waiting for them in the wood.

"Brave lads! And here is your reward," answered the forester, pushing open the door and pointing to the figure of a man, with a pale face and bandaged head, lying asleep beside the fire.

It was the count, sorely wounded, but alive, thanks to his devoted follower, who had saved him when the fight was over and, after weeks of concealment, suffering, and anxiety, had brought him so far toward home.

No need to tell of the happy meeting that night, nor of the glad return, for, though the château was in ruins and lives were still in danger, they were all together, and the trials they had passed through only made the ties of love and loyalty between high and low more true and tender. Good Dame Gillian housed them all and nursed her master back to health. Yvonne and Hoël had a gay wedding in the course of time, and Gaston went to the wars again. A new château rose on the ruins of the old, and, when the young lord took possession, he replaced the banner that was lost with one of fair linen, spun and woven by the two women who had been so faithful to him and his, but added a white dove above the clasped hands and golden legend, never so true as now:

En tout chemin loyauté.